THE ALBORUVIAN GARDENER

by

HELEN ROBEY

Visit us online at www.authorsonline.co.uk

A Bright Pen Book

Copyright © 2010 Helen Robey

Cover illustrations by © Jo Spaul 2010

Cover design by © Jamie Day 2010

All rights reserved. No part of this publication may be reproduced, stored in a retrieval system, or transmitted in any form or by any means, electronic, mechanical, photocopy, recording or otherwise, without prior written permission of the copyright owner. Nor can it be circulated in any form of binding or cover other than that in which it is published and without similar condition including this condition being imposed on a subsequent purchaser.

British Library Cataloguing Publication Data.
A catalogue record for this book is available from the British Library

ISBN 978 07552 1213 2

Authors OnLine Ltd
19 The Cinques
Gamlingay, Sandy
Bedfordshire SG19 3NU
England

This book is also available in ebook format, details of which are available at www.authorsonline.co.uk

This book is dedicated to the memory of my parents, who first encouraged me to write and introduced me to Wharfedale.

By the same author: "Art Circles".

"No Contracting State shall expel or return a refugee in any manner whatsoever to the frontiers of territories where his life or freedom would be threatened on account of his race, religion, nationality, membership of a particular social group or political opinion."

United Nations Convention relating to the Status of Refugees, 1951 (Article 33,1)

The author's main research sources for this novel were publications by Amnesty International and the Border and Immigration Agency of the Home Office.

Chapter 1

In the cold, dark interior, people sat or lay on the floor, separately or huddled for warmth in groups or couples, clutching the few possessions they had brought with them. There was little inclination to speak. Most were wary of their travelling companions and thought it best to tell nobody who they were or where they hoped to go and why. It was frightening to be so close to complete strangers yet unable to see them. A small dim light in the middle of the high roof did little more than indicate its own presence.

Maria shivered, clutched her jacket more tightly round her body, pulled her woolly hat further down over her ears, and wrapped her arms around her knees, as much for privacy as for warmth. Her canvas bag was stowed under her bent legs, where she could feel that it was safe, although its most important contents - her passport and most of her money - had been taken from her before she was allowed on this vehicle. She still had her precious photographs and newspaper cuttings, though, and the thought of them gave her a small measure of comfort. Of more immediate physical importance was the food she had packed. Warned in advance that there would be few stops on the journey where food would be obtainable, she had brought as much as she could fit into her bag, along with a change of clothing and some basic toiletries.

How long would the journey take? The driver had been vague about this - five days, if they were lucky, he'd said. It would depend on which of the EU countries they finally stopped in, and whether there were any problems on the way. Maria wondered about these 'problems' and prepared herself for a long and unpleasant ride in the smelly, airless container. How would she manage to sleep in these cramped conditions, as the old vehicle rattled and jerked on uneven roads, people talked or snored, and a small child wailed inconsolably? At least, she had only herself to look after. Would she have embarked on such an uncertain journey if she'd had a child to care for? What horrors must that baby's mother be fleeing from, to take such risks?

Maria thought of her last meeting with Pavel, just three days ago, and his final attempt to dissuade her from leaving Alborus. She had, briefly, been tempted to stay, but her mind was already made up. Now, with time for reflection, she shed a few tears for her relationship with Pavel. She would never see him again.

Sitting quietly alone, though disturbingly close to strangers, she heard snatches of conversation, mostly in Alboruvian, some in other Slavic languages she couldn't identify. How long had they been travelling? she wondered. With her watch gone, and the darkness in the container, there was no way of judging the time of day. Hearing quiet talk around her, she began to feel lonely. There must be other people travelling on their own, but it was impossible to see anyone clearly. When she noticed a few dim lights moving in the darkness, she wished that she, too, had thought to bring a torch. Once, she felt unnerved when a beam shone directly into her face for several moments.

She almost started when a woman's voice, quite close, spoke to her in Alboruvian.

'May I talk to you a little?' the voice said. 'It is sad to be alone on such a journey. It would help to make the time pass more quickly for us, I think.'

Maria turned to answer.

'Yes, please,' she said eagerly. 'I was feeling so lonely. My name is Maria.'

'Mine is Nina. I think I saw you, Maria, when we were waiting to hand in our passports. I did not like to do that - So hard to prove our identity without them.'

'Yes, I was very worried about it.'

'These are difficult circumstances,' Nina said, her voice quieter than before, 'I think it would be wise not to talk about our plans during this journey. Maybe you think I'm over-cautious, but I'm sure it's for the best.'

'No, I think you're right, and it will take our minds off the journey a bit if we talk about different things. Isn't it funny,' Maria added on a lighter note, 'to be having a conversation with someone we can't see? I've never done this before!'

The two women laughed briefly, then were silent for a while, but although each was absorbed in her own thoughts, both had shed the harrowing sense of isolation and the days ahead seemed less fearsome.

When she boarded the vehicle, Maria had been dismayed to be told by one of the two drivers that he could not guarantee that they would go as far as England. When she'd asked why, he had muttered something unintelligible, about trouble with the police. Maria was well aware that the men she had paid for her journey were not working within the law. They were 'people traffickers', making money from those desperate to leave their own country. Almost certainly, they were not to be trusted.

'I wonder if it's still snowing,' Nina's soft voice broke gently into Maria's thoughts, 'It sounds as if the road is very wet, doesn't it?'

'I hadn't noticed,' Maria answered, 'but yes, it does. I expect wet roads are safer than icy ones, though.'

'January!' Nina exclaimed. 'Not the best time of year for a journey of this kind!'

'No, but we seem to be going faster now,' Maria observed. 'Perhaps we've left the mountains behind.'

Silence fell. After a while, Maria dozed into a light sleep, but she was soon disturbed by a shuffling noise, and a man's voice said, 'Excuse me!' as he stumbled over her feet in the darkness.

'Sorry!' said the man, regaining his balance and lurching on towards the door at the rear of the container. This was the first of many such disturbances, and Maria dreaded the times when she would need to make her way to the one toilet. Before the journey began, one of the drivers had told the passengers that there would be stops on the way, where they could get out if they needed to. What the facilities would be like at the stopping places, he had not said.

Three hours later, the truck slowed down and stopped. The harsh noises of the metal doors at the back being opened roused everyone.

'Fifteen minutes' stop!' the driver shouted.

Stiffened limbs found flexibility at the mention of food, and everyone hurried to the rear exit to jump down onto the frozen ground. It was just beginning to get light and in the gloom Maria could see that they were in some kind of farmyard. A warm beam of light shone from the open door of a barn, onto the snow. There were other buildings, but they showed no lights, and it was difficult to see what kind of country they were in, though vague shapes suggested hills, or perhaps forests, beyond.

Everyone hurried to get inside and eat the soup and rolls that had been promised, in the short time allowed. The barn was furnished sparsely with trestle tables and spindly folding chairs, which the travellers had to collect from a stack against one of the walls and which provided little comfort. At one end there was a rudimentary kitchen with a counter in front, where two women stood behind cauldrons of soup. They looked resentful, as if they had been coerced into this duty, and addressed harsh words to each other in Alboruvian. The one who served Maria gave her a contemptuous glance, splashing the greasy liquid carelessly into her bowl, so that half of it spilt onto the counter.

The travellers had been told that the price they paid for the journey included a few meals on the way, and there were grumbles, mostly from the men, about the small servings of unidentifiable thin soup and the stale bread, which did not amount to a meal. Most people, though, were so dazed and disorientated by the light, after prolonged darkness in the container, that they lacked the energy to complain. The toilets, though rudimentary, were better than the overused one in the lorry.

Seeing Nina properly for the first time, in the light of the barn, Maria was surprised to realise that her new friend was much older than herself, her face very lined and her hair almost white. Her voice sounded young, rather like Maria's own, and she was twenty-three. She wondered why Nina was making such an arduous - possibly dangerous - journey, but both women kept to their agreement not to talk about their plans, although Nina once mentioned briefly her concern for her daughter in London, whom she had not heard from for many months.

The air in the container was fresher when they returned to it, and much colder, but for people who had begun to fear suffocation before the stop, the chilly conditions were welcome. Most passengers tried to get back to the places they had occupied before, the instinct to find and inhabit an individual space asserting itself even here, and there were several quarrels over territory before the doors were shut, darkness descended again, and the journey resumed.

Women were greatly outnumbered by men, Maria had noticed when they were all in the barn eating the frugal refreshments, and this, together with a smell of alcohol when they were back in the container, made her feel uneasy. She was grateful for Nina's companionship and nearness to her, but she remained alert and wary. Once the truck was on its way again, she became aware of someone shuffling about quite close to her, and a slurred male voice said:

'I know you, don't I? I saw you in a police station two months ago. You were there with your father.'

Maria froze. She had indeed been in a police station with her father, just before his imprisonment.

'I never forget a face!' said the man, or youth - Maria could not tell which - in a tone that made her tremble.

'Your father wrote those dirty books, didn't he?'

Maria had determined to keep silent, but this was too much for her.

'No, he did not! That was someone else with the same name. My father was a man of great humanity. He died protesting about injustice in our country. You should be proud of what he...'

She stopped abruptly. Nina had put a gently restraining hand on her arm, and she whispered urgently: 'Maria, dear, it is best to say nothing.'

Maria subsided immediately, regretting her indiscretion. She heard a loud chuckle: 'No luck there, Anton? Never mind; there'll be plenty more opportunities, plenty of time! And quite a few to choose from in here!'

Obscene laughter followed.

Another voice added, 'And it doesn't matter what they look like, in this bloody box!'

The youths guffawed again.

'Calm down, you lads,' an older male voice quietly intervened. 'Let's keep up some decent standards in here."

The youths subsided for a while. An uneasy quietness now prevailed, but there was never silence. Unable to sleep, Maria heard the whispering of couples, the rustling of paper when anyone opened a packet of food, suppressed sobbing, and restless shuffling as people tried to make themselves comfortable and inevitably disturbed others by doing so, sometimes provoking angry outbursts or just murmurs of annoyance. Sometimes she heard someone praying and the click of rosary beads.

Maria wondered what the container normally carried, when people were not its cargo. She'd noticed a smell when she first came on board, a bit like rotting vegetables.

During spells of wakefulness, she and Nina talked quietly, firstly about the places where they had lived and grown up. Later, discovering a shared interest in reading, they talked about books, recommended titles to each other, discussing novels they both knew well, compensating a little for the impossibility of reading here, in the dark.

The next time the truck stopped, one of the drivers came into the container to announce that they would soon be entering the European Union. He refused to say which country it was. Some delay was likely at the border, and the truck would probably be parked in a stationary queue for some time. Total silence would be vital until they were moving again, and no one would be allowed to move from where they were. If police or customs officers came on board, no one was to answer any questions, or to ask any. Knowing that this was one of the most risky stages of the whole venture, nobody raised any objection to these rules. But then a man's voice spoke:

'There's a two-year-old baby in here. It isn't right to risk all our lives for the sake of a kid who might start to cry at any moment! That child and its mother should be turned off the truck!'

A few murmurs of agreement followed, but most people waited in tense anguish, torn between humane feelings and the instinct for self-preservation.

'I will enforce silence in here myself,' their guard announced in a grim tone that no one would have dared to challenge. 'You can talk now until I tell you,' he added.

A rumour began to circulate. Some people swore that they'd seen the butt of a gun sticking out of the guard's pocket. Was it to threaten anyone who disobeyed his orders, or to shoot any official who showed curiosity about the container? Others wondered fearfully how the guard would silence the baby, if it should cry.

'There's always someone worse off than ourselves,' Nina said to Maria. 'Just imagine how that baby's mother must be feeling now!'

The period of silence at the border seemed never-ending, and it was made especially unnerving by their guard's use of a torch to look at the travellers. Sometimes he would focus his attention on one individual for several minutes at a time. But the baby never cried, no officials boarded the container, the driver-cum-guard got out and returned to the cab, and at last they were moving again. The successful crossing into a country of the European Union - Poland, most of the travellers assumed it to be - produced a marked relaxation from the almost unbearable tension of the last few hours. There was singing in the container as the journey got under way - almost a party atmosphere - and people began to talk more freely.

Several hundred miles further on, the truck stopped again, and after another frugal and unappetising meal in yet another unidentifiable place, some newcomers came on board. Their language was unlike any of those spoken in the container so far. But of much greater significance to the existing passengers was the obviously advanced stage of pregnancy of one of the new women.

'That's all we need!' exclaimed the man who had protested against the small child being allowed to travel.

All conversations stopped abruptly. The tension was almost palpable.

'Is she going to have a kid in here?'

The woman looked at him beseechingly, his meaning clear despite his unfamiliar language. The guard was standing impassively at the rear entrance, where he checked the people entering the container.

'Chuck her out!' the protester demanded.

'No,' the guard answered stolidly, 'She's paid her fare.'

A woman who always sat alone, and had been so unobtrusive that few people had noticed her, stood up and walked over to the terrified newcomer, put an arm round her, and led her to the place where she usually sat and, without a word, made a space for her, trying to make her as comfortable as she could. The man who had objected said no more. Another crisis had been averted.

On and on the truck travelled, until Maria lost all sense of how long it was since she'd left her home town, or how soon, if ever, she would reach England.

Chapter 2

Jason Entwistle closed the lid of his laptop and sighed. There just wasn't enough time to prepare adequately for the latest case he'd taken on. It was past midnight. Caroline had come into the study half an hour ago and asked, impatience only partly concealed, whether he remembered that he had to get up at six tomorrow morning, to drive to Glasgow in time to represent 'that refugee' at his asylum tribunal. She'd looked tired, slightly aggrieved, and he'd felt guilty, remembering how her sleep had been disrupted for hours the previous night by the crying of Benjie, the youngest of their three children, fractious with teething.

'Alborus - Where on earth is that?' Caroline had asked, peering at the computer screen.

'Eastern Europe - bordering on Russia, I think.'

Caroline looked puzzled.

'Just something I needed to look up, to help a woman with her asylum application. That's the country she's from.'

'Not another of those cases!' Caroline exclaimed. 'I can't understand why you take them on,' she added quietly. 'Surely you've enough regular work without those as well? And it seems so unrewarding.'

'Yes,' Jason conceded. 'It doesn't pay well. But I feel it's so worthwhile - helping people to present their case for seeking asylum in Britain. You'd be appalled if I told you about the horrific conditions some of them have fled from. And they have such trust that this country will take them in. It makes some of the cases I normally deal with seem utterly petty.'

Caroline took his hand and stroked it.

'You're such an idealist,' she said, ' And that's partly why I love you. But we've got the boys to think of now.'

Almost on cue, a whimpering sound from Benjie's room called Caroline from the study. Jason followed a few moments later. Caroline picked up the baby, cuddling him and patting his back gently, until eventually he gave a big yawn and dozed off. She put him in his cot and tucked the soft blanket around him. They both stood looking down at him for a while - round pink cheeks, dark eyelashes, and a tiny fist pointing out from the top of the blanket.

'I'll just go and finish what I was doing,' Jason said quietly. 'Won't be more than ten minutes.'

He had been considerably longer than that, scrolling through the BBC's country profiles to learn about the persecution of political dissidents in Alborus. His new client, Maria Petrova, who had telephoned him today to arrange an appointment, seemed to have a justifiable fear of persecution if she was sent back there. Her father had been imprisoned and had died, suspiciously soon after being taken into custody, and Maria had left Alborus for her own safety, after her job prospects had been drastically reduced and vague threats made against her. He must find some specific evidence to put forward. He decided to try and find someone with first-hand knowledge of that country - a foreign correspondent perhaps, or a diplomat or academic, or even a former refugee from Alborus who had been allowed to settle in Britain, if any had. He would work at it. But there wasn't much time. Maria's asylum interview - which would decide her fate - was due to take place in two weeks' time.

Abruptly, Jason's thoughts returned to his family - David and Christopher, seven and four, and the baby. Yes, they were his priority, of course they were; but he didn't see his duty to them mainly in terms of financial provision. He hoped to hand on to them his values of fairness, justice, and a concern for those less fortunate. When Caroline talked, as she often did, about sending the boys to the public school her brothers had attended, he felt uncomfortable. Jason had worked his way through comprehensive school and sixth-form college, gained a degree at one of the newer universities, then studied at law school and became a solicitor. He envisaged some similar career pathway for his sons, depending of course on their own career choices. To pay public-school fees for them, he would have to stick to the more lucrative aspects of the law, and give up the less profitable - many would say thankless - role of helping people like Maria and his Iraqi client. He would take no pride in such a career. A quotation came into his mind:

He that hath a wife and children hath given hostages to fortune; for they are impediments to great enterprises.

Francis Bacon had understood the problem - the same in 1625 as it was now - and this thought consoled Jason a little. Oh well, he concluded, he would have to try and find a compromise.

Meanwhile, there was tomorrow's appeal tribunal, which he was determined to attend, despite the disruption to his schedule. He'd been informed at very short notice, by the Border and Immigration Agency, that the Iraqi doctor, Ahmed, who had been living here in Bradford, had now been moved to Dungavel House, an Immigration Removal Centre near Glasgow. The tribunal at which he would appeal against the recent rejection of his application for asylum would now take place in Glasgow instead of Bradford, the voice on the telephone had told Jason.

'Sorry it's such short notice, but you'll have to travel to Glasgow - that is, if you still want to attend the tribunal.'

The casual implication that he need not bother to attend strengthened Jason's determination to do so, as did also Ahmed's transfer to a Removal Centre, whence rejected asylum seekers were normally sent back to their countries of origin - as if it were a foregone conclusion that his appeal would fail.

The few colleagues Jason knew who had done work with asylum seekers had warned him that their clients were often moved to different parts of the country. Lawyers often gave up such cases because of the disruption they involved. Another solicitor in the client's new area might take over the case but, by then, there was usually little time to prepare adequately.

'Between you and me,' Jason's colleague, Mike Barton had said, 'it looks very much as if there's a deliberate policy of making the whole process difficult for asylum applicants.'

'Why?' Jason asked naively.

'Well, it'd be embarrassing for the Home Office if large numbers of them qualified for refugee status and had to be allowed to stay in Britain! There's no mileage for this government - or any other government - in spending money on asylum seekers - just about the least popular cause among the electorate, one would imagine! The Home Office loves to be able to announce a reduction in the number of people accepted and an increase in those sent packing! So the Case Owners, who interview them and decide their fate, must be looking for any excuse to turn down the applications. They've got their job security to think of, after all.'

Jason had listened, appalled.

'And we need to think of ours too,' Mike had added. 'Asylum work won't advance your career, and you'll miss out on cases that would. Unless you're really committed to it, I'd pack it in after these two cases you're working on just now.'

'And what about Britain's commitment to the UN Convention on Refugees - that no one shall be returned to a country where he has a justifiable fear of persecution?'

Mike shrugged. 'Well, I'd say the Government's got an impossible task on its hands. This country just isn't big enough to take in unlimited numbers of refugees, however desperately they need help. I don't think it's possible for Britain to keep to that commitment any longer. The population's increased hugely since 1951 when that Convention was signed. I think you'll be wasting your time if you continue taking on asylum cases.'

There was a pause. Then Jason said quietly: 'Thanks for your advice, Mike, but I don't intend to act on it.'

'Good luck, then. You're going to need it,' his friend added.

Chapter 3

Maria walked through the gateway into the park, a short distance from the house where she was staying with a family of her compatriots. She didn't want to go back there immediately. She wanted to think over the interview.

As she was making her way towards one of the wooden benches that faced the pond, lively with the splashing of mallards, coots and moorhens, a large red ball bounced a short distance away and rolled towards her. Instinctively she picked it up and threw it to two young Asian boys who ran to retrieve it. They grinned their thanks and she smiled at the carefree pair. They didn't look as if they'd had to struggle to be accepted in this country. Long ago perhaps their parents, or maybe their grandparents, had made great efforts for acceptance here. There were many dark-skinned people in this city, Maria had noticed since she arrived in Bradford three weeks ago, and this encouraged her to think that foreigners were not unwelcome here.

She sat down on the bench and watched the ducks for a while, as they squabbled over pieces of bread that a woman was throwing for them, the spray of water-drops catching the sunlight as they splashed about. Then she took out of her pocket the paper she'd been given by her Case Owner, the woman who would decide whether Maria would be granted asylum. Two addresses were printed on it - a police station where she was instructed to report every week until further notice, and a lawyer who might be willing to help her present her case. She should telephone his office for an appointment to see him. She felt apprehensive about reporting to the police. Recent meetings with police in her own country had been frightening, but she reminded herself that things were better here.

She had found the first meeting with her Case Owner worrying, partly because the woman had spoken rather too quickly for her, so that several times Maria had had to ask her to repeat things. She'd been dismayed, though not surprised, when told that she would need to produce proof of her identity at her formal asylum interview and bitterly regretted the unavoidable surrender of her passport before boarding the container vehicle. The Case Owner had made one or two notes, before looking at her watch, telling Maria she had five more clients to see after her and concluding the meeting briskly. Maria would be notified when her asylum interview would take place. She was not told how soon this was likely to be.

She wondered what impression she had made on the Case Owner. It had been impossible to tell. The woman had shown little reaction to her answers, and had barely smiled to greet her, or at the end of the meeting. She'd looked very tired, Maria thought. Perhaps she was overworked with so many people seeking asylum.

Anyway, there was one positive step that Maria could take. She would telephone the solicitor's office today and make an appointment with... She looked at the name on the paper she'd been given... Mr Entwistle. How was that pronounced? she wondered.

She was pleased, too, that she now had some good news for the family of Alboruvians with whom she was living in Bradford. They would now be paid an allowance for her board and lodging, until a decision was made about her asylum claim. This was a relief. These people were only very remotely related to Maria and their house was quite small, so that she felt she was a burden to them. Ursula and her husband had come to Britain many years ago, and spoke English most of the time. Their two teenaged daughters had been born here and spoke only English. So it was not easy to regard the family as her compatriots. But Ursula had already shown Maria great kindness. She had accompanied her to the Asylum Screening Unit in Liverpool on the day after her arrival, as it was vital that she register her application for asylum in person immediately. Other than certain ports and airports, the only such units were in Croydon and Liverpool. How would she have managed to do this without Ursula's help and her generosity in paying her train fare?

Maria tried to spend as much time as possible out of the house, to intrude as little as possible on the family's privacy. This park and the nearby public library had become her favourite haunts, and it was to the library that she now walked - a wonderful warm place with friendly, helpful staff, where she could sit as long as she liked, reading the newspapers and learning all she could about the country where she hoped to make her home. She spent hours looking at maps, to familiarise herself with the geography of Britain and the location of towns she heard or read about, and she browsed through books on British history and literature. And all this at no cost! For this she was deeply thankful, having no money to spend on herself. Maria had an excellent reading knowledge of English, and she spoke it well, though not yet fluently. Understanding the spoken language was the hardest part, especially the northern accent - very different from the pronunciation she'd been taught in Alborus.

Arriving in the library, she looked first at the newspaper and magazine racks. Her attention was caught by a small magazine with a cover photograph of what she thought the most beautiful landscape she had ever seen. It showed a hillside, partly wooded, lightly sprinkled with snow, above a flat green valley, through which a river meandered placidly, clearly visible here and there, elsewhere glimpsed fleetingly between trees which lined its course. Sheep grazed in some of the fields, which were marked out by simple grey stone walls, and each had a small building, also of stone, which matched the houses and church of a village just visible in the distance. The whole scene spoke to Maria of peace, order and beauty. It looked like a place where man and nature could live in harmony, like all the elements of this view, where nothing clashed and everything seemed to have its rightful place.

Maria took the magazine to a nearby table, sat down, and flicked through its pages until she found more pictures of the same area, which she learned was called Wharfedale. These, too, conveyed to her the same feeling of serenity as the cover illustration. One showed two walkers with backpacks, a signpost pointing their way to Kettlewell, a village nestling between green hills; another a ruined abbey beside a river which people were crossing by stepping stones. Maria was especially moved by a photo of a cluster of old farm buildings, sheltered by a group of protecting trees from a wild moor rising behind it.

She found an atlas in the reference library, and discovered that part of Wharfedale was not very far from Bradford. But the places named in the photos' captions were further north, towards the source of the River Wharfe. If only she could go there and see those beautiful places! If she was allowed to stay in England, and if she could find work there, that is where she would choose to live.

Chapter 4

The young woman who faced Jason across his desk was thin, pale and rather frail-looking. She was going to need all the support she could get, he thought, if her asylum claim was to succeed. She even looked frightened of him at first, and spoke hesitantly in answer to his initial pleasantries and simple questions.

He began by reassuring her that his role was to help her to put forward her case at the forthcoming interview, which would determine whether she would be allowed to stay in Britain. They would work together to make sure that everything relevant was presented to the Case Owner. As the conversation progressed, Jason realised that he had underestimated Maria. Once she had overcome her initial nervousness, he realised that her English was good, and that she had prepared well for this meeting.

'It is very important to be able to prove the claims you make,' he said. 'Have you anything which proves your identity? Your passport would be the best thing.'

She looked crestfallen at first and explained that she'd had no choice but to surrender it as a condition of her journey.

'But,' she added, 'I have here a photograph, two newspaper cuttings and a letter, which may help to prove who I am.'

She opened her bag, took out a very worn brown envelope, from which she produced first a photograph of a tall middle-aged man with thick dark hair, standing beside a girl, whom Jason immediately recognised as Maria herself, slightly younger and obviously in better times, for both were smiling happily at the camera.

'My father,' Maria said, pushing the photo across the desk towards Jason. He looked at it courteously, but could see no value in this family snapshot for substantiating her claimed identity.

'My father, Alexis Petrov, was very well-known in Alborus. He was an important journalist. Anyone in Alborus would recognise him from this picture. He became famous, and later notorious, for his political writings which criticised the injustice of our government.'

She then unfolded a yellowed newspaper cutting - a longish article headed by a small photograph of the same man, but considerably younger.

'This was earlier in my father's career. He wrote articles for this newspaper. This piece is about the opening of a new football stadium.

'But here,' she added, opening a newer page of newsprint, 'is something much more recent. I will translate the headline - "Alexis Petrov arrested for seditious writing against the State of Alborus".'

Her voice quavered as she showed the page to Jason. He noticed the accompanying photograph, recognisable, but the face very lined, the hair much thinner.

Looking up Jason saw the distress in Maria's face.

'My father died very soon after he was imprisoned,' she explained. 'I believe he was murdered.'

'I'm sorry,' Jason said, embarrassed, and waited a few moments. Maria was the next to speak.

'I also have a letter to show you,' she said.

She handed him a small envelope. He was glad to see that the town and the date of posting were clearly stamped on it. He hesitated to take out the letter.

"Yes - you can look at it,' Maria said. 'It is the last letter my father sent me, from the prison. I will keep it until the day I die, but I show it to you because it is further proof that I am his daughter, and that I tell the truth about my father. Shall I translate it for you?'

'No. I don't want to read your private correspondence, but tell me anything you think would be helpful for me to know.'

'He says he is not at all well in the prison. The conditions there are not good. He is in solitary confinement...'

Here she broke off, unable to speak. The tears she had mastered so far began to flow. Jason passed her a box of tissues and asked if she wanted a drink of water. She shook her head, impatient to continue and ashamed of her weakness. With an effort, she continued.

'Father wrote that it would be best if I did not visit him again. At the end he wrote, "Be brave, Maria. Keep up our good work. Go to England, if you can. You can speak and write freely there." '

'Your father was a courageous man,' Jason said. 'Now, these documents could be very useful as proof of your identity and to corroborate your story. May I take photocopies of these? I'm sure you want to keep the originals, so it will be useful to have copies to refer to. But,' he added after a moment's thought, ' do bring yours to the asylum interview. It's possible your Case Owner will only accept original documents. We mustn't leave anything to chance.'

'Yes, of course,' Maria said.

'Excuse me while I get these copied. I'll be back in a few minutes.'

While Jason was out of the room, Maria looked around. Glass-fronted bookcases contained heavy volumes of what she supposed was the English law, as well as reference books and encyclopedias. She was intrigued by one title - *Who's Who*. Files and folders were piled up on a table under the window and stacks of papers occupied much of the remaining space. On the desk itself, besides what she assumed were papers relating to cases Jason was currently working on, there was a laptop computer, a telephone and a bowl of blue hyacinths whose heady scent seemed incongruous in such a place. They made her think of spring - would it come earlier here than in her own country? Her journey from Alborus had begun at the end of January and it was now mid-February. Already she'd seen crocuses in gardens and the park. On a small table near the desk stood a photograph in a silver frame - a woman sitting in a garden chair, holding a baby and watching two little boys playing with a ball. Maria tried to imagine Jason in that informal setting, taking the photograph of his family.

'Sorry about that,' he said, coming back into the room, then handing her documents back to her and sitting down. 'Now, you'll probably be asked some questions about your country. Unfortunately, some asylum seekers tell lies in their efforts to get accepted in Britain, so your Case Owner may well test your knowledge about Alborus - about the town you lived in, for instance, the name of the President, geography, recent history, currency etc. etc. So let's have a little practice now. It may show you some areas you need to check up on.'

He asked her a few questions: How would she travel from her home town to the capital? How much would a loaf of bread cost in Alborus? What's the name of its principal airline? What is the school-leaving age? She answered them all fully and confidently.

'Try to have clearly in your mind the details of your journey to Britain. The Border and Immigration Agency are meticulous about dates, so I'm told. Make sure you know the dates when you left Alborus and when you arrived in England.'

Maria nodded.

'It might help if you knew which countries you travelled through in that container lorry.'

'This I do not know. The truck only stopped a few times, usually when it was dark, and of course I couldn't see out at all. I have looked at maps in the library here. I think the shortest route would be through

Poland first, then Germany, then maybe Holland or Belgium, or perhaps France.'

'Well, if you're not sure, do say so. Don't guess in the interview. If you came via France, it could have been through the Channel Tunnel or by ferry. You'd have felt some movement if you were on the sea. Can you remember?'

'Yes. It was definitely a ferry. There was a time when the floor seemed to move up and down. I had to hold on to something to avoid falling. Some people were sick. It seemed a long time because it was so unpleasant, but maybe it was only an hour or two.'

'Well,' Jason said, after answering a few questions Maria asked, 'We've covered quite a lot of ground. I think you have a very sound case for seeking asylum here and I'll do all I can to help. I'm afraid you might have quite a long wait before you're given an appointment for your interview, but you've got somewhere to stay haven't you?'

'Oh yes - with a couple from Alborus and their daughters. I'm very lucky.'

'You won't feel homesick, then!'

'No. And I feel more confident now, with you help,' she said as she stood up and walked towards the door. Goodbye, and thank you very much.'

After she had gone, although his next client had been sitting some time in the waiting room, Jason carefully wrote himself some reminders of points that had arisen, then sat for a few minutes thinking about Maria. Despite her distress about her father and the horrors of her journey - barely hinted at by her, but easily envisaged by his sharp imagination - she had kept strictly to the facts of her story, never indulging in emotional digressions. She deserved all the help and support he could provide.

Chapter 5

Jason was shocked by the failure of his Iraqi client Ahmed's appeal against his asylum rejection, and especially by the role played in this by incompetence and what looked to him like sheer callousness. From the start, the proceedings were rushed. Ahmed was not given enough time to answer questions, and the interpreter, an Iraqi student, was inaccurate and omitted several important points.

The worst blow was that the immigration judge disallowed the use of an important document, on the grounds that it was in Arabic and was a photocopy. The document was a testimonial bearing the letterhead of a major hospital in Baghdad where Ahmed had worked, recommending him as a highly competent and trustworthy doctor. The judge refused to have it translated by the interpreter present. The original letter had been sent to a translation agency by a previous lawyer who had soon abandoned Ahmed's case as unprofitable. Repeated phone calls by Jason to this agency had at length been rewarded by a promise on the morning of the tribunal to have the letter and its English translation available to him by the following day. Jason had requested an adjournment to allow for their arrival, but this was refused on grounds of lack of time.

By now, Jason reflected a fortnight later, Ahmed had probably been deported to Iraq, where he would no doubt continue to be harassed by the extremist gang whose persecution and death threats had been his reason for fleeing his country.

Ahmed had shown the judge the scars on his hands and arms, inflicted when the gang attacked him in their efforts to make him unable to continue his work as a cardiac surgeon. The judge had discounted this evidence because there was no proof of how the injuries had been caused.

Jason had worked long hours to make up for his day at Glasgow, but eventually he picked up his notes on Maria, the young woman from Alborus. Many phone calls and internet searches to try to find someone with first-hand knowledge of that country had at last put him in contact with Dr Frank Lawson, a lecturer in the Department of Slavonic Studies at the University of Harrogate, who had spent six months in Alborus. Dr Lawson's specialism was in Slavonic languages and literature, but he had learned a great deal about the present-day politics and social conditions of the country. He confirmed Maria's account of the repressive régime which had replaced, after only a few years, the freedom and stability which Alborus had enjoyed in the immediate post-Soviet period. The President, he said, ruled virtually as a dictator. The press were muzzled and any opposition to the authorities was mercilessly suppressed. When Jason had mentioned Alexis Petrov, Lawson had immediately recognized the name. He had in fact met the courageous writer and admired his fearless campaigning. He had been dismayed, though hardly surprised, when Petrov's death had been announced soon after his imprisonment.

Maria was deeply touched to learn of this English academic's admiration for her father, when Jason telephoned her with the news. A copy of an article Dr Lawson had written for the Journal of East Slavonic Studies, describing the conditions in Alborus and the repression of the press, which mentioned Maria's father by name, could be useful evidence to present to her Case Owner.

Chapter 6

Almost as soon as Maria entered the house, Ursula knew that her asylum interview had gone badly. She heard her going up the stairs, each step slower than the last. Usually, Maria would come into the kitchen and have a chat with her, or at least exchange a greeting, when she arrived home. She never went straight upstairs to her room without a word, until today. It was the 20th of April, and Ursula knew how important the date was to Maria, how long she'd had to wait for the appointment, and how she'd pinned her hopes on its outcome.

'How was the interview?' Ursula asked gently when Maria came down half an hour later.

When she looked up, she saw the answer in Maria's face. She had obviously been crying.

'It was horrible. I am sure they will not allow me to stay in England.'

'Did they say that?'

'No, but the Case Owner didn't seem to believe me, about the danger of going back to Alborus.'

'Didn't you tell her what it's like there now? Surely she would take notice of that? '

'I thought she would. Mr Entwistle, my lawyer, showed her an article from a journal, by a specialist in Slavonic studies at Harrogate University. It described the ways critics of the régime are treated there. Best of all, I thought, my father was mentioned in the article - his imprisonment and his death. But the Case Owner just glanced at it. She even said she'd never heard of any trouble in Alborus!'

'Well, it's hardly ever mentioned in the newspapers here, you know.'

'But she just ignored our evidence! It was the same with the photos and newspaper cuttings I showed her. She looked at them and handed them straight back.'

'Was the interpreter helpful?'

'That was another problem. I'd asked for an interpreter, in case the questions were too quick for me to understand them. But I could tell he wasn't accurate. So I asked to continue without him. It was a bit better after that. But I was not allowed enough time to answer the questions properly. The Case Owner kept asking about my journey to England - questions I couldn't answer - what countries we went through, where we stopped on the way. She didn't seem to believe me that there were no windows to see out of, and that the stops were all in the dark.'

'She must have realised that you couldn't tell where you were.'

'Well, she didn't seem to care. I got that feeling right from the start of the interview.'

Ursula, though shocked, tried to be reassuring.

'I think it probably seemed like that because you were so anxious. That woman must have known you were being truthful, from the way you answered her.'

'Well, I hope so. I have to wait for the decision now. She did tell me, though, that if my application is rejected, I might be able to appeal - Then my case would be considered by a judge.'

'Well then, I don't think you need worry, Maria. The judge will see that you are treated fairly. He will be independent. You'll see. It will turn out right in the end. Now, let's have some tea, and talk about something different.'

Comforted by tea and cake, Maria was at last able to think of other matters.

"Do you know a place called Wharfedale?' she asked.

Ursula thought for a moment.

'I've heard of it. There's a part of Yorkshire - north of here - called the Dales. It's just countryside and villages, I think.'

'I saw some pictures of Wharfedale in a magazine in the library,' Maria said. 'It looks such a beautiful place - hills and valleys - so green and peaceful.'

'Lev and I haven't travelled around very much,' Ursula said. 'He works long hours at the garage, you know. And at the weekends he's so tired, he just wants to relax in front of the television. And the girls have their homework to do. They're a bit lazy, though - You've heard me telling them to get on with it! Still, it would do us all good to walk in the country sometime, for a change. Maybe we could all go up there one Sunday, in the car, and have a look round - since you think it's so nice.'

'That would be lovely,' Maria said. But, somehow, she couldn't imagine this outing really taking place.

Chapter 7

'Don't say I didn't warn you!'

Mike Barton had listened to Jason's account of his client Maria Petrova's failure to have her asylum refusal overturned at her appeal tribunal.

'It's a travesty of justice!' Jason exclaimed.

He had been seething with fury since receiving the news this morning.

'I don't think she really stood any chance, right from the start, now that I look back on the whole procedure!' he said. 'I'd like to know who does manage to get asylum if she couldn't! She has a justifiable fear of persecution in Alborus - which alone qualifies her to stay here. And besides that, she's got a good command of English, and she's a qualified teacher. She'd be self-supporting and contributing to this country's economy - an ideal citizen, in fact. We could do with more like her!'

'Don't get carried away by righteous indignation!' Mike answered. 'You did your best; much more than some lawyers I've heard of - giving up on asylum cases half-way through, or spoiling a client's case through carelessness, sending vital documents to the wrong address, or too late for an appeal tribunal.'

'All the more reason why...'

'You can't expect to win every case, Jason! If you do, you'll never be happy in this profession!'

'More than three months it's taken since Maria first registered as an asylum seeker and this is the result!' Jason stabbed his forefinger viciously at the letter bearing the news.

'Well, in many cases, it takes much longer than that,' said Mike. 'What reason was given by the judge?'

'Inadequate proof! And the same reason was given for refusing the Iraqi doctor I represented before Maria. It's been a total waste of effort!'

'And very little pay for your trouble too, for these legal aid cases.'

' If just one of them had been successful, I'd have been satisfied with achieving something worthwhile, but I'm beginning to agree with you. If there's no hope of success, it's futile to try.'

'There was a programme on Radio 4 last December about the asylum process,' Mike said. 'I don't suppose you heard it or you wouldn't be so surprised by what's happened. *Unreliable Evidence*, it was called, if I remember rightly. I can't remember much of the detail, but one phrase stuck in my memory. One of the speakers - a lawyer, I think - said that there's a *culture of disbelief* working against asylum seekers.'

'That certainly rings true, from my brief experience of the system,' said Jason.

Mike nodded. 'And you and I aren't likely to be able to change prejudices like that,' he added.

A glum silence followed.

'What does Caroline think about it?' Mike asked after a while.

'She's not at all happy - torn between idealism and practical sense - and I suppose I'm about the same. Which means I'll stop doing asylum cases, for a while at least. I don't imagine there'll be fewer cases in years to come! It seems to me it can only get worse, with thousands fleeing from brutal wars and repressive régimes. I don't envy the Home Office - having to deal with the problem. It seems insuperable.'

'It does indeed.' said Mike.

'So,' Jason added, in a ruefully humorous tone: 'By the time the boys have grown up and are independent, maybe I'll be able to afford to return to this kind of work! Or even take it up as a retirement hobby!'

Chapter 8

'I am going away tomorrow,' Maria said quietly.

Ursula looked up from the vegetables she was slicing for a casserole.

'But why?' she asked.

'I don't want to leave you, Ursula. You have been a good friend to me - my first friend in England,'

'So what's made you suddenly decide to leave us?'

'The result of my appeal tribunal. It's final now. The judge decided there wasn't enough evidence to support my claim for asylum. This letter,' she said, showing Ursula the one she had received that morning, ' tells me that I must leave this country and return to Alborus within twenty-one days. If I don't go voluntarily, I will be deported as soon as transport is arranged. I will probably be taken from this house to what they call a Removal Centre - what a horrible name! - and kept there until I am deported...'

Ursula, appalled, interrupted, 'I can't believe what you are telling me! Such things don't happen in England! I'm sure you've misunderstood what they tell you.'

'I wish so much that I could believe you, but it's true. Your allowance for my lodging here will be stopped soon...'

'Maria!' Ursula again interrupted her, 'Don't think about that money. We're not going to turn you out if you can't pay us. We'll manage somehow. You could get a job, couldn't you?'

'No. They tell me it would be illegal for anyone to employ me! They said I would not be able to get a number that everyone needs if they want to have a job.'

'A National Insurance number,' Ursula said, 'But you must have misunderstood that letter...'

'Ursula, what I've told you is true. You can read the letter if you want to. I have to decide whether to let them send me to Alborus, or to go away, so that the immigration officials can't find me.'

'But where will you go? What will happen to you? - You will starve! Maria, you mustn't do this!'

Maria was touched by her friend's concern and distress on her behalf, but she almost wished that she had simply walked out of the house, leaving a letter of explanation and thanks, rather than face Ursula's opposition to her plan.

'You have been so good to me, Ursula,' she said. 'I will never forget your kindness to me, from when I first arrived in February, and you took me to Liverpool to register as an asylum seeker.'

But Ursula was thinking of something else.

'There might be something we could do to help you,' she said, 'I will talk with Lev when he comes home from the garage.'

When the rest of the family were watching television and Maria was helping Ursula with the washing-up, Ursula said, 'If you're really sure you want to go away from here, there's someone Lev knows through his work who runs a bed and breakfast place in Skipton. He's always saying he can't get staff to work there. So when I told Lev about your problem, he rang him up just before dinner, and said he knew someone who wanted work - He meant you, of course, but he didn't say you were an asylum seeker. If you don't mind low pay, he can give you a job, with board and lodging provided. It's only short-term, of course. The holiday season will be starting soon. There wouldn't be any problem about insurance, he said.'

'Would it be legal for me to work there, on those terms?' Maria asked cautiously.

Ursula looked worried.

'Well, if it isn't legal, nobody will know. He and his wife wouldn't report you. They'd be in trouble themselves if they did - paying less than the minimum wage, employing an asylum seeker.'

Maria nodded, though she was still doubtful.

'Well,' Ursula said, 'as you know, I'm not happy about you going off on your own like this but, if that's what you intend to do, you'll be more secure there than if you just wander off, hoping to find work. I'm not advising you to go, but if you must, I think this is your best hope. If you don't like the job, you can leave at any time - There'll be no employment contract to sign. But that means, of course, that you won't have any job security. Anyway, it's up to you, Maria. It's the only thing Lev and I can think of to help you. We don't know this man very well, or his wife, but they want staff, and you want a job - so, why not try it?'

'What would I be doing there?'

'Cleaning rooms, washing up, serving meals.'

Maria thought for a few moments.

'Yes,' she said, 'I would like that job.'

'If you like, then, Lev will phone the place and say when you'll be arriving.'

'Thank you so much,' Maria said, but her lip trembled as she spoke.

'There's one thing you'll like about that place,' Ursula added. 'Skipton is called *The Gateway to the Dales* - and that's the area you said you wanted to visit, after you saw those pictures - remember?'

'Oh, yes!' Maria said, smiling for the first time that day.

Chapter 9

Claire Martindale awoke with a start. The telephone in the office below her flat was ringing insistently. She was tempted to let it continue until the recorded message facility came on after twelve rings. She had been late getting to bed last night when the guests had departed after the inaugural dinner. She could hardly have pleaded tiredness and slipped away while Professor Edgeworth, the Mayor and Mayoress, the Trustees of Wildwood House College, and eight of the tutors she had engaged to give courses in the summer were still chatting in the reception hall.

Today, the College would swing into action - the fulfilment of Claire's long-cherished dream. She jumped out of bed, shoving feet into slippers and slinging a sensible dressing-gown over her shoulders, dashed out of the flat onto the gallery which lined three sides of the hall below, ran down the polished wooden stairs to the office door and unlocked it swiftly - just as the ringing stopped. A slight qualm disturbed her optimistic mood. No one would telephone the College before eight o'clock unless they had an urgent reason - a tutor suddenly unable to start a course or give a lecture that day, or, worse still, the secretary, Diane, needing time off because her child was ill. This was not to be thought of; Claire couldn't cope without Diane... Probably a wrong number. She waited a few moments to check whether the caller had left a message. They hadn't, nor was their number available to ring back. Claire shrugged and turned to go upstairs. Then she noticed a quantity of mail which had landed on the floor behind the big oak door. She sifted out a few items addressed to herself in handwriting she recognised, before depositing the rest on Diane's desk in the office and carrying her personal letters upstairs.

She lingered, just briefly this time, at the big landing window, to gaze across the garden and the field beyond, to where the River Wharfe flowed, sparkling in the sunlight of this June morning, spanned by the understated grace of a sturdy five-arched stone bridge. The early-morning mist was lifting slowly to unveil the hillside opposite, with its pattern of dry-stone walls, its stone barns and its sheep.

Yes, this is my place! - The words came unbidden into her mind.

In the flat, Claire tore open an envelope with a Canadian stamp,

postmarked Toronto. Opening the card inside, after a brief glance at the elegant flower design on the cover, she read in Jonquil's stylish hand;
'Congratulations, Mum! I *know* the College will be a *huge* success!' The words know and huge were underlined. 'I'll be thinking of you on opening day. Hope this arrives in time.'
In a modest PS Jonquil had added, 'The concerts went well. Back in York on Saturday.'
She'd timed it perfectly and, amazingly, so had Rory, though almost certainly by chance. His postcard of the Mayan Temple of the Great Jaguar in Guatemela, written three weeks ago, carried a similar message. Claire was one of the very few people who could read Rory's scrawl - and he spent most of his time deciphering ancient scripts!
These, and cards from two old friends from her school and university days, gave Claire a warm glow of joy,which she feared to spoil by opening the envelope that she had left till the last. Its message was harmless enough:
'Well done, Claire! I'll be in touch again soon.'
After the huge signature, a tiny - apologetic or stingy? - kiss was appended.
She wanted to believe that Aidan was truly pleased about the College, but their relationship had changed when she first embarked on the project and she feared that problems lay ahead.

Chapter 10

Around midday, checking with Diane the names of students who had arrived and been shown to their rooms, Claire glanced through the office window. She saw a tall figure walking energetically up the drive. Briefly, she thought of a huge dark bird, wings flapping at its sides, as the man drew nearer. He wore a long brown raincoat of vaguely old-fashioned cut which, left unfastened, flared out as he strode. Of course - Hugh Armstrong! - the tree man, and lynch-pin of this first course to be held at Wildwood House. She greeted him in the porch, as he slung his backpack off his shoulders.

'Did you find somewhere to park on the road?' she asked. 'Our parking area is almost full now.'

'I walked here, from Grassington.'

'Practising what you preach?'

'Not specially. I couldn't resist a walk on a day like this! - curlews calling, trees still showing all their different shades of green. This is a wonderful time of the year! I've just been watching a dipper foraging about on the pebbles in the Wharfe - just down there.'

He pointed to the spot.

'Sorry to drag you indoors! There's coffee and light lunches in the dining room, but some people have taken their refreshments outside. We've put a few tables and chairs on the terrace.'

'Sounds great! Talking of food, that was quite a feast last night, Claire!'

'Yes. The local catering firm did us proud - to my great relief, with the dignitaries being present!'

'I thought your idea was to soften up the tutors! We'll be like putty in your hands now, after that!'

'I hope so!' she said, laughing. 'I'll have to go now, Hugh. There's so much to keep an eye on today...Oh, by the way, we sorted out that problem I told you about with the projector. It should be OK now.'

'Thanks, Claire. Don't worry. I could improvise if need be.'

'Good. How I envy your relaxed approach to life!'

****

Sandy wished she hadn't come. It was much too early to start socialising again. All those people chatting and laughing down there in the hall when she arrived! It had been an ordeal to weave her way between them, to get to the office and check in. She could have turned round at that moment and gone back home, while there was still time. But now, she'd committed herself, and was half-heartedly unpacking her small suitcase and hanging her clothes in the wardrobe, hoping the things she'd brought would be suitable - two pairs of jeans, several tee-shirts and a jumper. At the last minute, she'd added her green linen dress, for the evenings, just in case there was any need to dress up a bit. Well, you never know!, she thought.

The lunch buffet, set out in the dining room, had looked tempting, but she couldn't face having to talk to strangers just yet. So she'd had to content herself with the welcome tray in her room, which offered tea or coffee and two chocolate biscuits, supplemented by an apple she had intended to eat on the train.

Her window looked out onto a broad stretch of lawn, dotted with a few shrubs. Nearby, a constant succession of greenfinches, goldfinches and blue tits visited feeders which hung from a venerable oak tree. Sandy watched their fluttery comings and goings for a while, completely absorbed, until she realised that it was time to go down and hear the Principal's Welcome followed by the first lecture, according to the printed schedule she'd found on her bed.

Val had told her about this course, many months ago. She had read about Hugh Armstrong in one of her ecology magazines and had persuaded Sandy to come with her. It was painful to be here on her own, but she had felt, obscurely but intensely, that this would be some way of keeping Val's spirit alive. Putting it into words made the idea sound mawkish, even superstitious. Sandy couldn't have explained it to anyone. But that was why she was here.

****

'Could I have your attention for a few moments, Ladies and Gentlemen?'

Conversations quickly subsided and very soon all faces were turned to where Claire stood, half-way up the staircase which led to the gallery.

'Nearly everyone seems to have arrived by now, so I'd like to welcome you to the first course to be held at Wildwood House. This is a very special moment for me. You can't imagine the thrill it gives me to see you all here.'

She paused and looked round the reception hall, taking in the range of expressions, mostly relaxed and curious, but a few slightly apprehensive, or perhaps just tired after their journeys.

'It has taken two years to make the necessary alterations to this lovely Georgian house, whilst retaining its original character, and many people have put in a lot of hard work to make sure everything is in order. Only three months ago, I had doubts whether we would be open on time. But here we are!' she said, spreading her arms in a brief expansive gesture that seemed to embrace the house, the people present and the surrounding countryside.

'I hope you like your rooms.'

She was relieved to hear murmurs of pleasure.

'I'm very pleased that we have several people here who live locally or just a few miles away, attending the course on a daily basis. You are especially welcome because I want this college to have a strong connection with the local community.

'Now, as you all know, the subject of our inaugural course is *Trees in Britain*, chosen partly as a tribute to the name of this house. We are exceptionally lucky to have Hugh Armstrong here as our principal tutor for this course. Some of you may have read his books. What Hugh doesn't know about trees probably isn't worth knowing! Tomorrow he will take you on a guided walk through Skipton Woods, near the castle.

'I'll mention just a few other things on the programme. You will find a schedule for each day in your rooms the previous evening. Rachel Williams, who lectures at a London art college, will talk to us about trees featured in paintings. My own contribution will be to share with you some poems and passages from novels in which trees are important. Perhaps you can think of some you'd like to add to the discussion. It will be quite informal.

'I was delighted to see quite a few of you arrive armed with easels, folding chairs, sketch pads, cameras etc. It looks as if our creative sessions will be popular! There will be plenty of opportunities to express yourselves as you wish - drawing, painting, photography, writing. Even if you haven't done anything like this before, I'm sure you'll feel inspired to try something. We have a range of art materials available, and Grace Weatherby, a local artist, will be here on Sunday to give useful tips about painting trees.

'Just one more thing. I'm sure you will have noticed that we are in a most beautiful part of England. Several walks have been included in the programme and you can explore the Dales on you own, if you wish. We have a good supply of maps and you are welcome to borrow them. Finally, if you have any queries or problems, I or our secretary, Diane, will be happy to help. Well, Hugh is waiting to give his introductory talk in the lecture room, so I won't delay you any longer. Enjoy the course!'

****

After introducing Hugh to the group, Claire found a vacant chair towards the back of the room and began to relax as Hugh launched into his talk. It was clear, right from the start, that trees were his passion.

He began with an overview of the history of trees in Britain, from the ending of the last Ice Age, around twelve thousand years ago, when the treeline began its northward advance as the climate gradually warmed. He showed maps to illustrate the march of the tree varieties - first the birches and aspens, followed by pines and hazel; then oak, lime, elm, and later ash, beech, maple, yew and holly - until the country was almost covered with forest - before man began clearing land for settled cultivation. He spoke of the ships of the English navy, built from native oak, of the *Victory* at Trafalgar, and the special affection the English have for the oak tree and all that it symbolises. He talked about woodland management and forestry, of coppicing and pollarding, of the construction of great barns, of homes - from the simplest to the grandest - based on wooden structures, of furniture-making, wood carving and forest sculptures...

...Jonquil had been right; the College would be a success. For the first time since the inception of her project, Claire felt confident, and while Hugh infused his audience with his unquenchable enthusiasm, she allowed herself to bask briefly in the joy of a dream fulfilled.

All this would have been impossible until two years ago when, on impulse, she had bought her first-ever National Lottery ticket. *HUGE WIN FOR LOCAL TEACHER CLAIRE!* the *Reporter* had crowed. Skimming through the article, she had winced at the inaccuracy: *Claire is the separated wife of Aidan Martindale, former Editor of this newspaper.* Until then, luck and coincidence had not played a conspicuous part in Claire's life. She had, in fact, won what was to her an unthinkable amount of money, enough perhaps - she really had no idea - to set up a college where adults could pursue their leisure interests, on short residential courses, with like-minded companions. Long sessions with her accountant brother, Charles, inspections of numerous properties, (suitable for conversion and pleasantly located), discussions with builders and later with decorators and furnishers, interviews with experts on many subjects to build up a panel of tutors, and recruitment of domestic staff, had dominated the last two years...

...Hugh was now answering questions from his audience.

'Is it true,' asked an earnest-looking elderly man, - the only person present wearing a suit - 'that sick and convalescent patients can recover more quickly if there are trees outside their hospital windows? I heard this claim made on a news broadcast recently.'

Claire smiled to herself. She knew what Hugh's opinion would be, but also that he would give sound reasons to support his view, whilst disclaiming any medical knowledge. A lively informality was developing now, as anecdotes were exchanged and a consensus reached - everyone felt better for seeing trees!...

...All the time Claire had devoted to establishing this college was now justified, and yet a niggle of guilt - pushed aside for many months - now surfaced in her mind. She could not remember giving the twins any support, or feeling much concern for them when they were preparing for their A levels last year. Still, they had emerged with high grades and would soon be finishing their gap years. Perhaps it was a good thing that she had been absorbed in her own project; Rory wouldn't have appreciated her fussing about whether he would be safe in Guatemala. Growing up in York, his imagination had been aroused at an early age by the *Jorvik* Viking Centre, and he had set his heart on becoming an archaeologist. He had been thrilled to be accepted to help with excavations on a Mayan temple for a year, before starting a degree course at Durham University.

Jonquil would begin her music studies at the Royal Northern College of Music in the autumn. A talented viola player, she was spending a year with a youth orchestra, at present giving concerts in Canada. Claire's guilt about neglecting her children was soothed by the rueful realisation that they were both doing very well with the minimum of attention from her. In three years' time, they would be independent adults.

On the sideboard in her flat at the College, she had an enlarged photograph of the twins which she had taken the day before Rory left for Guatemala. They were so alike, each with a mop of fair curly hair, freckles and expressive large blue eyes, and the same generous smile radiated from them both. She could see little of herself in either. Their visible inheritance was all from Aidan - but it was a long time since she'd seen that smile on his face.

****

'Tree hugging?'

'That's what he said.'

'I thought this was going to be a serious course - not an invitation to some weird cult! If that's what it is, I suggest we leave first thing tomorrow morning - and claim a refund for the fee before we go!'

The speaker, a stout man of sixty or so, was red in the face. He had driven from Grimsby with his wife, and, delayed by an accident on the M62, they had arrived too late to attend more than the last five minutes of the introductory talk on *Trees in Britain*.

'But Ted,' his wife said quietly, 'there must be a mistake. Remember the information in the brochure about the tutor - all those letters after his name?'

'I expect this chap's a substitute. I wouldn't be surprised if they advertised a well-qualified tutor to attract people, then replaced him by someone inferior!'

'I'm sure they wouldn't do that! Anyway, he introduced himself to us as Hugh Armstrong when he spoke to us on his way out. It's definitely him! He seemed very friendly, I thought.'

'Friendliness is not the point, Rhoda! I came here to learn something. Whatever your motives might be,' he added darkly.

Rhoda subsided. Ted was right about that. Her motives were different. Since they sold the shop and retired two years ago, she had felt a need for them to get out more, take up new interests, make new friends together. She had been disappointed to find that she felt relieved when Ted went out to play golf on Fridays, even though it meant that she was free to go into town and meet her cousin Liz for a long chat over coffee or to see a film. She wanted their life as a couple to be more enjoyable, but when she talked about making new friends, Ted always seemed suspicious, perhaps even jealous. She'd been delighted when he agreed to come on this course with her, but she had some misgivings nonetheless...

At five o'clock, the sun was still shining generously over the dale. The twelve people who had attended Hugh's talk had spilled out of the house and spread themselves over the lawn, standing or seated on the grass, drinking their tea, getting acquainted. Rhoda was looking for Hugh. He was easily found, his tall stature making him instantly recognisable, but he was surrounded by eager questioners. When she got her chance to speak, she felt almost overawed despite Hugh's easy and approachable manner.

'We arrived late - that is, my husband Ted and I. We only heard the last bit of your talk. Ted's a bit worried! You mentioned *tree-hugging*. Isn't that something a bit weird?' she said in a breathless rush.

Hugh and several people in the group laughed, but not unkindly.

'Not the way we do it!' Hugh answered, smiling. 'There's a lot of interest in very ancient trees just now, and an important part of the study is to measure them. Unless you're in the habit of carrying a tape measure around with you, when you walk in the woods, a good way to get an idea of the girth of one of those giants is by using what we call *adult hugs*. It does sound odd, doesn't it? All it means is that several people stand round the tree, reaching their arms out till they touch each other's fingertips. It's a useful way of getting an approximate measurement. I'll demonstrate the technique tomorrow in Skipton Woods.'

Rhoda smiled with relief.

'Ted!' she cried, hurrying across the grass to where he sat alone on a bench seat on the terrace, looking rather forlorn, she thought. She would be able to enjoy the course now.

Chapter 11

'I suppose we should all be planting trees in our gardens now, shouldn't we?'

Members of the course were relaxing in the lounge, drinking their after-dinner coffee. The speaker was Jessica, a woman in her early forties with short dark hair.

'Yes, Hugh answered,' provided that you don't pull out any shrubs to make way for them!'

'This carbon problem seems very complicated,' Rhoda sighed.

'Yes, it is. I've prepared some handouts giving a few suggestions about ways we can reduce our carbon footprints. It's a hugely important subject, and we're heading for real trouble if we don't all do our bit to help. But I don't want to overload this tree course in that direction.'

After a few moments' thought, Hugh added, 'But simply being aware of the beauty and value of trees - and talking about them to our friends, and most importantly of all, to children, will go a long way towards ensuring that trees are cultivated and conserved.'

'I'm sure that's true,' Jessica said. 'I think we take trees too much for granted.'

'Not in spring and autumn though, surely,' said Sandy, who had hardly spoken during dinner. 'Not when they look so fresh after the winter, and so spectacular in autumn - especially the horse chestnuts'.

'Yes, but most of the time we just regard them as part of the view, don't we? We don't notice how lovely they are, until someone cuts one down,' said Claire.

'You're right,' Rhoda agreed. 'I was really upset when our cherry tree was cut down, just before we had the front garden paved last year.'

'Don't I remember that!' said Ted. 'You cried all evening after it happened. But that tree had to go. It was in the way!'

There was a pause in the conversation. Then Jessica asked, 'How did you get interested in trees, Hugh?'

'I can't remember a time when I wasn't! But I certainly started young. I was about eleven when I discovered a hollow oak tree in a wood near where we lived. I used to take my books there to read, and my dog for company, and I'd be happy for hours sitting in the hollow tree - noticing the insect life, and seeing the birds and sometimes a squirrel or two, coming really close if I kept very still. I remember how I loved the smell of the wood and the texture of the bark - everything about it. My parents always knew where to find me if I didn't come home in time for meals. Often, I'd climb up into the highest branches - I still do, occasionally! It can feel quite dramatic when the wind is blowing - the noise of the leaves rushing about and the creaking of the branches, and the glimpses of the surrounding country and the feeling of moving with the wind instead of resisting it as we do on the ground. It's wonderful!'

Hugh's eyes shone with enthusiasm. After a short pause for breath, he resumed: 'A big tree is a marvellous ecosystem in itself. It supports a vast range of life - from mosses and lichens, fungi, ivy twining round its trunk, innumerable insect varieties and, of course, many kinds of birds, besides squirrels and other mammals.'

Unexpectedly, Ted spoke next. 'I've just remembered,' he said in a tone of surprise, 'the tree house I made with my brother when we were kids - about ten, I think I was,'

Rhoda looked at him in astonishment and said, 'I didn't think I'd be finding out new things about you after thirty-five years of marriage!'

'Well,' Ted added, 'I have to admit my motives weren't anything to be proud of. We went up there to eat food we'd helped ourselves to from the kitchen. When we got a bit older and more daring, to smoke cigarettes and look at some rather dubious magazines!'

'Your equivalent of the bicycle sheds, I suppose!' Sandy laughed, surprised to realise that she was enjoying herself.

'I never had a tree house,' said Jessica, 'but I remember reading a book about children who made one, and feeling very envious!'

'So did I! The Secret Seven, weren't they?'

Something about Jessica seemed familiar to Claire, and she was beginning to wonder where she had met her before, when the door opened and Claire saw Geoff Hunter, the caretaker, indicating that he needed to speak to her. She stood up reluctantly and went out of the lounge.

'Sorry to interrupt,' Geoff said in a confidential tone, ' but I thought I'd better consult you. There's a chap just arrived - seems a bit agitated - said his name's Peter Holmes. He was a bit vague about why he's come. Were you expecting anyone else for the course?'

Claire thought for a moment.

'The name doesn't ring a bell... There is one man who hasn't turned up. Quite a different name, though - Banks, Tim or Tom Banks, I think. I'll have a word with this man - Peter Holmes, did you say? Where is he?'

'He's in the hallway. I offered him a chair but he said he'd stay standing. He seemed a bit on edge.'

'Thanks, Geoff,' Claire said, and she walked to the front porch where the stranger was waiting.

'Mr Holmes? I'm Claire Martindale, the College Principal. What can I do for you?'

She gestured to a pair of chairs and they sat down.

'It's about Sandy Marlowe. She's come here on the course about trees.'

He paused. Claire smiled and nodded.

'I'm not sure if she's really able to cope.'

'Well, we don't put any pressure on people who come here. There's no exam or anything like that. And nobody need attend all the sessions if they don't want to. The emphasis is on learning through enjoyment.'

Claire hoped that didn't sound like a prepared speech. She'd said it so many times recently!

'Yes, she told me that, but... This is a bit awkward. I feel I'm breaking her confidence, but I'm quite worried about her.'

'You are a friend...a relative of Sandy's?'

'Well, partner, really. We've been together, on and off, for a couple of years. I feel responsible for her...you know?'

'Well, Sandy seems to be settling in quite happily, so far as I can judge. She's with the others in the lounge. You can go in and talk to her, or I could go in and tell her you're here, then she could come and talk to you out here.'

'No - not yet anyway. Please keep this confidential, won't you?'

'Of course.'

'Some months ago, Sandy had a terrible experience. A close friend of hers, called Val, was killed in a car accident.'

'How dreadful!'

'Yes. She's been in a terrible state - weeks and weeks off work, on strong medication. But she was determined to come on this course. It's the only thing she's shown any real interest in for a long time.'

He seemed uncertain whether to say more.

'Well,' Claire said, 'maybe this will be a turning point for her.'

'It might. But I'm afraid the associations might be too much for her.'

'Associations? I don't understand.'

'Well, she and Val had booked to come on this course together. It was Val's idea in the first place. She'd persuaded Sandy to come along. So there'll be painful feelings involved for her, won't there?'

'Well, you can judge that better than I can, obviously. But perhaps Sandy herself knows what's best for her?'

There was a silence during which Claire wondered. Had Peter travelled here just to tell her this, so that she would understand if Sandy should break down during her stay at Wildwood House? Or had he a more specific purpose?

'I had to come immediately.' He answered her unspoken question. 'Because she forgot these. I found them in the bathroom.'

He handed Claire a small brown bottle of tablets with Sandy's name printed on the label.

'I'll give them to her as soon as she emerges from the lounge,' Claire said.

'Thanks very much,' Peter said, but he seemed in no hurry to leave.

'It's rather late. Have you somewhere to stay tonight?'

'Well, I'd intended to drive straight back...'

'We could give you a bed for the night, in one of our cottages. You may have noticed them on your way up the drive. - Oh, but perhaps...'

Claire broke off, embarrassed, wondering whether Sandy would want Peter to share her room. Again, he seemed to read her thoughts.

'I want Sandy to feel she's doing exactly what she herself planned, so the cottage will be fine for me, thank you. Frankly, I'd have liked to be around all the time the course is on, just in the background, you know, but I have a business that can't be left for more than a day or two.'

Just then they heard movement from the lounge and the door opened. Peter caught a glimpse of Sandy, smiling as he hadn't seen her smile for a long time, in a group standing round a tall man he took to be Hugh Armstrong. Then he wondered, not for the first time, if Sandy was finding the twelve years' age difference between himself and her too great.

Claire handed the bottle of tablets back to Peter saying, 'You can give these to Sandy yourself.' Then she went quickly forward to break the news of his arrival to Sandy.

Chapter 12

At five o'clock, Sandy realised that further sleep was impossible. She felt too tense and agitated. She switched on the bedside lamp and reached for a paperback novel she had bought at the station bookstall yesterday morning. She had gone to sleep almost immediately last night but had woken, as she often did nowadays, around three a.m. - the deadest time of night - when she always saw everything in the worst possible light. Some writer had associated this time with the *dark night of the soul* and she agreed with him. She had heard that more people died around then than at any other hour. After about an hour, she had dozed off again, but not for very long. Now, noticing daylight between the curtains, she got out of bed and crossed the room to draw them back. Already, birds were pecking at the feeders, while further away, the *peewit* cry of lapwings and the thrilling, bubbling call of a curlew raised her spirits a little. She wondered how Peter was getting on in the cottage. No doubt he was fast asleep now. She felt gratitude to him for coming all that way to bring her pills. Without his support, she could never have got through the trauma she had experienced since Val's death.

She dressed in the warmest clothes she'd brought and stole downstairs for an early walk. The heavy bolts on the front door responded reluctantly to her cold fingers, and the noises of her exit resonated in the empty hall. The chill air struck her in the face and she hurried to pull from the pockets of her fleece the gloves she'd thought would be unnecessary. It was June, after all! Thick dew lay on the grass and her boots changed from light to dark brown within minutes. She walked briskly down the driveway and between the big stone gateposts into a lane which took her downhill. Then she climbed over a stile on her right and onto a footpath beside the river.

Sandy couldn't remember ever having been out so early in the day. She felt like an intruder on nature's private time, and slowed her pace instinctively. Cows turned and looked at her disdainfully, while sheep moved out of her way, bleating to their lambs which scampered in a flurry of white tails to their mothers' protection. Looking up the opposite hillside, she noticed a huge bird of prey hovering, almost stationary, until it swooped to the ground and flew off with some poor creature between its claws. She shuddered. Nature always reminded you of its fundamental cruelty, she thought, howerver lovely it appeared.

In the river, she watched fishes darting about, but soon it was the endlessly swirling movement of the water between the rocks close to the bank that intrigued her. The activity seemed random but, as she watched, she noticed that there was a definite pattern. After about six swirls, the pattern would change, maybe twice, and then the whole sequence would be repeated. It reminded her of what Peter had told her about Chaos Theory. He had studied physics at University, but had given up his degree course when his father died and he took over the family business. She'd been puzzled that Chaos Theory seemed to be about patterns, and what she was looking at now appeared to be an example of that.

Looking ahead, Sandy saw that she was approaching a farm and that her path skirted the farmyard wall. There was some activity going on and she could hear a hum of machinery coming from the buildings. Dogs barked as she approached, but no people were visible.

Beyond the farm, the river narrowed to pass through a rocky gorge below the path, which now continued through a small copse of alders and willows, full of the chirping of birds. Emerging from the wood, Sandy found a seat beside the path and sat down to enjoy the view. Val would have loved this. Tears welled up, but she told herself sternly, as she had done countless times since the accident, that Val was dead, and the only thing she could do for her was to enjoy the interests and causes that she had shared with her and try to promote them. She was unsure how to do this, but Hugh's suggestions for bringing trees to people's attention had given her some ideas to work on, and would help her to come to terms with what had happened... But it wouldn't help Val. At best it would only help her to feel less guilty about her own survival... Recognising the familiar negative pattern of her thought, she pulled herself together, stood up, and started walking briskly back towards Wildwood House.

Once she was in the lane again, she saw someone walking towards her - no doubt one of the locals, Sandy assumed. It was a woman, younger than herself, dressed in jeans and a sweatshirt. As she approached, Sandy noticed that the girl's clothes were shabby and none too clean. Instinctively she moved to the other side of the lane, but the girl crossed over too and came up to her.

'Good morning,' she said, articulating the words carefully, her accent a far cry from the Yorkshire speech Sandy had expected to hear.

'Hello,' she replied with a faint smile, stopping reluctantly.

The girl's face was pale, almost grey, and there was a look of supplication in her face and manner.

'I have not eaten,' she said, her voice tremulous now, as if she were close to tears. Then she raised a hand to her mouth.

Sandy could easily believe what she said. The girl was almost distressingly thin.

'I'm sorry,' Sandy began. Then, groping in the deep pockets of her fleece jacket, she found a cereal bar that she'd forgotten about and handed it to her, ashamed that this was all she had to offer. The girl took it, with such a look of gratitude that Sandy felt even more embarrassed, though wondering all the while why she was in such a plight. The last place she would have expected to find someone begging was in the Yorkshire Dales.

'Do you live near here?' she asked, careful to speak distinctly.

'No, no. Far, very far away.' An eloquent wave of the arm spoke to Sandy of infinite distance.

Then she added, 'Thank you! Thank you!'

She clearly did not want to talk. No doubt she just couldn't wait to eat the totally inadequate cereal bar, Sandy thought, as she heard the wrapper being ripped off immediately after they parted.

A few minutes later, Sandy saw Peter coming down the lane.

'I thought you must have gone for a walk, when I couldn't find you,' he said. 'What a glorious morning!' he added after a kiss.

'Did you sleep well in the cottage?'

'Pretty well - a few noises from next door in the small hours - water running, toilet being flushed. But I soon got off to sleep again. If we go back to the House now, we can have breakfast together, then I really must get a move on.'

'It was so good of you to come all that way, Peter. I know it wasn't just to give me the tablets - you could have put them in the post yesterday'.

'I couldn't stop myself, Sandy. I hate to have to leave you now. You will phone me, won't you? I'll be thinking about you all the time.'

'Yes, of course I will. But don't worry - I'll be fine.'

The house had come to life by the time they walked in, and with appetites sharpened by the fresh air, they did justice to the cooked breakfast before Peter drove away.

****

'Is something bothering you, Claire?' Diane asked.

She'd noticed Claire coming in and out of the office several times for no apparent reason, looking out of the window, then at her watch, frowning.

'No...no,' Claire replied rather abstractedly, 'I just wish they'd get on their way and let us have the place to ourselves.'

Something was definitely wrong. The impatience in Claire's voice was so untypical.

'Yes,' Diane said, 'but I expect they'll be away for a good while. Some of them will want to go round the Castle after Hugh's guided tour of the woods. They'll probably make a day of it.'

'I expect you're right,' Claire answered, and out she strode again.

Her disquiet had begun when she spoke to Peter at breakfast time and, asking if he had slept well in *Curlews* cottage, had learned about the noises next door.

'Oh, no! Not rats again!' she had exclaimed, but when he had explained about running water and a flushing toilet, she'd become seriously alarmed, and just managed to stop herself from saying that there should not have been anyone in the adjoining cottage last night. This was something she must investigate promptly and discuss with Geoff Hunter, the caretaker. No doubt there was a logical explanation - perhaps noises from the main house were audible in the cottages, although that seemed unlikely in view of the distance between them.

Hugh was now leading his group down the drive at last, so Claire followed them as far as the two cottages, anxious to solve the mystery and in some trepidation lest she should confront an intruder. She opened the door of *Swifts*, the right-hand cottage, and entered warily.

'Anyone in here?' she called.

The main room, with its small table, chairs and sofa, looked immaculate - cushions plumped and neatly arranged. She glanced into the kitchen. Nothing seemed to have been moved. She climbed the stairs to the bedroom. The bed looked exactly as she had told the cleaner to leave it - not made up, but with the pillows, and blankets folded on top. Clean sheets and pillowcases lay folded on the bedside chair. The bathroom, too, showed no signs of use, just a few drops of water in the shower tray, but they could easily have leaked from the nozzle. She concluded that the noises Peter had heard had been caused by the hot water tank which served both cottages, refilling after his own ablutions - it was slow to fill up. Perhaps he had been half asleep and misinterpreted what he had heard.

Then Claire noticed the small guest soap on the wash basin. It had clearly been used - only about half the bar remained. She hurried downstairs to take a closer look at the kitchen. The basic supply of tea and coffee bags and sachets of sugar were still there and looked untouched, though Claire couldn't be sure how many had been provided.

She looked in the pedal bin - nothing there. The kettle stood on the worktop. She touched its side - and felt a slight warmth. Someone had indeed spent the night - or part of it - here, and had been at pains to conceal the fact.

The front door had been secure, but what about the kitchen door? - Locked as usual, its key in place on the inside. A window next to the door looked closed but it was not fastened down, its catch rather flimsy. It would have been possible for someone to squeeze through the window, she thought, imagining how she herself might have climbed in. Geoff should have replaced the catch with a more reliable one - and he was the next person she must see.

'What time did you check the cottages last night?' she asked when she found Geoff.

'About ten-thirty. That chap who arrived late was in *Curlews* by then - the lights were on. I checked the door of *Swifts* - nothing untoward there.'

'No lights on?'

'Not a sign of life.'

'The kitchen window wasn't properly fastened.'

'It's a bit loose. I'll put a new catch on it today.'

'Yes. Do that as soon as possible. Someone has been in that cottage during the night. The man who arrived late last night was in *Curlews*, and he just happened to mention noises next door! - Running water etc. If I hadn't had a word with him before he left this morning, I'd never have known we'd had an intruder. And there was hardly any evidence in the cottage. Whoever it was, he covered his tracks very well.'

'I'll keep a thorough watch on the place from now on,' said Geoff. 'I'll stay around till eleven-thirty tonight, in case there's any trouble.'

'I'd appreciate that, Geoff.'

After a pause, Claire said, 'You know this district well, don't you?'

'Lived in the Dales all my life - I should think I do!'

'Are there some tramps in these parts?'

'If there are, they don't draw attention to themselves. They'd much more likely sleep in a barn than go inside a house. That's why they're vagrants, I suppose. Anyway, they'd be very unlikely to sleep in the same place two nights running, so I don't think we've much to worry about. Whoever that was, he's probably miles away by now.'

****

On the bus to Skipton, cars having been left - reluctantly by some - at Wildwood House, Sandy found herself sitting next to a tall, burly American, fortyish, she guessed.

'Hi!' he greeted her, with a warm handshake, 'Rex Blomberg - and you are...?'

'Sandy Marlowe...How do you do?'

His voice was surprisingly quiet.

'We were at different tables at dinner last night, of course; and afterwards those two guys at the front insisted on taking me to a real English pub - *The Blue Bell* at Kettlewell - the first one I've ever been in.'

'Did you like it?'

'Sure I did - steeped in history - the old coaching days! They told me that the little road through the village used to be a major route through Yorkshire - must have been a good while ago! There's another inn built almost at right angles. We sat outside with our drinks, looking at the patrons of *The Racehorses* across the way, and they sat looking at us!'

'I expect you'll find some of our ways rather quaint and old-fashioned,' Sandy said, smiling. 'And how do you come to be on a course like this, Rex?'

'I'm a lecturer in dendrology at Blakes University, Connecticut. I've just arrived to begin a year's sabbatical in Britain. This course seemed a pleasant way to start, before the new academic year begins. I know Hugh slightly - met him when he came lecturing in the States. How about you, Sandy?'

'Well, I live in Southport. I'm a librarian in Liverpool.'

'And how did you get interested in trees?'

'Well, it was partly through a friend of mine. She suggested coming on this course, but....'

Even before she faltered, Rex noticed a change in her tone and an expression of distress on her face. A change of topic seemed necessary, and he was about to comment on the Dales scenery, when Sandy spoke.

'How did you travel here?'

'Flew to Manchester, then picked up a hired car I'd booked in advance. The drive came as rather a shock - specially when I got to this Yorkshire countryside. It took a lot longer than I'd expected - these narrow, winding roads you have over here! We Americans just aren't used to them!'

'And we British don't usually relish the prospect of travelling those vast distances on your freeways!'

They laughed.

'Which way did you travel?' Rex asked. 'I'm not sure where Southport is.'

'It's about fifteen miles from Liverpool, on the west coast. I came by train actually, then by bus the last few miles. I don't drive nowadays.'

'Well, good for you! It's time more of us - that includes myself - gave up motoring to lessen global warming.'

Sandy gave a weak smile. Rex had attributed a virtuous motive to what really amounted to cowardice. She should explain - but no, she couldn't do that.

'Henceforward!' Hugh proclaimed, with a histrionic gesture towards Skipton Castle. The Wildwood House party had left the bus and now stood in the main street, gazing up at the two massive towers that flanked the gatehouse, where its French motto, *DÉSORMAIS*, dating from Norman times, declared in stone the confidence of the ancient, influential Clifford family.

****

Most of the time in Skipton Woods was spent in learning to identify the different varieties. Hugh told his students to look at the overall shape of the tree, its bark, the shape of its leaves, its flowers, fruit or method of seed dispersal, depending on the season.

'The only ones I'm sure about are oak and horse chestnut,' Rhoda said, 'Their leaves are so distinctive.'

'Sycamore is easy, too. Its leaves are shaped like the maple leaf on the Canadian flag,' said Hugh.

'They're the ones that get covered in black spots in the autumn, aren't they?'

'Listen!' Les exclaimed a few minutes later, 'What's that drumming sound?'

'A woodpecker, isn't it?' Jessica asked. 'Which kind, though? Aren't there several?'

'That's a Great Spotted, most likely,' said Hugh. 'The green ones rarely drum.'

'What causes the drumming?'

'It's how they announce their presence - very effectively, too! - hammering the tree trunk with their bill. They feed by digging out insects from under the bark, but drumming isn't part of that. Their colouring is very striking - black, white and red. So we may well see that one we can hear now.'

They walked on carpets of bluebells and wild garlic with its tiny star-like flowers and its characteristic smell, quite unlike the better-known cooking variety. When Hugh had pointed out some less well-known tree varieties - hornbeam, sweet chestnut - and explained something of the history of these woods, which had been owned by Skipton Castle for almost a thousand years, the party gradually broke up into smaller groups. Rhoda and Jessica were eager to collect some leaves, useful for tomorrow's art session, most wanted to have a look round the Castle, and they could all return to Wildwood in their own time, using the local bus service.

Strolling along a path that overlooked the Eller Beck, Sandy saw a flash of brilliant blue below.

'Kingfisher, wasn't it?' exclaimed Rex, who was just behind her.

'I've never seen one before, except in photos and films - What a gorgeous colour!' Sandy exclaimed. 'I'm glad I didn't blink just then, or I'd have missed it! I'll never forget that moment.'

'Nor I,' Rex said, taking her hand.

She looked up at him, suddenly shy. They walked on in silence for several minutes. Then Rex spoke.

'I don't know if you've heard of Henry Thoreau', he said.

'I know where to find him on the library shelves! But I don't know his work, I'm ashamed to admit.'

'He was one of our great writers about nature. He spent two years living in a hut he built out in the wilds - place called Walden Pond, near Concord, Massachusetts. It was an experiment in self-sufficiency. Then he wrote about the experience in a book called *Walden, a Life in the Woods*, describing his life there - farming, plants, and philosophy, too. Unfortunately, his best-known saying is *Most men lead lives of quiet desperation*. Not a very cheerful thought!'

Immediately he wished he hadn't said it. Sandy's face had clouded. He'd noticed how animated she looked when she was interested in something but, caught off guard, her habitual expression was sad, anxious.

'Sorry!' he said, 'I've spoilt this beautiful place for you with that dismal quote!'

'I'm all right,' she said, rather brusquely, disengaging her hand from his. 'Let's walk on,'

She went ahead. After a few minutes, she stopped suddenly and turned to him.

'Oh, look!' she said in an awestruck whisper.

A few metres ahead of them, almost on the path, stood a roe deer, looking straight at them, eyes bright and ears twitching. Then, with a brief glimpse of white rump and a flick of its tail, it fled into the tree cover..

'Aren't we lucky?' Sandy exclaimed.

'We are indeed.'

They were walking side by side again now, mostly in silence, broken occasionally by comments on the flora and fauna they noticed.

'This walk has done me a lot of good,' Sandy said after some minutes' silence. 'I nearly didn't come on this course. In fact I nearly turned back when I got here yesterday. I didn't think I could face it.'

Rex waited. They had stopped walking.

'Something awful happened last winter. A friend of mine told me about this course - I mentioned that before...'

Rex nodded.

'We were going to come here together, but then ...I killed her!'

It was some moments before Rex spoke.

'No!' he said vehemently, 'No! I don't believe it! I don't believe you would kill anyone! No! I won't believe it!' Each *No!* was said with greater emphasis.

'Well, that's what it amounted to. We were in my car. I was driving, heading for Liverpool from Southport on a dual carriageway - a route I used to take every day to work. We were just passing an airfield on our right. Suddenly, there was this terrible noise, from behind us, I thought. Then I saw a helicopter coming in very low over the road - coming in to land, I suppose. I must have been so distracted by it that I didn't see a van that must have stopped suddenly on the left, just in front of us. We went straight into the van. I was completely unhurt and so was the van driver, but Val....'

She couldn't finish. Tears which seemed as if they had been dammed up for weeks now poured down her cheeks. A few minutes later, the present moment imposed itself over her memories.

'I do apologise, Rex. I don't know what came over me to say all this to someone I hardly know.'

'No need to apologise,' he said gently. 'I'm glad you thought I was someone you could talk to about it. I don't suppose this is any consolation, but there must be lots of people around who've had similar experiences, and feel as you do.'

She was glad that he didn't start suggesting ways to try and forget about the tragedy. She'd heard them all from well-meaning friends.

'Now,' he said as they were approaching the exit from the woods, 'let's go and have a look round this castle!'

****

'Would you like to see *The Guardian?*' Hugh asked Sandy. 'I've finished with it now.'

'No, thanks. I've just read enough gloom and doom in this paper. Teenagers stabbing each other!' she answered.

Everyone had now returned from Skipton and most of the group were in the lounge enjoying a drink from the bar before dinner.

"Did you find anything interesting in the paper?' Rex asked Hugh.

'There's a piece about asylum seekers,' Hugh answered. 'The Government is planning to speed up the asylum process - apparently they're months behind schedule.'

'They should stop them getting into Britain in the first place, ' said Ted. 'This country's too small to take in all these foreigners.'

'I agree,' Les Harvey said. 'They should be turned back at the ports before they even set foot here. Britain's become a soft touch for asylum seekers.'

'I would like to believe that our country was a safe haven for refugees, but we seem to be letting them down nowadays,' Jessica said quietly in the pause that followed Les's outburst.

'What a difference a word makes!' Sandy said. '*Refugee* arouses sympathy much more than *asylum seeker*, doesn't it?'

'These aren't real refugees, though, are they?' Les continued. 'Most of them come here to take advantage of our health and social services. They're looking for a cushy life, if you ask me. My Dad died because he couldn't get his cancer operation soon enough. If you ask me, these hospital waiting lists are due to all these foreigners blocking up the system.'

There was an uncomfortable pause, then Jessica said:

'I'm sorry about your father, Les. I can understand how you must feel. I'm not sure if asylum seekers can get operations, though, except in emergencies.'

Then Ted took up Les's theme:

'They sneak in illegally in the backs of lorries, don't they? If they were above board, they'd go through the customs, show their passports, visas or whatever. - Probably criminals, some of them.'

'I think it's very risky letting all those people in, with the danger of terrorism nowadays,' Rhoda added, 'But I do feel sorry for the genuine refugees. Some of them are escaping from dreadful conditions in their own countries.'

'Well, don't get too sentimental about them,' Les replied. 'The reason we have better conditions here is because of all the efforts people made in the past. That's what we've inherited from our ancestors. We don't have to share it with all and sundry!'

'And look at that lot who came to Morecambe Bay to steal work from the local cockle pickers!' Tony added.

At this there was an outcry from those who had seen a television documentary on the subject.

'Those people had come all the way from China in horrible conditions!' Sandy interrupted angrily. 'They didn't have any choice where they worked. They were taken to Morecambe by gang masters. Blame them, not those poor refugees! And nearly all of them were drowned. The tide came in so fast, they couldn't escape.'

'Yes,' said Rhoda, 'I saw that programme. That woman who survived, she'd come from China because her husband had deserted her and their baby, and she couldn't earn enough money to support the child. Just imagine how desperate she must have been, to leave her baby with relatives and travel all that way? She was a genuine refugee, surely?'

'What do you think, Rex?' Sandy asked him, after a pause in the discussion.

'I don't know enough about the subject to comment. But Britain seems a very small country to have so many more people coming to live here. In the States, the situation's different. Many thousands of people cross the Rio Grande from Mexico into the US every year. But that's a far cry from Connecticut, where I live.'

There was a lull in the conversation. People were beginning to feel that enough had been said on that topic, and were looking at the clock, hoping dinner would be announced soon. Then Jessica held up a newspaper she'd been reading and said,

'Did anyone see this news item? *Asylum Seeker rescues Toddler from Lake,*' she read, *'Four-year-old Amy Thomas was paddling at the edge of a boating lake in Scarborough yesterday, while her mother chatted to a friend nearby, when she ventured too far out, lost her footing and screamed as she disappeared below the surface. Before Amy's mother had time to react, a young man who was fishing nearby strode rapidly into the water, then swam to the rescue. Amy's mother, Debbie Thomas, told our reporter, "I thanked the man for saving Amy's life, and asked his name, but he would only tell me his first name, Joe. He said he was an asylum seeker. Then he grabbed his fishing gear and ran off." '*

'Well,' Hugh said, 'That seems a good note to end our discussion of that subject,' as the gong sounded for dinner.

Chapter 13

Six o'clock on Sunday morning.

Claire awoke with a headache, decided she needed a couple of aspirins and went into the small kitchen of her flat, which overlooked the vegetable garden at the back of the house. She put the kettle on to make a cup of tea, and gazed out of the window while waiting for the water to boil. It had rained heavily during the night and the earth looked sodden, with small puddles in places, but in the early-morning sunlight the freshly washed grass looked inviting, and when she had swallowed her aspirins and drunk half the mug of tea, she dressed and went down to take a closer look at the vegetable patch. The fresh air would help dispel the headache.

The broad beans were already producing tiny pods, and the mange tout looked beautiful when Claire squatted down to inspect the plants closely, translucent with the sunlight behind them, clearly showing the tiny peas within. One or two yellow flowers were just beginning to show on the courgette plants. They would need care; in this year's wet conditions, courgettes could easily be spoiled by mould.

Claire walked along the narrow crazy-paved path which led to the greenhouse and was looking at the tomatoes within, just beginning to set, when her attention was distracted by a slight sound which seemed to come from the garden shed, just beyond the greenhouse. Probably the cat, she thought. Then it came again, unmistakeably human this time, however unlikely. Someone was crying - a child, perhaps - and trying to stifle their sobs. The despair which the sounds conveyed sent a chill through Claire, as she walked quietly to the door of the shed and tapped gently, fearing to startle the occupant. The crying stopped immediately and there was silence. Gently she opened the door and saw a figure huddled on the floor, under the potting bench - a young woman, who slowly raised her head and looked at Claire, like a cornered animal that realises it cannot escape its captor.

'Don't be frightened,' Claire said, 'I won't harm you.'

The girl's expression changed to one of supplication, but she did not speak. Claire knelt down on the wooden floor, lessening the impression of dominance, though the gesture was instinctive.

'Please,' the girl said in a foreign accent unfamiliar to Claire. 'Will you help me, please?'

She was shivering.

'I can take you somewhere warm, and get you something to eat. But who are you?'

'My name is Maria. I had to leave my country...'

She broke off momentarily, her face contorted, then continued:

'I came to England to ask for asylum. I waited a long time for a decision. The decision was no - I must return to my own country.' Her voice rose. 'I cannot return! I will be sent to prison! I think they will kill me!'

Claire took one of Maria's cold hands in hers, hoping to reassure her, though wondering what grave crime the girl had committed to make her fear such consequences if she went home. But the immediate problem dominated Claire's thoughts. To avoid arousing curiosity, she would take Maria to one of the cottages and bring her some food. Then she would decide what should be done.

'My name is Claire. Come with me, Maria.'

Claire stood up, and Maria emerged from below the bench, getting up with some difficulty from the discomfort she had endured all night.

'You can bring your bag with you,' Claire added, on noticing a shabby canvas holdall on the bench. She led the way out of the shed and along the path which brought them to the two cottages. Producing her bunch of keys, Claire opened the door of *Swifts*.

'I think you've been in here already, haven't you?' Claire asked, 'The night before last?'

Maria's pale cheeks flushed.

'Yes. I am sorry. I was so afraid...'

'You left it very clean and tidy, anyway.'

The cottage felt chilly. Claire switched on the heating and the hot water system. Then she put the kettle on to make a pot of tea, which she placed with a cup and saucer and a sachet of sugar on the sitting-room table.

'Now,' she said, speaking slowly and clearly, 'I'm going to the main house to fetch some food for you. Please do not go outside. I will come back soon. Don't be frightened. You are safe here,' she added, with a reassuring smile, noticing Maria's look of dismay at being left alone.

'I understand. You are a kind lady. Thank you very much.'

From the kitchen in her flat, Claire quickly collected bread, milk, eggs, butter, cheese, a carton of orange juice, a pot of jam, an apple and a slab of date and walnut cake and put them in a bag. Feeling furtive in her own domain, she stole along the corridor to the linen room and took out a woollen blanket, a bath towel and a large tablet of soap. Thankful that none of the guests or staff were around yet, she hurried back to the cottage, where she found Maria looking at a book she had picked up from a row on the windowsill.

'Ah! You've found something to read!' Claire said, smiling. 'Which one is that?'

'*Jane Eyre,*' Maria answered. 'I know this - I read it in my own language in my country. It is a very good book! Perhaps I can read it in English now.'

'Yes. It's one of my favourites, too,' said Claire, glad to have established some common ground, as she set out the food on the worktop.

'Now I'm going to cook you a breakfast. When you've finished it, you can tell me your story.'

She cut a thick slice of bread, spread butter generously on it, handed it on a plate to Maria, and poured her a glass of orange juice. While Maria satisfied her immediate hunger, Claire cooked her an omelette, adding tomatoes and some grated cheese, laid a place on the table and set the meal, together with toast and jam, before Maria. At first, the girl seemed too overcome to eat, until Claire went upstairs to make up the bed and put towels and soap in the bathroom.

'Now,' said Claire, when Maria had finished eating, 'I've made us a fresh pot of tea. Let's sit on the sofa, and you can tell me more about yourself.'

'Thank you for this food, Claire. It is very good. I have not eaten such things for a long time.'

Claire smiled encouragingly, forcing herself to wait patiently for the girl to tell her story, aware that the main house would be coming to life and someone would want to speak to her very soon.

'I am a refused asylum seeker,' Maria began. 'I have nowhere to go. My country, Alborus, is in eastern Europe - not a member of the European Union.' She paused. 'My father was a journalist. His name was well-known. He was imprisoned for criticising the injustice of our government. He said to me, "Maria, go to England, if you can, and write about our country. The world should hear of our troubles." Soon after he went to prison, my father died - killed, I think - he was not ill before. So I wrote for newspapers about injustice, and I was threatened with prison if I wrote about politics. They told me to write about clothes, health, gardening in magazines for women. So I took Father's advice.'

'How did you get to England, Maria?'

'At first, I thought it was impossible. Father had been banned from travelling abroad, and I would not be allowed to go either. I tried for jobs on women's magazines, but they knew my name and thought I would bring trouble to them - even though I would only be writing about domestic subjects. I am a qualified schoolteacher, and I taught young children before I started writing, but I was no longer allowed to work in a school, except as a cleaner - very little money and no chance of better work.'

Maria paused in her narrative.

'So you felt that you had to get away, somehow?'

'Yes. Then someone told me about an organisation which helps people to go to EU countries - no choice of which country. All very secret. I thought it was worth taking the risk. I paid a lot of money to travel in a truck with a lot of other people. Our papers were taken from us, so we had no way to prove our identity - very worrying. It was a horrible journey. I thought it would never end. But at last I was in England!'

She paused and drank some more tea.

'What did you do then?'

'When we arrived in London, there was another container truck going north. I went on this as far as Bradford, to stay with a family distantly related to mine. Then I applied for asylum in Britain.'

Maria yawned.

'Sorry, I am so tired! I cannot tell all the details yet. I waited from early February until the middle of May, and then received my final refusal. The British Government told me to go back home!'

A choking sob interrupted Maria's narrative for a few moments. Claire was at a loss for words. Then Maria resumed, her tone suddenly loud with anger:

'The law of England says no refugee who faces danger in his own country will be sent back there. I trusted this country, but it has betrayed me!'

She paused, her thin shoulders shaking, and tears trickled down her pale cheeks, which she wiped with a sodden handkerchief. Claire handed her a packet of tissues which she had brought from her flat.

'You won't betray me, Claire?' Maria asked in a strangled voice.

'No, of course I won't betray you,' Claire answered warmly. Then she wondered what this promise, so readily given, might have committed her to. She was out of her depth. Like most people, she knew little about the asylum system. She realised that she needed more information, quickly.

'I have to go now,' she said, more abruptly than she'd intended, and Maria looked startled.

'I will see what I can do to help you. But please don't go out of this cottage. The main house here is a residential college for adults, so there are quite a lot of people about.'

'Yes. I saw the notice near the gate.'

'They're nice people, but it is best not to draw attention to yourself.'

'That has become my way of life in England! But,' she added, looking around the cottage sitting room, and smiling bravely, 'Here you have given me warmth, and food and books! I will stay in here until you tell me to go.'

****

Claire took refuge in her flat, where she paced about, deploring her ignorance, wishing she'd taken more notice of news items and discussions about asylum seekers. The term evoked for her, as for most people, a negative image - people coming to Britain in search of a better life, arriving here illegally, causing problems for the Government and local authorities, resented by the established population. What were the legal implications of providing accommodation for a failed asylum seeker? She must get information, she thought, eyeing her recently-bought laptop on the sideboard and wishing that she'd spent more time learning how to use it. She could, perhaps, ask Diane to do an internet search on the office computer. Diane was very obliging, but... This line of thought was suddenly blocked by the urgent need to tell Geoff about Maria, before he started his morning round, which would involve especially a check on the cottages! She looked at the clock - 7.45. He was probably on the premises already.

She found him in the hallway.

'There's something I need to tell you,' she said. 'Let's go outside.'

She led the way along the footpath across the front lawn, so that they would not be overheard.

'The person who slept in *Swifts* cottage on Friday night spent last night in the garden shed. She's a young woman - an asylum seeker. I found her there early this morning.'

'Hell!' Geoff exclaimed. 'Sorry, Claire. But you'd better report her to the police at once!'

'I'm not going to do that. She's very distressed, and half-starved by the look of her. I've taken her back to *Swifts* and cooked her a breakfast. She can stay there for the time being. She speaks English quite well. She's had a terrible time.'

'In a few days' time, that cottage will be full of asylum seekers! She'll let her friends know she's found a safe billet and we'll be overrun with them!'

'You must be exaggerating, Geoff. I can't believe that would happen.'

'If it does, I'll be the one who has to deal with them, won't I? It'll be too late then to start debating about it. Think about the security angle, Claire. I'm responsible for the safety of this place and the people in it.'

'Geoff, we're not talking about criminals. This girl, Maria, she's a refugee. Her father died in prison for criticising their country's government. She's in danger for writing about politics too.'

'Well, if people stick their necks out like that, they have to accept the consequences - not expect other countries to bail them out. Anyway, she may have made up that story to persuade you to take her in. You're too soft-hearted, Claire. Some of these people are just scroungers - out for what they can get, I shouldn't wonder.'

'Maybe some of them are. But I'm sure Maria isn't like that. Just think what courage it must take to leave your own country and put yourself at the mercy of a foreign country's officials.'

'Well, as caretaker here, I've got to put my foot down. I can't put the people here at risk. It's when people get desperate that they turn to crime - stealing food, to start with, then worse things. There is real danger in letting asylum seekers in here. If you won't call the police, I will!'

Looking him straight in the eye, fully aware of what this would mean to him, she said quietly, 'If you do that, it will cost you your job!'

Six months ago, Geoff had been accused of molesting a small girl at a school where he worked as caretaker. He had been suspended from work while the accusation was investigated, and although he had been completely exonerated and the accusations proved to have been malicious, he had had no success in finding another job until Clare appointed him caretaker at Wildwood House. Without a word, he turned but, just as he was about to walk back to the house, Claire said, 'Can I have your word that you won't contact the police for the next twenty-four hours?'

'Yes,' he said tersely, and strode briskly away.

Claire turned her back to Wildwood and leant on the drystone wall, looking over the valley at the hillside beyond, as if unable to cope with the complexity of her responsibilities. Just a few days earlier, she had questioned her capability to run the College, but compared with this totally unexpected problem, the role of College Principal seemed well within her competence. The pivot round which Wildwood's students, tutors and domestic staff functioned smoothly so far, Claire now felt disorientated and ignorant through the arrival of one helpless stranger!

Five minutes later, she turned and walked resolutely back to the house. The cheerful breakfast sounds of conversation and of cutlery on china greeted her as she passed the dining room. She looked in at the office and said 'Good morning' to Diane whose confident smile reassured her a little, but who looked at Claire rather strangely when she said that she would be in the flat and must not be disturbed for an hour or so, except in emergency.

The moment before Claire had turned back towards the house, she had made a decision. Once in her safe haven, she closed the door and picked up the telephone. Aidan would be surprised. They hadn't spoken to each other for nearly a month, but in the present crisis, it was to him that her thoughts instinctively turned. They had lived disconnected lives for several years now, but had occasionally poured out their troubles to each other, and on this occasion, he could give her some specific help.

'Martindale.'

His glum tone contrasted with the beauty of the name, which Claire had been delighted to adopt when she married him. He hadn't been glum then.

'Aidan, it's Claire.'

'Well, well!' he said in the sarcastic tone she had grown to hate, 'Fancy remembering me in your hour of glory! Something's gone wrong, has it?'

'No - well, it isn't really about the College.'

He noticed the strain in her voice.

'What's up, Claire?'

'I need some information, some advice.'

She paused, wondering how to begin.

'Didn't you write an article about asylum seekers sometime last year?'

'I did. It was in *The Guardian* - one of my more successful projects, in a lifetime of mediocrity.'

Aidan hadn't changed much. What others took for ironic self-deprecation, Claire knew to be bitterness - made all the worse by her own recent success.

'But why bring that up?'

'A destitute young woman has turned up here at the College. She applied for asylum in Britain months ago, but was refused, and she tells me there's no financial support for failed asylum seekers. Can this be true?'

'If I remember rightly, financial support stops twenty-one days after an asylum claim is refused. They're supposed to return to their country of origin by then, and they're not allowed to get employment here. It's an iniquitous system. I'll get that article up on the computer and print a copy for you.'

'Thanks, Aidan, I'd be very glad of that. I'm worried about the legal position. Geoff Hunter, the caretaker here, says I should report Maria to the police. Am I doing anything illegal letting her stay here for a while?'

'Strictly speaking, I think you probably should tell the police, but I don't think they'd want to know about her. Nobody knows what to do with failed asylum seekers. They're an embarrassment to the Government, local authorities etc. Many asylum seekers can't be deported because their countries of origin won't issue visas, and many of them have lost, or been robbed of passports etc. on their way here. Some would do anything rather than return home to brutality, civil war, death threats. All of which means that there are many thousands of these unfortunate people living in destitution in this country.'

'How dreadful,' Claire said, 'Anyway, you think I won't be breaking the law?'

'The law seems to be very vague on the subject. I very much doubt if anyone will care. She'll be one person fewer to embarrass the authorities. But you wouldn't be able to give her paid employment. She won't be entitled to National Insurance.'

'I hadn't got as far as thinking about employment for Maria. I just want to provide food and shelter, and to make her feel safe and know that somebody cares for her.'

'I don't think you'll get into any trouble for just doing that. Anyway, can you download this article onto your computer?'

Download! - Oh no! Claire thought.

'Sorry, I haven't learned how to do that yet!'

She felt helpless and foolish.

'I'll send it as an email attachment. Then you can read it on the screen and print a copy, if you want to.'

'How do I do that?'

She heard a sigh of exasperation.

'Have you noticed there's sometimes a paperclip symbol next to an email title?'

He was laughing at her, she felt sure.

'Yes - I wondered what they were for.'

'Now you know! Just click on the paperclip, and the attachment comes up.'

'I hope I'll be able to do that.'

'Course you will! Just take it slowly, and don't panic!'

'Couldn't you just put a copy in the post?'

'You need the info quickly, though. Best try email.'

'OK - Thanks, Aidan. I just haven't had time to get to grips with computers yet. I absolutely dread my secretary being absent from work. She's got everything on the computer and I wouldn't be able to operate it! And how are things at home?' she asked.

'You still think of the old place as home, then, do you?'

She didn't answer this.

'Jonquil's back. Did you know?'

Claire was shocked. She'd forgotten her daughter's card announcing her imminent return to York, when the youth orchestra returned from Canada.

'Is she there now?'

'Yes - but fast asleep! Or she was when I tapped on her door half an hour ago. Jetlagged, I imagine.'

'Give her my love. I'll ring her soon. Aidan, I'll have to go now, but thanks again for your help.'

'Bye, Claire. I hope things work out all right.'

Which things? Claire wondered, as she switched the phone off.

****

Claire and Maria were not the only early risers at Wildwood House on Sunday morning. Jessica had been to early communion at the nearest Anglican church and she returned in meditative mood. Being responsible for three churches in rural East Yorkshire had proved more challenging than she had imagined. Less than three years since her ordination, she wondered, sometimes, whether she could cope much longer. Practicalities such as the urgent need to raise money to mend the tower at St. James's before it collapsed - 'Only a matter of time,' the diocesan architect had warned her - got in the way of the work she had felt strongly called to do - the pastoral duties of a parish priest, the counselling she had believed herself to be especially suited to, after her experience with the Samaritans, helping troubled people to work through their problems. The logistics of taking three services in each church every Sunday, dependent on her ten-year-old Fiesta, no longer the reliable workhorse it had been in its youth, was a constant worry; and a recent spate of robberies at churches in the area had left her wondering how to keep her three open to parishioners and visitors, yet secure against theft and vandalism.

But there were also the great imponderables to contend with. She found it hard to look Alan and Josie Barnes, whose farm was a model of good land stewardship, in the eye. Their twelve-year-old daughter, Becky, had died of a brain tumour a month ago. The whole village was stricken. 'Why does God allow such things to happen?' Alan had asked her. Jessica had felt ashamed, uttering what seemed like platitudes, especially when the couple thanked her for her kindness. Taking Becky's funeral had been one of the most distressing experiences of her life.

People asked the same question about incidents further afield - natural disasters - earthquakes, tsunamis, devastating floods and fires, and man-made horrors - acts of terrorism, a child stabbed to death by a schoolmate. Jessica seemed to be making excuses for God all too often. She would point out that, sometimes, good would come out of tragedy. There were indeed shining examples of this; stricken individuals had set up charities, or run in marathons, to support people who had suffered similar disasters. Their lives had a sense of ongoing purpose. In some cases, faith had been kindled or strengthened through adversity.

Jessica's own community, the residents of her three parishes, included several people who were heroically coping with terrible illness or family tragedy, and there was a real feeling of mutual support amongst neighbours - more so than was usual among urban communities. Nevertheless, she had been disappointed to find a noticeable hardheartedness towards outsiders. Without any evidence, local people had agreed that burglaries at two houses in the district had been carried out either by gypsies whose caravan was parked on some waste ground just outside the village, or by 'those foreigners' employed at the vegetable-packing station down the road.

****

'Jessica? May I talk to you for a few minutes?'
Jessica was sitting alone eating muesli. She had been gazing out of the dining-room window while these thoughts went through her mind. She turned, said almost automatically, 'Yes, of course.' Then, seeing Claire, she said, smiling,
'I don't think you've recognised me yet, have you?'
Claire looked puzzled, delving into her memory.
'Your face is familiar... Were you Jess Hooper?'
'Yes! And you were Claire Mills! In the Upper Sixth for our last term at the High School!'
'I'd never have dreamed that you'd go into the Church!' said Claire. 'At school you were so bolshie - always going on protest demos and such like! I am right, aren't I? There's a Rev. before your name on your enrolment form, I think?'
'Yes, there is, but it's relatively recent - since Stephen died - my husband. He was killed in a fall in the Cairngorms eight years ago. We used to go climbing a lot. We had some wonderful times - in the French Alps, the Dolomites. the Lake District, Scotland... It was ironic, how it happened. Stephen and I wanted to start a family, so we decided to give up these dangerous activities. That was to be our last climbing holiday.' She paused, then resumed, her voice reduced almost to a whisper, 'Well, I lost Stephen, and the shock brought on a miscarriage. We hadn't even known that I was already pregnant.'
Jessica's usual calm self-possession deserted her for a few moments.
'That's awfully sad,' Claire said, after a pause.
'Yes - Well, it set me thinking a lot and, in the end I found something else to put my heart and soul into. I'm finding it quite a challenge, actually. And it isn't really so inconsistent with my angry girlhood! Just

another way of trying to make a difference.'

Claire pondered this.

'And what's been happening to you?' Jessica asked, in a brighter tone, 'apart from this wonderful College - a tremendous achievement!'

'Oh, I married Aidan Martindale twenty years ago. We're still married, but only just, I sometimes think. We've got twins - a boy and a girl - both coming to the end of their gap years. But, Jess, I wanted to consult you about something. I heard part of that conversation in the lounge last night, before dinner, about asylum seekers. I noticed your comments - more sympathetic than some people's! The thing is, an asylum seeker, a young woman, has turned up here, at the College, and I just don't know what I should do about her! I found her in the garden shed very early this morning. I'm letting her stay in one of our cottages for the time being. I've cooked her a breakfast, and I've asked her not to go outside - I expect she's catching up on her sleep now. I've telephoned Aidan. He's a journalist, and he wrote an article about asylum seekers last year. He's going to send me some information by email.'

Jessica nodded, but said nothing.

'I wondered whether you'd been involved with any asylum seekers - through your work, I mean.'

'There are quite a number of them in my area - especially just now when farmers and market gardeners are taking on temporary staff for the summer. It's illegal to employ asylum seekers, but it suits a few of these growers not to enquire too closely about their seasonal staff, and perhaps the police are turning a blind eye. At least, if refugees are working, they're not destitute, so they're less likely to resort to crime.'

'Do you know any asylum seekers personally?'

'Yes! In fact, I have a young couple from Somalia living in my house right now! Their asylum application was turned down, then their appeal against the refusal was rejected too. I was quite shocked. They had what seemed to me a very justifiable case for being allowed to remain here.'

'Are they working on a farm?'

'No. I told them that I couldn't let them stay at the vicarage if they worked illegally. But they hate to be dependent on me. The result is that my house is cleaner and tidier than it's ever been, the garden is beautiful, and my old car is positively gleaming! This is how they pay me for their accommodation, food etc. They feel uncomfortable about the situation, but, as I keep telling them, I'm doing very well out of the arrangement! They shouldn't be doing menial work, though. He was a University lecturer in Mogadishu, and his wife was a nursing sister.'

'What do your parishioners think about this?'

'Some of them seemed a bit shocked at first, but the fact that the couple attend church regularly on Sundays has helped a lot in getting them accepted! I'm not sure whether they are believers, or whether it's just a courteous gesture to me, but they seemed familiar with the morning service right from the first time.'

'Would you be willing to talk to Maria, later today, when she's had a good rest? I want her to know that there are people here that she can trust. - She's had such a bleak, lonely time since she left home.'

'Of course, Claire. I'll be happy to do that. Don't expect an instant solution to her problems, though!'

****

After breakfast, the atmosphere at Wildwood House was quite different from that of the two previous days. There was a great bustling up and down stairs with paraphernalia - easels, folding chairs, sketchbooks, boxes containing paints, brushes, pencils, besides cameras and tripods, and collections of leaves, twigs and other evidence of arboreal interests. A delightful mix of earnestness and lighthearted banter prevailed, as people discussed how they would spend the day. But first, most of them would listen to a few hints on tree painting in watercolours from Grace Weatherby, a local artist who was chatting with Claire and Hugh while the students deposited their belongings in the studio and sat down.

'What colour are tree trunks?' Grace asked abruptly, to engage their attention.

'Brown', Ted offered, then added,' Maybe grey, some of them.'

'Have a look at some of those, just outside,' Grace said, pointing to three oaks clearly visible through the big patio doors.

'Those look more like a greenish grey,' said Sandy.

'That one's got a bit of yellow in it'.

'There's a reddish-orangey colour, too, and a bit of white just there. Look!'

Suddenly, they were all laughing, including Grace, who added, 'Yes - and a bit of purple, too, isn't there?'

'Are we all seeing the same things differently, or what?' asked Ted, who liked to get things straight.

'Partly that,' Grace answered, 'but it's also a question of how the light falls, and whether it's warm sunlight or the colder light of a winter's day. So long as you really look at your tree before applying any colour, it will be more realistic. If you're not in too great a hurry to start painting outside, you can have a go at mixing the colours you can see in these tree trunks.'

Fifteen minutes later, Grace gave some useful hints on technique.

'Besides colour, there's texture to notice before you start painting. Most trees have rather rough bark - not easy to paint unless you try dry brush work, and preferably use rough-textured paper. We have some sheets of it here, if you want to try it out,' she added, as people began rummaging through their equipment. Grace demonstrated as she spoke - 'Dip your brush in the colour you've mixed, then drag the brush sideways quickly over the paper, at a very slight angle to it. Can you see how the paint has missed some areas so it looks more natural? Just practise that for a few minutes.'

She walked round, looking, showing, encouraging.

'Now for foliage. Whatever you do, don't try to paint every leaf! You'll never finish your tree! A good trick is to half-close your eyes, so that you can't see the detail - just the effect of the foliage as a whole. You'll see areas of different colour and of light and shade. Again, you'll find that using the side of the brush, rather than the tip, will produce a more natural effect.'

Grace explained how to make use of two or three washes of colour to paint trees in full leaf, applying the lightest first, then dropping in a deeper tone while the first is still wet.

'I'm getting quite absorbed in this!' Sandy said to Rex. 'It's wonderful how you can create textures with this dry brush method, isn't it?'

Rex wasn't so sure. 'I think I'm more of an Impressionist,' he declared. 'Sloshing on big areas of contrasting colour is more my thing - and not necessarily the real colours of the objects themselves!'

'Isn't that more what the Fauves did?' Les asked. 'Artists like Derain. His colours were really startling.'

'We'll all be demanding to see your work later, Rex!' Jessica said playfully. 'It sounds as if yours will be the most original picture!'

****

Maria was woken by a tap on the front door of the cottage. Wariness had become a habit, ever since she left home, and she waited, uncertain whether to go downstairs and see who was there. She heard two female voices outside, speaking quietly. Then the door opened gently and Claire's voice called, 'Maria? May I come in?'

Maria got quickly off the bed and made a hasty attempt to tidy herself. She felt crumpled and frowsty after her long sleep, but clean at last, having wallowed in the long-missed luxury of a hot bath before she lay down on the bed, mid-morning, and sank thankfully into oblivion. It was now five o'clock in the afternoon.

'Yes,' she called. 'Please come in. I have just wakened.'

'Did you sleep well?'

'Oh!' Maria said with feeling, as she came downstairs, 'The best sleep since I left my country - beautiful sleep!'

'That's good to know! I've brought a friend to talk to you. She's just outside.' Maria's face clouded. Was this an official of some kind, come to disturb her new-found but precarious peace of mind?

'It's all right, Maria. She's just an old school friend of mine. She might be able to help you.'

Maria smiled and nodded.

It was Jessica's face that showed Maria she had nothing to fear - the face of someone who had experienced a share of suffering in her own life, but had come to terms with it and emerged calm and relaxed.. She looked friendly in a quiet way. After introducing them, Claire went back to the main building.

'Claire is so busy!' Jessica said when they were alone. 'The College only opened on Friday. She's had such a lot to do, getting everything organised. She told you that we were at school together, but we hadn't seen each other for years and we only got reacquainted this morning!'

'Where are the students?' Maria asked. 'I see only older people out there.'

'I'm a student! Just for this week. It's a college for adults. People come on short courses - just for enjoyment. We're studying trees. It's more like a holiday for me. And this is such a beautiful place.'

'Yes,' Maria agreed. 'It is so peaceful. I feel safe here - as if nothing bad can happen.'

She smiled, but after a moment her face clouded and she added: 'But I think I must not stay. I cannot pay for living here. I have no money. I do not know what I can do.' She broke off, her voice constricted by despair.

'Well now,' Jessica said, 'I may have some good news for you! Let's make a pot of tea, and I'll tell you about something Claire has suggested.'

Maria still looked absorbed in anxiety, but she showed Jessica into the small kitchen, put the kettle on and set out cups and saucers on a tray, while Jessica cut two slices from a cake Claire had provided earlier and put them on little plates.

The simple gestures promoted an atmosphere of calm normality between the two strangers. Maria carried the tray into the sitting room and they sat together on the sofa, enjoying their refreshments, saying little until Maria had eaten a second piece of cake and both had finished their tea.

'Now,' Jessica began, 'Claire told me that she needs someone to look after the College garden - just to keep everything tidy, weeding the flowerbeds, dead-heading the roses, cutting the grass - that sort of thing. Claire wondered if you would be interested in doing this job, in exchange for living here, plus a little money to buy things you need. Do you think you would like to do that, Maria?'

It was some time before Maria answered. She seemed to be turning the idea over in her mind.

'Claire is a very kind lady,' she said at last, 'But I could not do enough work to pay for all this!' she added, indicating with a gesture the cottage and its amenities.

'Well, if you don't accept her offer, Claire will have to pay a gardener to do the work - so you needn't feel bad about this arrangement! But you can think about it for a while, if you like. You don't have to decide in a hurry.'

'Yes, I decide now! This is the best thing that has happened to me in England! Please say to Claire that I accept this work and I will keep the garden as beautiful as I can!'

'That's good. If the weather stays nice, I think you'll enjoy the work. But English weather is unpredictable, I'm afraid! Still, if it rains, you won't have to water the pot plants!'

'Unpred...? What is this word, please?'

'Unpredictable. It means you can't know what it will be like. Our weather here is difficult to forecast - It changes so often.'

'Thank you. I must improve my English,' Maria said earnestly. 'I will write this word - one moment, please.'

She rummaged in her old canvas bag and produced a small, dog-eared notebook and a ball-point pen.

'How is the word spelled, please?'

She wrote it carefully, as Jessica dictated.

'My things are still in this bag,' she said apologetically. 'I never unpacked since I left home! I keep everything in here.'

She patted the shabby bag, as if it were a faithful dog, the gesture eloquent of recent deprivation, human as well as material.

'Would you like to tell me about your journey to England?' Jessica asked gently. 'Claire told me you travelled in some sort of a lorry.'

Maria shuddered.

'It was horrible - too many people crowded together, in total darkness most of the time. I felt very uneasy. I did not like the attitude of some of the men. I did not feel safe. I was very distressed when one man, who must have recognised me when we got out at a stopping place, said bad things about my father. I had tried to keep silent, but this I could not endure, and I spoke up. Now that time has passed since that journey, I can think of us all in that container as a kind of society in miniature. There were selfish people, like a man who said a woman and her baby should be thrown out, because the baby might cry at a customs post, and our journey would be stopped and we would all be arrested. And there were kind people, like a woman who made space for a pregnant lady to sit, when people wanted her to be sent away in case she had the baby in the container. I learnt things about myself, too. I never criticised those unfortunate people, but I was worried that their presence with us would put an end to my hope of getting to England. If people had tried to send them away, would I have dared to intervene? It worries me to think about that.'

Maria paused.

Jessica said, 'I think the concern you felt for those unfortunate people, and that you still feel, after all this time, strongly suggests that you would have intervened if necessary. I think you'll be able to stop worrying about that now, Maria.'

She spoke with quiet conviction, and smiled. Maria relaxed.

'I did make one friend on that journey,' Maria added in a more cheerful tone. 'A woman much older than me. She was called Nina. We sat together and talked about books we had read. She was going to look for her daughter in London. I hope she has found her. I don't think I will see Nina again, but that journey would have been unbearable without her companionship. I gave her the address of my relations in Bradford, but she did not know where she would be living.'

'Well, it's quite possible you'll get a letter from her, through those people, isn't it?'

'Not unless I send them my new address - but I must keep my address secret. I am expected to leave this country, because I have been refused asylum in Britain. I should not be here at all!'

'All you need do now, Maria, is live quietly here, and look after the garden. Let the future take care of itself for a while.'

Chapter 14

'My artistic inspiration had run out by about two o'clock!' Sandy said apologetically.

'Mine did too, but much sooner than that!' said Rex. 'I'd done all I could long before lunchtime.'

'You looked very confident - splashing on those vivid colours, before I'd even chosen the view I wanted to paint!'

'Well, I've just invented the Look and Paint School! Though when I stood back and gave my effort a cool appraisal, I thought Look, Paint and Tear-it-up seemed a more apt name!'

'You haven't torn it up, have you?' Sandy cried, with mock horror. 'Didn't you know we've all got to put our paintings up round the walls of the studio, for everyone to see?'

'Then mine will serve as a horrible example! It'll cheer people up. They'll all think, "Well, at least mine's better than that one!" I'll take care not to sign it, though!'

Rex and Sandy were strolling across a field that sloped gently down to the river, sparkling in the late afternoon sunlight. Late picnickers were packing up their belongings. Two small children stepped unsteadily on the pebbly beach, trying to retrieve a plastic duck they had dropped at the water's edge. A black and white dog splashed exuberantly into the water to fetch a stick thrown by its master, and emerged in a flurry of iridescent spray on the shallow bank. Rex chose a handful of flat pebbles and skimmed them across the water, seeing how many times each would bounce.

Then he and Sandy strolled into the village of Burnsall with its mellow stone houses, many with mullioned windows. They had a look round the church, impressed to read a commemorative tablet to Sir William Craven who had *repaired and butified* the church in the early seventeenth century, as well as founding the local school and rebuilding the bridge.

'It's lovely to see them all still standing, so long afterwards,' Sandy commented, as they emerged into the brightness outside and headed for the riverside path beyond the bridge, now shaded by trees, the river narrower as it flowed through a rocky gorge where local boys were daring each other to leap into the water from increasingly high points, their shrieks resounding off the rocks.

'Tell me about Connecticut,' Sandy asked, after they'd been walking single-file where the path was narrow, but now had more space. 'I've never been to America - not yet, anyway. I think I only know about spectacular sights like the Grand Canyon, Niagara Falls - oh and New England in the fall - That's nearer to you, isn't it?'

'You're more interested in our natural features than our man-made ones then, are you?' Rex asked with a smile. 'Well, so am I. You can tell that from my job. I can see we're getting back to the theme of the week! There's no getting away from trees! Sure, our autumn colours are spectacular - not just yellow, gold, red, but bright pink, too! You'll have to come over and see them for yourself one day.'

'Am I right in thinking that Connecticut is called the Nutmeg State? I seem to have heard or read that somewhere.' He nodded.

'Why?'

'Well, it doesn't reflect very well on us! The early inhabitants are said to have been so shrewd that they could fool people into buying wooden nutmegs!'

Sandy laughed.

'But we're not like that nowadays!' He grinned. 'Not all of us, anyway.'

'Does the name Connecticut mean anything?'

'It's an Indian name. It means "beyond the long tidal river", or something like that. Oh, and we have an official State Tree - the white oak; and the robin is our official bird!'

Sandy laughed.

'There are big areas of forest inland, but the coast, where most of us live, is very urbanised. Most of our cities are on the coast - Hartford - that's the capital, New Haven, where Yale University is...'

'Is that your university?'

He laughed. 'No chance of that! No, I'm not in the Ivy League. I lecture at Blakes - one of the newer universities. The dendrology department is highly regarded, though - since I joined it,' he added with a wink.

'Have you a family, Rex?'

He didn't answer at once, as if he was wondering what to say.

'Hard to answer that question! A year ago, I'd have said an enthusiastic "Yes", but my wife left me for another man six months ago. Our daughter, Becky, lives with her - a lovely girl. She's still in high school. I don't get to see her as often as I'd like to nowadays.'

Sandy said nothing. After a few moments, Rex added: 'This shouldn't have happened. I don't know what Judy sees in this new man. - But there it is! It's mainly because of all this mess that I applied for a sabbatical year in Britain.'

'What a shame!' Sandy said. 'It looks as if we're both here to try and recover from something.'

They walked on in silence for some minutes, then Sandy glanced at her watch.

'Let's turn back now,' she said, 'or we'll be late for dinner.'

****

Claire put a mug of cocoa on the coffee table. Then she selected a disc and put it into the music player. The plangent tones of a Celtic harp filled her small living room.

'Ah! That's better!' she thought, as she sat down on the sofa and the music began to beguile her into a relaxed mood.

The telephone rang.

'Hi, Mum!'

'Jonquil, love! I was going to phone you. Dad told me you'd arrived, when I rang earlier, but he said you were sleeping off your jet-lag. How did the tour go?'

'Oh, it was wonderful, Mum! The audiences seemed to enjoy our efforts. We were so nervous - most of us very inexperienced, as you know, but Laurence kept our morale up, as usual, and everyone was so kind to us. And there was a lovely atmosphere among us all - except for one or two bursts of temper, due to nerves and quickly over. I've made some good friends.'

'I'm so glad, Jonnie. What was the travelling like?'

'OK. No one lost their instrument! But you wouldn't believe what it was like going through the security checks at the airports. The staff seemed specially suspicious of the string section. I'm sure they thought there was a bomb concealed inside my viola!'

'Goodness! I hope it didn't get damaged in the process?'

'It survived. - What's that gorgeous music, Mum?'

'Hilary Rushmer playing the Celtic harp - one of my favourites to relax with.'

'I'm forgetting - You must have been so busy this weekend, getting the College started. I'm sorry to phone so late.'

'I'll sleep much better for having had this chat with you. It was nice of you to send me that card, love, amid all your own excitement. We've got the course up and running now - nice group of people. Oh! and one of the students turned out to be Jess Hooper, an old school friend of mine! But the biggest surprise - quite a shock really - was the discovery of an asylum seeker on the premises! I found her very early this morning, in the tool shed, where she'd spent the night.'

'Dad told me about that. Did you get his email, by the way - the article he said he'd send you?'

'Eventually - after one of my heroic struggles with the computer this afternoon! Thank Dad for me, won't you?'

'Of course I will.'

After a few moments hesitation, Jonquil spoke again, sounding less confident:

'Speaking of Dad ... Well, I don't want to worry you, Mum, but he doesn't look at all well. I don't think he's been looking after himself properly - I mean, eating proper meals etc. And...'

Was there a reproach in her daughter's tone? Claire wondered, or was her own sense of guilt making it sound like reproach?

'What is it, Jonnie?' she asked gently.

'Well - he seems to be drinking again.'

Claire said nothing.

'Mum?'

'Yes, love. Sorry, I was just thinking. I'll try and get over to York one day this week. I'm sorry you've come home to all this. But I think Dad will feel better for having you at home. And Rory should be back very soon, too.'

'Mmm...' Jonquil sounded unconvinced.

'Come if you can, Mum. I'll let you go now. You must be tired out after the day's exertions. Good night.'

'Good night, darling.'

Claire sighed, and picked up the now cold mug of chocolate.

Chapter 15

Maria shuddered as she approached the garden shed - the scene of one of the worst nights she'd spent since she arrived in England. Her morale had then been at its lowest point, as she'd tried hopelessly to make herself comfortable for the night under the potting bench, after several days of near-starvation. Unbelievably, that had only been the night before last, and now her luck had turned immeasurably for the better. Claire had told her that the caretaker would show her the tools she would need to use, and show her round the garden, pointing out the work that needed to be done, in her new role as unofficial gardener at Wildwood House. She tried the shed door.

'It's locked,' a man's voice said, just behind her. 'To keep out vagrants,' Geoff added in an uncompromising tone, almost rude.

Maria blushed with shame, but she said nothing.

'I'm the caretaker - the name's Geoff,' he said. 'So you're Maria, are you?'

She nodded, uncomfortable under his appraising gaze. She wondered how much Claire had told him about her. He was not a man whose approval would easily be won by a stranger, she felt.

He unlocked the door and stood back to let her go in first.

'You'll find most of the things you need in here - spade, fork, rake, hoe, watering can, hosepipe and so forth.' He gestured vaguely to the implements leaning against the wooden walls or lying on the bench.

Maria felt at a loss. Her English vocabulary was inadequate on the subject of horticulture. Nor, she realised, did she know more than a few English names for plants and flowers.

'There's a wheelbarrow just outside. It'll save you a few journeys when you're working at the far end of the garden.'

'Thank you. I will remember.'

'Now I'll show you round the garden,' he offered, and they stepped into the sunshine. 'This part, at the back of the main house, is the kitchen garden - vegetables, mostly. Claire's trying to make this place self-sufficient in veg. See - broad beans here, a few in flower already, one or two pods starting to form. There are the peas, starting to climb those canes. Lettuces coming on nicely over there. There'll be soft fruit later - strawberries, raspberries. And those,' he said, pointing to a bed separate from the rest, 'are courgettes. They'll be like tiny marrows in a few weeks.'

Maria nodded. It was hard work trying to take in all this information and to memorise the unfamiliar names.

'Now we'll go round to the front and I'll show you the flowerbeds.'

The clatter of metal utensils and the sound of resonant voices told Maria they were nearing the kitchen. Here, Geoff showed her a socket, just inside the door to the kitchen porch, where she could plug in the lawn mower, then an outside tap for attaching the hosepipe.

'Yes, I see, thank you.'

'Right, well, the lawn could do with cutting fairly soon,' he said, as they came in sight of the front garden. 'And the rose bed in the middle of the lawn needs weeding. Those buds'll be opening soon, if this sunshine keeps up.'

'Plenty for me to do!' Maria said.

'Aye, you'll have your work cut out!' he said, with a certain relish.

Whatever did that mean? she wondered. This man puzzled her. His unfriendly manner had repelled her at first. Unlike Claire and Jessica, he made no concessions to her unfamiliarity with English speech, and his accent added to her difficulty in understanding what he said. But he was being quite helpful, despite his uncompromising manner. This must be the Yorkshire characteristic Ursula had told her about at Bradford. Geoff was the first person she'd come across who fitted the description. She was relieved that her lack of garden vocabulary hadn't made her seem foolish. With the garden before them, it was easy to understand most of what he was saying, until he began naming the flowers that were not yet visible.

'Then there are these borders,' he continued. 'Claire wants this one to be a cottage-style bed - delphiniums and hollyhocks against the wall, then a mixture of marigolds, geraniums, busy lizzies, pansies, violas in front...'

'I'm sorry. I don't know any of these names!' Maria interrupted, out of her depth.

'I expect you'll recognise some of them when you take a closer look. But some of the plants Claire's chosen won't do well in the soil we have here - No sign of hollyhocks or delphiniums, of course! I could have told her that. Anyway, I'll leave you to it now. I've got work to do - checking the door locks, for one thing!' he added with a grim smile.

****

Maria had thought that mowing the lawn would be hard work, so she'd tackled that job first. Now, she stood back and looked at the results with relief, even satisfaction, and a sense of well-being she'd not felt since that last long walk she'd had with Pavel. - But she wouldn't think of him now. She would rejoice in her good fortune at last - a beautiful place to live, pleasant healthy work, two new friends who cared about her, and safety - above all, safety. Could it last, though? Maybe not, but she would live in the present, make the most of being here.

The edges of the lawn could do with trimming. She'd seen the tool for this in the shed. After putting away the mower, with its extraordinarily long flex, she would do that next.

****

Coffee time! Members of the *Trees* course came spilling out onto the terrace with their drinks, exclaiming, or gazing silently, according to character, at the serene view that was now familiar to them but always gave delight.

Sandy felt a need for exercise, so she went down the steps onto the lawn below and began walking round it. A girl was trimming the grass where it had encroached on the driveway. As Sandy approached, she looked up - the girl she'd met in the lane on Saturday morning!

'Hello!' Sandy said.

The girl smiled, but Sandy noticed a flicker of anxiety cross her face.

'You were kind to me,' she said simply and looked away for a moment, embarrassed. 'I work here now - my first day,' she added.

'Good! I'm on a course here, about trees. I'm Sandy.'

'And I, Maria,' she said, offering a dusty hand, which Sandy shook warmly.

There was something tense about Maria's manner that puzzled Sandy - as if she was afraid to get into personal conversation. But then she smiled.

'I try to improve my English - learning names of tools and plants now - spade, hoe, rake, trowel,' she recited, waving towards a selection she had wheeled in the barrow from the shed. 'I don't know this one which I am using to cut the edge of this grass. Can you tell me?'

'I'm not sure I can!' Sandy answered. 'I think we call it a half-moon - because of its shape, but that's probably not its official name.'

'Half-moon', Maria repeated. She laughed, gesturing skywards. 'I won't forget this word!'

They spent a few minutes looking at the main border, Sandy telling Maria the names of some of the flowers, before it was time for her to return to the house, to hear more of Hugh's talk entitled *Trees in a Landscape*.

'I've been learning about garden designers in the eighteenth century who made the grounds of big country houses look like natural scenery, instead of copying the traditional French style, with very formal gardens. It's really interesting,' Sandy said, 'But I'll have to go in for the next session now.'

Maria looked puzzled. 'There is so much that I do not know about this country!'

'Well, if you want to know anything about trees in Britain, you must meet our tutor, Hugh Armstrong! People call him the Tree Man. That's him, look! just going up the steps.'

Maria looked towards the entrance and saw a tall man, striding energetically into the house. She could not see his face.

****

Claire's meeting was scheduled for 2pm, straight after lunch, in the Tutorial Room. Sandy had been surprised by the invitation and wondered what the meeting could be about. She hadn't heard of anyone else among the students being invited.

As its name suggested, the Tutorial Room was small - intended for one-to-one discussions between a student and tutor - with a large desk and a chair on each side of it, but three extra chairs had been brought in for this occasion. Claire sat in the tutor's chair. Forming a semicircle in front of her were Hugh, Geoff and Jessica. Sandy took the fourth chair, still puzzled. The others were all older than herself and seemed more senior, though, of course, Jessica was a student here, like herself. Claire stood up, went to the door, took a look outside, then closed it and returned to her place.

'Thank you for coming, all of you. I hope you didn't have to rush your lunch, but this is rather important. Something totally unexpected has occurred, though Jessica and Geoff already know about it. The reason I decided to speak to you four is that you are people I feel I can trust. I need to have your cooperation in a slightly tricky situation.'

Claire paused. Geoff's face looked grim; he shuffled restlessly in his chair. Hugh's expression showed lively curiosity. Jessica looked calm.

Sandy was clearly bewildered - Whatever was Claire going to ask them to do? she wondered.

'You've probably all noticed the young woman who is now looking after the garden here,' Claire resumed. 'Her name is Maria. She arrived here at the weekend. In fact, she's an asylum seeker and her application to stay in this country has been refused. Her presence in Britain now is officially illegal. She had been living with a family of her compatriots in Bradford, but when she received this news, she left them and stopped reporting regularly to the police there as required. She believed that she would be removed to a detention centre and would then be sent back to her country of origin - even though she has good reason to fear ill-treatment, and possibly execution, if she returned there. Her father, a writer, died soon after being imprisoned for criticising their government in the press. She believes he was murdered. She would have been entitled to some financial support for up to twenty-one days after the final rejection of her asylum application, but couldn't get this without the authorities knowing where she was.'

Again, Claire paused.

'How did she end up here?' Hugh asked.

'First, she found a job at a bed and breakfast place in Skipton. The landlord was glad to find someone he could pay considerably less than the statutory minimum wage, but he let her sleep in an old caravan in the grounds, sharing with another girl who worked there. - I gather that the conditions were pretty rudimentary. But she was suddenly sacked, without even a day's notice, when the landlord's daughter came home from college for the vacation to work there. So Maria searched for work again - reading notices in job centres and postcards in newsagents' windows. No luck anywhere.'

'But why did she end up in this particular part of Yorkshire?' Sandy almost interrupted.

'That's what intrigued me, too,' Claire answered. 'Well, it's strange, but a few pictures changed her course. Maria told me how she saw some photographs of Upper Wharfedale in a little magazine - probably the *Dalesman*, I should think - in the library near where she was staying in Bradford. She seems to have fallen in love with those pictures. She even remembers the names of some of the villages up here - Buckden, Starbotton, Hubberholme. She told me she felt sure she'd be safe if she went to that area. So when she lost the job at Skipton, she just packed her few belongings again and set off walking. She'd managed to make a sketch-map by copying one displayed in a bookshop window. It wouldn't be difficult to find the way, once she got onto the B6265 or the B6160, would it?'

'She'd manage to get here in a day, I should think,' said Hugh, 'Though she probably wasn't very fit, and she could have lost the way, though it's very straightforward when you know it.'

'I'd agree with that,' Geoff said.

'Well, it actually took her nearly three days, because she wasn't just walking. She was looking for work, stopping at every shop, guest house, b.& b. and farm along the way, enquiring about jobs.'

'People aren't too keen to take on casual callers, are they?' said Jessica. 'Maria must have had a dreadful time, getting rejected by everyone.'

'Yes,' Claire continued, 'It was a fruitless quest. She must have reached her lowest point by the time she turned up here. She'd run out of money and she'd spent two nights sleeping in barns. From what she told me, she was on the verge of desperation when she turned into our driveway in the dark, found *Swifts* cottage empty, and stayed the night. And that brings you just about up to date with Maria's story.'

There was a silence, eventually broken by Geoff.

'Not a very practical choice of area, was it?' he said. 'There's very little work available round here - and less still further up the Dale, where she was heading for. Sheep farmers can't afford to employ anyone - with the price for sheep being so low as it is. I'm amazed they haven't all given up farming by now!'

'It's in their blood, isn't it?' Hugh said. 'Most of them come of a long line of men who've farmed the same acreage for generations. There's much more involved than the price of sheep.'

Claire looked at her watch. She hadn't much time for digressions.

'Rather a romantic view, if you ask me!' Geoff replied. 'Anyway, Maria would hardly have fared any better in catering. The further you go up the Dale, the fewer pubs or b.& bs there are that might need staff. That girl should have thought things over before she even left home, then she wouldn't have got into the mess she's in now, and lumbered you with her problems, Claire.' After a moment, he added, 'I will say, though, she's made a good job of the front lawn.'

'I can understand her falling in love with the Dales,' Jessica said.

'So can I,' said Sandy, and Hugh nodded.

After a pause, Claire resumed, 'As I said earlier, I've taken you people into my confidence about Maria because I feel I can trust you. I must admit, when I found Maria in the garden shed early yesterday morning, I knew very little about the position of asylum seekers in this country, but I've learned a lot in a very short time.' She added, with a smile, 'In the process, I managed to become a bit more adept at using my computer! I was almost afraid of it until yesterday, when I desperately needed information in a hurry.'

Claire's admission enabled the others to relax a bit. It was reassuring to learn that there was an area of activity with which she was not already quite competent!

'I downloaded information from the websites of the Home Office's Border and Immigration Agency, and reports from Amnesty International about the experiences of failed asylum seekers in London. I also re-read an article my husband, Aidan, published last year on the subject. I can print out more copies from these transcripts if any of you would like them. I've also learned a lot from Jessica here, who has asylum seekers in the parish where she is the vicar.'

The other three looked surprised at the last piece of information. Jessica smiled.

'I'll just mention a few points that are useful to know as regards Maria's presence here at Wildwood,' Claire continued. 'Decisions about whether or not asylum seekers are granted permission to stay in Britain seem very arbitrary. Some find themselves being deported to their countries of origin even if this puts them at grave risk of persecution or death when they arrive there, despite the fact that it is against this country's law to deport people in such circumstances.'

'But this country will be overrun by foreigners if we let them all stay here!' Geoff exclaimed. 'And they're living at our expense, too!'

'I'm afraid we haven't time to debate such a huge issue just now,' Claire replied, 'But to help get things in perspective, I should point out that although asylum seekers do get a small subsistence allowance, this stops after twenty-one days if their application is refused - and the majority are refused. Add to this the fact that they are forbidden to take paid employment, and the result is that there are many thousands of people in Britain literally starving and living rough, or totally dependent on the charity of others.'

'I never knew anything about this,' Hugh said, shocked.

'Is there any risk that you'll be breaking the law - letting Maria stay here?' Sandy asked.

'This is a grey area, I know,' Claire answered, ' but apparently the police may turn a blind eye. They may well be glad that some asylum seekers are being provided with a roof over their heads when there's a shortage of secure accommodation to put them in. I'm letting Maria stay in *Swifts* cottage for the time being, in exchange for working in the garden. Very little actual money will change hands - just pocket money really.'

'Seems a good arrangement,' said Hugh, 'probably the best in the circumstances.'

Sandy and Jessica agreed.

'I must emphasise that I'm not asking anyone to do anything illegal! But I thought it might be helpful if you bore in mind - and perhaps told any of the students here who might comment about Maria, seeing her working out there - that she is a young friend of mine from Eastern Europe, that she's had some distressing experiences, so it would be best not to risk upsetting her by asking her any personal questions. All of this is true - Maria *is* now a friend of mine. Could you agree to this, do you think?'

Jessica, Sandy and Hugh agreed readily. Geoff looked very doubtful for some moments, but at lenght nodded his assent.

'Thank you all, very much indeed,' Claire said. 'That's the end of the meeting. I feel much better for having shared all this with you. It's a great weight off my mind. I do hope I haven't delayed the start of your work.'

Chapter 16

Diane was checking booking forms from people wanting to register for courses later in the summer, when she was disturbed by a sudden loud noise in the reception hall - a man's voice, harsh and angry. She got up promptly from her desk and opened the door from the office. 'Where's my wife? - Anyone know where she is?' the voice demanded.

Two members of the course, who had been studying the notice board, made themselves scarce, hurrying across the hall and leaving by the nearest door, looking shocked.

'Can I help you, sir?' Diane asked, as pleasantly as she could.

She saw a man of medium height, rather overweight, his face red and his hair dishevelled.

'Yes - my wife, Claire! Are you the secretary?' he demanded.

'Yes. I'm afraid Mrs Martindale isn't usually available at this time of the afternoon, but I'll put a call through to the flat. She may still be in...'

Diane went back into the office and Aidan stamped about unsteadily in the hall, muttering incoherently, until Claire appeared at the top of the staircase, pale and shocked.

'Aidan!' she exclaimed.

'Not much of a welcome, this, is it?' he called to her loudly. 'You don't look very pleased to see me!'

'Well, I am. But this is a bit of a surprise. - Come up to the flat, Aidan. Then we can talk properly. It's very public here and you're talking rather loudly.'

Claire watched him as he climbed the stairs, cursing and stumbling.

'Sit down and I'll make some coffee,' she said as soon as they were in the flat with the door closed.

'Why so tight-lipped?'

She said nothing.

'Coffee! Haven't you got anything stronger than coffee?'

'Aidan, you've had too much alcohol! - It's only too obvious,' she added as he feigned innocence. 'Coffee, tea, or fruit juice?'

'All right,' he said sulkily, 'coffee then.'

He subsided while she went into the kitchen.

'How did you get here?' she asked suddenly. He couldn't have driven from York in this state, could he?

'Jonquil drove me.'

'Where is Jonquil?'

'She's waiting in the car. - Said she'd give us a few minutes to ourselves before she came up.'

'She told me she was worried about you when she rang me last night - about you drinking too much.'

'Jonquil worries too much. She should relax more! - And so should you! Anyway, Rory'll be back from Guatemala soon. He'll go down the pub with me, if you two are too prim and proper!'

'I hate it when you talk like this, Aidan!'

Claire was on the verge of tears. It occurred to her, though, that Aidan would be less likely to overdo the alcohol if she or one of the children went with him to the pub.

The coffee and a generous piece of date and walnut cake seemed to sober him a bit.

'Nice place, this. How's it going, the College?'

'Quite a good start - good tutors, nice group of students. The food's excellent. I'm very lucky with the catering team - a mother and daughter who live locally. People used to tell me that the success of the College would depend more on the food than anything else!'

He nodded, almost smiled.

'Did you get my email and the attachments?'

'Yes. Oh, Aidan, I'm forgetting! Thanks very much for them. I managed to download them without too much trouble. And they were really helpful. I spent an intensive session on them yesterday, trying to digest all the info.'

'Any more of that cake?' he asked. 'Best thing I've eaten for weeks!'

'What have you been living on?' Claire asked, as she cut him another slice.

'Oh, this and that, you know. But Jonquil went out early this morning to Tesco, and stocked up the fridge for us - ready-meals, of course. She hasn't time to cook.'

He was making Claire feel guilty again. She rallied.

'You could have made one of your famous curries, for yourself and Jonquil, couldn't you?'

'Oh, those! I haven't cooked a curry for years! Can't remember what spices I used.'

'No excuses! Unless you've moved it, that recipe is on a card in the yellow box in the kichen drawer at home.'

'Oh, well, I might try it sometime,' he said, unconvincingly.

'I might even come over to York for lunch one Sunday, if you invited me for a curry - maybe when Rory gets home. We could all eat together.'

Aidan yawned. 'Well, we'll see.'

A tap on the door heralded Jonquil's entrance. Claire sprang up, and mother and daughter hugged each other, speechless for a while. Then questions and answers followed in rapid succession.

'Dad's asleep!' Jonquil noticed after a few minutes, 'even with us talking at the tops of our voices!'

'Come into the kitchen. We can carry on talking in here, without disturbing him, though I doubt if he'd wake up easily now.'

Jonquil noticed a wistfulness in her mother's expression as she looked at Aidan, and she felt sad for her parents' strained relationship.

They sat down at the table in the flat's tiny kitchen.

'Did Dad ask you to drive him here?'

'No! He was going to drive himself. I tried to persuade him not to go. He'd been drinking. I was terrified he'd have an accident. In the end, he agreed to let me drive him. I had to phone Lucy and Max at Pocklington to say I couldn't meet them as planned. I'm going there tomorrow afternoon instead.'

'Has Dad come here for any special reason, do you know?'

'I don't know. Just a spur-of-the-moment decision, I think. He was very happy when I arrived home, but he's been very glum since then. I think he's bored with not having a proper job. He didn't say so, but he can't pick up a newspaper without getting furious about the way the reports and articles are written - "slapdash and badly researched" is his usual comment. I don't read the papers enough to form my own opinion, so I haven't made any comment. I think he's wishing he hadn't given up that editorship - But that was ages ago, wasn't it? Rory and I must have been about twelve when that happened!'

'He resigned from the newspaper to give more time to his novel. That's how confident he was in those days! As he was quite a well-known journalist, he had no difficulty getting freelance articles accepted, so he still had an income from journalism, though much less than he'd been used to.'

'Was that when you started teaching evening classes?'

'Yes. It was a rather hectic time for me, with the daytime supply teaching in schools. But that's how I discovered the delight of teaching adults! I couldn't believe my luck that there were people out there who wanted to listen to me enthusing about English literature and who enjoyed discussing poetry with me! That's why I gradually took on more adult classes, and dropped most of the schoolteaching.'

'And that's what led to this College!'

'Yes. Winning the Lottery helped a bit, too!'

They laughed.

'Dad must feel I have all the luck,' Claire said after a while. 'I do wish he could find something to absorb his energy and his talents.'

'Could he do any teaching here?'

'It's an idea. I might suggest that to him. He used to be good at giving talks.'

She didn't sound too optimistic, though, Jonquil thought.

'Tell me all about the College, Mum,' Jonquil said, and Claire spent the next half-hour relating all the events of the long weekend.

'I can't believe we only opened on Friday - well, Thursday really, when we had the inaugural dinner. That seems ages ago now, and yet it's only Monday afternoon!'

Jonquil was engrossed in thought for a few minutes, then she said, 'This refugee, Maria. You said she wanted to write, didn't you?'

'Yes. She seems to want to take over the role her father had, before he was imprisoned and - well, murdered, she believes; writing about the abuse of power, the lack of freedom of expression in her country, Alborus.'

'D'you think Dad might be able to help her with that?'

'How do you mean?'

'Well, maybe he could help her to put what she wants to say into good English style.'

'Yes. Yes, I see what you mean. It might be a very good idea,' Claire said, 'But would people here want to know what goes on in Alborus, d'you think? It's not a country many of us have even heard of. Had you heard of it before?'

'No, I don't think so. It sounds vaguely familiar, though.'

'It was part of the Soviet Union until the communist régime collapsed,' Aidan said, coming into the kitchen. 'Are there any aspirins? I've got a splitting headache.'

Claire took a packet from a cupboard and handed it to him with a glass of water.

'Thanks. Alborus is independent now, but it's virtually a dictatorship. Why were you talking about it?'

'It's the country Maria comes from.'

'Oh, yes - your tame refugee!'

'Don't call her that! I'm trying to help her,' Claire protested.

'Some people would view her employment here as exploitation. D'you realise that? - Payment below the minimum wage....'

'But you told me yourself that asylum seekers aren't allowed to have proper jobs! I'm providing accommodation, plus a small amount of cash. I'm doing the best I can for her in the circumstances. You seemed to think it was a good idea when we talked on the phone yesterday.'

'So long as you realise the risks. Have you heard about the new law coming into effect soon? - Anyone who employs refused asylum seekers will be liable to imprisonment. So think on, Claire!'

Claire looked grave.

'I could never forgive myself if I abandoned Maria now,' she said quietly.

Jonquil's eyes were brimming with tears, but she was smiling. 'I think you're wonderful, Mum,' she said.

'Well,' said Aidan, in a quieter tone than before, 'I just thought I should warn you. But, as I said on the phone, I don't think the police are actively searching for asylum seekers - unless the Home Office are looking for particular ones, such as terrorist suspects. So you'll probably be all right.'

After a moment, he added, 'And I think you're wonderful, too.'

All three were silent and still for a while. Jonquil was wishing that Rory was here, to share this rare moment of family harmony.

'Shall I go down and give Maria a hand with those plants?' Jonquil suggested a few minutes later.

'Yes, do,' Claire answered. 'It will be nice for her to talk to someone nearer her own age. I think she's about twenty-three. Most people here are a lot older'

****

'Hello,' Jonquil said.

Maria was firming in a pink-flowered plant she had just added to about a dozen already planted.

'Those busy lizzies look lovely and bright! I like the way you've arranged them in front of those green plants. They show up really well.'

Maria, at first wary of the stranger, looked up.

'Thank you,' she said simply. Then she asked, 'What is the name of these flowers, please?'

'Busy lizzies.'

Maria looked puzzled. 'Why this name?'

Jonquil smiled. 'Well, busy means very active. These plants keep flowering through the summer, I think, so maybe that's why they're called that, and lizzy just because it rhymes, I suppose. Lizzy is a girl's name, short for Elizabeth.'

Maria smiled, then her face turned sad.

'I had a sister with the same name, Elizaveta. She had a very slow brain - not busy at all - something wrong in her head. She died when very young.'

'I'm sorry, Maria,' Jonquil said, wishing her words had not evoked such an unhappy memory. 'That's very sad.' After a pause, she said, 'I haven't introduced myself. I'm Claire's daughter. My name's Jonquil. That's another flower name!'

'Do you live here?' Maria asked.

'No, I live at York with my father. We've both come on a short visit to my mum. She told me how you came here. You are very brave.'

'But now very lucky!' Maria answered, gesturing to the house, the garden and the hillside beyond.

'Mum told me you're a journalist.'

'Yes, and my father was also. But in my country, there is not freedom of the press.'

'My father is a journalist, too,' Jonquil went on. 'He knows about asylum seekers. He's written about them for a newspaper....Quite a coincidence,' she added when Maria made no reply. She looked uncertain whether this was good news or not.

'Your father - he criticised asylum seekers?'

'Oh, no! He understands the problems our Government has with so many people seeking refuge here, of course. But he knows that a lot of refugees are being told to go back to their own countries even though they face great danger there. There is a law against that, but it is being ignored. Dad wrote an article about all this, to try and help people like you.'

'Then your father is a very good man,' Maria said.

'Let me help you,' Jonquil said, when all the busy lizzies were in. 'What will you put in next?'

'These, I think.' Maria pointed to some trays of blue and yellow pansies. 'Will they look nice here, at the front?'

'I'm sure they will,' Jonquil enthused, 'But you're the gardener! It's your decision!'

****

They caught the bus in Burnsall, heading for Kettlewell further up the Dale. Hugh seemed preoccupied, sitting by himself, less eager than he usually was to point out landmarks on the way. Jessica and Sandy sat together, bound by an unconscious complicity following Claire's meeting, but they said little. Rex was puzzled. Sandy had seemed evasive when he asked her what the meeting had been about. He turned and chatted sporadically with Les and Tony, his drinking companions at *the Blue Bell* a couple of nights ago. Maybe they would drop in there again later today. Rhoda fussed quietly about whether it was likely to rain, wishing she'd brought her waterproof jacket. Ted gazed out of the window.

The journey proceeded quietly until the massive limestone outcrop of Kilnsey Crag appeared on their left. Now Hugh emerged from his introspection, explaining how, in the later stages of the Ice Age, the Wharfedale glacier had scoured back the base of the cliff, to form the menacing forty-foot overhang at the top. The Crag, a magnet to rock climbers, was 170 feet high, dwarfing the *Tennant Arms* hotel below.

Alighting at Kettlewell, the group walked through the village, passing three inns, a reminder of the village's importance when the road had been a major thoroughfare for stagecoaches. After a short climb, they left Kettlewell by a field path, 'centuries old' according to Hugh, which ran above and parallel with the Wharfe and the road to Starbotton on their left, giving beautiful views of the green valley ahead, with woods and little groups of trees by the river, and the fields, each with its stone barn.

The easy rhythm of walking promoted a more relaxed ambience among the group. Sheep and lambs were grazing, a lark poured out its joyous song, and clumps of wild flowers grew among the roots of straggly trees clinging to the hillside. Tony and Les were busy with sophisticated cameras, photography being their main reason for joining Hugh's course.

'Look!' Jessica said, pointing upwards over the valley.

A hawk was hovering, wings outstretched and tail spread like a fan.

'A kestrel,' Hugh said. 'He'll be focusing on his prey - a vole, maybe.'

Moments later, the bird dived straight to the ground and rose at once, a small creature clutched beween its claws.

'Magnificent!' Les cried.

'Amazing eyesight it must have,' said Rex.

'It reminds me of that poem by Gerard Manley Hopkins - *The Windhover*,' said Jessica. 'It's another name for a kestrel.'

Sandy looked troubled. 'But it's so cruel!' she exclaimed. 'I saw one when I went for an early walk the other day. It spoilt the walk for me!'

'Cruelty doesn't come into it,' Tony said. 'Birds kill instinctively, because they're hungry, or to feed their young.'

'Human beings are much worse,' Rex opined, 'killing for greed, revenge, jealousy. Animals only kill from necessity, to stay alive.'

'This is your area of expertise, Jessica, isn't it?' Hugh asked.

She laughed, then looked serious. 'Well, not expertise!' she answered, 'But, yes, my "subject" - as you call it, Hugh - does include morality, but only as regards humans! We're the only creatures - so far as is known - who have a sense of right and wrong. But we have free will. So there are more options open to us, aren't there? So it's harder for us, though our brains are more capable of dealing with choices. We can usually distinguish right from wrong. Animals are innocent, living by instinct. Morality doesn't really concern them, I think. End of sermon!'

Rhoda said, 'The human race seems to be getting worse and worse nowadays - such cruel things being done to people, even by children. And all these terrible wars going on and on! I find the news programmes really distressing nowadays.'

'Yes,' Jessica answered, 'I often feel the same, Rhoda. I think we all do, at least sometimes. But we do still hear of amazing acts of selfless bravery and little kindnesses happen every day. There's always the potential for good, isn't there?'

'Public morale would be better if the news media told us more about the good things being done,' Sandy said, to general agreement.

The path now led downhill to the tiny village of Starbotton, so quiet in the mid-afternoon that it almost seemed deserted. But its cottages were well cared for, with colourful plants brightening small flights of stone steps here and there. The walkers lingered for a few minutes on the footbridge, gazing into the clear water of the Wharfe, before crossing the river, to return to Kettlewell along a stretch of the Dales way, on the other side.

About half-way back to Kettlewell, Rhoda said, 'I'd like to take a photo of the group before we get back. I like to have a picture of each place we visit, to remember the place and the people by. I've nearly finished this film.' The others were obligingly arranging themselves, when Rhoda exclaimed, 'But where is my camera?'

She began feeling in pockets and rummaging in her small backpack.

'I must have left it when we stopped to look at the kestrel. I do remember putting it down on a rock when you handed me the binoculars, Ted. Oh, how stupid of me!'

The others stood round, sympathetic; several offered to go back and look for the camera.

'Oh, no! I really couldn't let you do that!' she answered. 'After all, it was only one of those cheap disposable cameras - not worth the trouble, really.'

They walked on, most feeling embarrassed. Rhoda put on a pretence of exaggerated unconcern, taking out her wildflower book and busily identifying varieties they'd seen in the hay meadows.

'Most of the farmers here don't cut the hay before July,' Hugh told them, 'so that the flowers have a chance to set seed for next year.'

'And it prolongs this lovely sight for summer visitors like us!' Sandy said.

'It's curious how almost every field has its own barn,' Ted commented. 'I've not seen so many in other parts of the country.'

'Yes, it's absolutely typical of these dales,' Hugh answered.

'What are they used for?'

'Farmers used to keep the cows in them, in stalls, over winter. They were fed on hay which was stored in the loft above. A very practical arrangement. I think they're used for storing equipment nowadays.'

'Where's Les?' Rex asked Tony, as they headed for Kettlewell.

'Dunno - call of nature, I expect. Oh no, I've just remembered. He went to get some shots of a heron he'd seen at the water's edge, about ten minutes ago.'

'Pity he didn't tell us all about the heron.'

'Oh, well, he probably thought we'd scare it away if we all went down there to look. Photography's his livelihood, so I suppose he can't risk missing an opportunity. We belong to the same photographic society. I'm just an amateur, though I've learnt a lot from Les.'

Two hours later, the walkers were back at Wildwood house, relaxing with drinks before dinner.

'Has Les got back yet?' Hugh asked.

'Yes. He's out on the terrace, chatting with Ted and Rhoda.' Rex sounded surprised.

'I can't thank you enough , Les!' Rhoda was saying. 'Going to all that trouble, just for my cheap little camera!'

'It was no trouble at all. Worth it just to see how pleased you were to get it back! But don't embarrass me with gratitude! Anyway, I began with disposable cameras, and now I do wildlife photos for magazines. So, who knows?'

Chapter 17

It was very late on Monday evening but Maria felt wide awake. Over the weekend, she'd had many hours' sleep, which by now had dispelled the exhaustion she had suffered from for so long. Her work in the garden had already contributed to this feeling of well-being which she'd thought would never be hers again. Her mind was too active for her to go to bed yet. She opened the door of the cottage and looked out. The garden was now in deep darkness. The trees and shrubs had merged together into the background of the hillside opposite. Looking up, though, she saw that the sky was brilliant with stars. She could make out constellations familiar to her since her childhood in Alborus and this moved her almost to tears. She had often stood with her father when she was a young girl, and he had shown her how to recognise Cassiopeia, Orion and the Plough. She stepped out across the lawn, still looking at the sky.

Suddenly, the air was rent by a shriek, and a ghostly white presence moved with flapping wings, so close to her that she thought she felt it brush her shoulder. She must have cried out, because a man's voice, startlingly near, said:

'It's only an owl! Don't be frightened!'

The tone was amused, but reassuring - not mocking - and she relaxed.

'Who is that?' he asked.

Maria wished he would identify himself first, and hesitated.

'Maria, isn't it?'

'Yes.'

'I'm Hugh. I've seen you working in the garden sometimes.'

'The Tree Man! But where are you?'

It was disconcerting talking with someone invisible but very close by.

'Here!'

She felt a warm hand on her elbow and turned towards him. She could now make out his face, light in the frame of his dark hair.

'I came out to see the barn owls,' he explained. 'Why are you out here?'

'I am too awake to go to bed. The air is cool here.'

After a pause, she said, 'The stars are very bright - I feel closer to my home - the same stars as we see there.'

'Yes,' Hugh said after a few moments. 'It's reassuring to see them, always the same, when so much is changing all around us.'

Maria wondered for a moment what 'reassuring ' meant, but she understood from the words that followed it.

There was a quality of stillness in their conversation, due in part to Hugh's care to avoid asking Maria personal questions, as Claire had requested, and to Maria's attentive listening and forming her own comments in English. But the silences seemed a part of the dialogue, and neither of them felt a need to fill them with words, while their limited view of each other freed them from self-consciousness.

'I think you like trees very much?' Maria asked, 'teaching about them here.'

'Yes, I've loved trees since I was a boy.'

'Where I lived, there are great forests of pine trees. They cover great spaces, grown for timber, for the building industry and furniture. But I love trees with silver-coloured stems...No. What is the word for the stem of a tree?'

'Trunk,' he answered, 'Stems are for flowers.'

'Yes. Thank you. I like trees with silver trunks, with little green leaves that change to gold in autumn. Those are my favourite trees.'

'Silver birches!'

'Silver birches!' she echoed, savouring the sound of the words, as if visualising the trees at the same time. 'I have seen silver birches here in England, but also many other kinds. I must learn their names.'

'I can lend you a book, if you like, to help you to recognise them. I'll bring it for you tomorrow. Would you like that?'

'Yes, thank you...Hoo,' she answered, taking great care with his name.

'No!' he laughed, 'That's what the owls say! Try again - "Hugh".'

'Huh-yoo! No, that is wrong also! So sorry. It is bad to say a person's name wrong.'   She was relieved to realise that he was not offended, but was, on the contrary, suppressing laughter.

'Have another go!' he said. 'Just say it the way you did last time, but a bit quicker.'

'Hugh!'

'Bravo!' he said heartily.

'I think, Hugh,' she said with exaggerated carefulness and a note of mischief in her voice, 'If I try to teach you my own language, Alboruvian, I shall laugh very much!'

'Yes, I'm sure you would! I'm hopeless at languages - specially the pronunciation!'

When they stopped laughing, they stood silent again in the dark, then Maria said: 'That bird that came here - what did you call him?'

'An owl.'

'Owl,' she repeated slowly and carefully. 'It sounds funny - do you think?'

'Yes I suppose it does. I hadn't thought so before, Maria, but it was the way you said it!'

'I think you laugh at me, Hugh!'

'No, no,' he said gently.

'That owl is one of a pair that are nesting in a ruined house just down the lane from here,' he said, after a short silence. 'I hope no one's going to demolish it, or they'll be homeless. Barn owls are having a hard time.'

Maria thought about this, then she said, 'Many creatures are having a hard time. People also. I was homeless until Claire let me stay here.'

Hugh wished he hadn't inadvertently raised the topic of homelessness. Maria was puzzled, almost disappointed, that he showed no interest.

'I asked for asylum in Britain,' she said. 'I was told to return to my country. Do you know about this?'

'Yes, Claire told me. I think you were very brave to make that journey. You must have been very distressed when your asylum appeal was refused.'

'Oh, I was so disappointed! I cannot tell you how I felt. I wanted to die!'

In the faint light, he saw the despair on her face - tears gleaming in her eyes. He put an arm round her thin waist and drew her close to him.

'Well, you're safe now. I don't think you could be in a safer place than this.'

'People here are so kind! And such beautiful country! When I was in Bradford, I saw pictures of Wharfedale. I longed to be there. At least I achieved that little ambition! But I fear this will not last.'

'I wonder,' Hugh said, 'Do you like walking? You could come on one of the walks with people on the course. Then you'd see more of the upper part of the Dale. It's my favourite part of England.'

'Oh yes, please, Hugh! I would like that so much!'

Her eyes were now bright with enthusiasm.

'Good,' said Hugh, 'I'll see what I can arrange.'

'Thank you, Hugh. I will enjoy a walk so much. I think I shall go indoors now. A bit cold,' she added with a slight shiver. 'Good night!' she said and held out a hand to him. He clasped it warmly, held it for a few seconds.

'Good night! Sleep well,' he said.

He watched her open the door of *Swifts* cottage, step inside and close the door. Then he turned and walked to the main house, and went up to his own room.

Maria felt less capable of sleeping than before she had gone outside. She put the kettle on and made herself some tea, wondering if she should have offered Hugh a cup. Was he now walking somewhere in the dark? She knew he avoided using transport whenever possible. Or did he have a room in the main house while teaching at the College? She hadn't thought to ask him. What an extraordinary meeting it had been! Talking so long, yet barely able to see each other in the darkness; as if that conversation had been out of time and place, with the presiding constellations giving a timeless ambience to those minutes. Kind, interesting, funny too, in a gentle sort of way, he was the first person who had made her laugh since she left home - the most decisive step she'd ever taken and which now seemed much longer ago.

But then, Pavel came vividly into her thoughts. Three days before her departure, he had tried, for the last time, to persuade her to stay in Alborus. She'd been disappointed earlier by his refusal to go with her despite the values they shared. Since her arrival in England, she had often thought of his arguments. The British, he'd said, would not welcome her with open arms, in spite of their traditional reputation for protecting refugees. They not only had needy citizens of their own to provide for but, just now, people from the countries which had recently joined the European Union were arriving in Britain in large numbers, as they were legally entitled to do. And Britain was not a country with endless space to absorb large numbers of foreigners. So, Pavel argued, refugees from other countries couldn't expect much help or sympathy. In his opinion, Maria's hope of being granted asylum was over-optimistic. She had quoted the United Nations convention relating to the status of refugees, signed by Great Britain, that no refugee would be returned to his own country if he had a justifiable fear of death or persecution there. Surely, Maria had argued, Great Britain would not break such a promise? Pavel, however, had little faith in declarations, or in any country's trustworthiness. He had tried, one last time, to persuade her to stay in her home country. As long as she was careful to avoid writing anything critical of its Government, she would be safe staying there.

'What is life without freedom of expression?' she had replied, quoting the title of her father's last published article before he was arrested.

It had been painful to realise that she might never see Pavel again. His own decision to stay in Alborus had seemed like a rejection of herself, so that she had not, at the time, considered objectively enough the reasons he gave, or appreciated the concern for her safety which partly motivated his efforts to persuade her to stay. Much of what he had said had proved true, and although she had found great kindness at Wildwood House, she could not let her present dependence on Claire continue indefinitely.

Chapter 18

The clothes were in remarkably good condition, Maria noticed, as she took them out of the box which she found on her doorstep on Tuesday morning. There was an accompanying note from Claire:
   'These are some clothes that Jonquil no longer needs. We think you are about the same size.'
   If these were Jonquil's cast-offs, the family must be quite wealthy. They looked brand-new to her. Was the message a white lie, to spare her the embarrassment of knowing that Claire had bought these clothes for her? Simple, practical garments - a pair of blue denim jeans, three tee-shirts - bright pink, blue and yellow, a pair of trainers - the classless clothing of young people everywhere. Also a warm green pullover and a lightweight waterproof jacket. There were two plastic bags at the bottom of the box. One, with the name *Marks and Spencer*, contained a pack of four pairs of pants. In the other, with the *Boots* logo, were a face flannel, a toothbrush and tube of paste, deodorant and a large box of tampons.
   Overwhelmed by the thoughtfulness all this represented, Maria burst into tears. She had resolutely not asked for anything, and had been worried how to obtain these latter necessities. Claire and her daughter had thought of everything.

****

Tuesday's programme began with Claire's talk on *Trees in Literature*.
   'Far in a western brookland
   That bred me long ago
   The poplars stand and tremble
   By pools I used to know.

   There in the windless night-time,
   The wanderer, marvelling why,
   Halts on his way to hearken
   How soft the poplars sigh...'
   Claire had made no introductory statement. Instead, she read these verses, very quietly, to the group. Then she paused for a few moments.

The poem, she felt, deserved, or perhaps imposed, this treatment; and indeed none of her listeners interrupted the silence and stillness that followed.

'This was the first poem that came into my mind when I decided to talk to you about trees in literature,' she resumed. 'I'm sure some of you knew it before?'

She looked round. Several people nodded or smiled. 'By A.E. Housman, isn't it?' asked the quiet man in the grey suit.

'Yes,' Claire answered. 'Those are the first two verses of a poem from *A Shropshire Lad*, his long cycle of poems, published in 1896. - By the way,' she added, 'do, please, feel free to comment and tell us your views. This isn't a formal talk; that's why we're here in the lounge, rather than the lecture room.' She smiled encouragingly, then she asked, 'Did you like these verses?'

Rhoda said, 'Yes, but it seemed very sad.'

Claire nodded.

'It seems to be full of longing for a place the writer used to know,' Jessica said, 'as if he were in exile from his home.'

'I just love the sound of it! - words like *soft, sigh,* and *tremble,*' Sandy said. 'Poplars really do sound like that - like whispering voices. There are three tall old poplars in a nature reserve where I live at Southport. I often walk there and I sometimes stand and listen to the poplars for a few minutes, murmuring that first verse to myself - or to a friend,' she added quietly, almost to herself.

'I thought of Housman last month,' said Hugh: '*Loveliest of trees, the cherry now/ Is hung with blossom on the bough...*'

'Oh, yes,' Rhoda agreed. 'The cherry blossom was specially wonderful this year. But it never lasts long - just about two weeks, then we always seem to get a few very windy days, and all the blossom's gone in no time. Quite sad!'

'Yes. It's the transience of the blossom that makes it seem so magical. I think Housman uses it as a metaphor for life, in that poem,' Jessica added.

'Let's move on to something else, now,' said Claire. 'Most of the poems and prose we're going to read today are in these handouts,' she added, issuing a copy to everyone. 'Now, look at page two please. Here's an old favourite of mine, *The Way through the Woods* by Kipling. I've always found woods rather mysterious places, and this poem expresses that feeling. Would anyone like to read it for us?'

'I would,' Sandy offered:

'They shut the road through the woods
Seventy years ago.
Weather and rain have undone it again
And now you would never know
There was once a road through the woods
Before they planted the trees.
It is underneath the coppice and heath
And the thin anemones.
Only the keeper sees
That, where the ring-dove broods,
And the badgers roll at ease,
There was once a road through the woods.

Yet, if you enter the woods
Of a summer evening late,
When the night-air cools on the trout-ringed pools
Where the otter whistles his mate
(They fear not men in the woods
Because they see so few.)
You will hear the beat of a horse's feet,
And the swish of a skirt in the dew,
Steadily cantering through
The misty solitudes,
As though they perfectly knew
The old lost road through the woods...
But there is no road through the woods.'

'Lovely!' said Jessica. 'I love the way he describes the animals in the wood, and that *swish of a skirt in the dew*, suggesting some romantic incident long ago.'

'My compatriot, Robert Frost, wrote well about woods,' said Rex. 'I'm glad you've included *Stopping by Woods on a Snowy Evening*, Claire. May I read it?'

'I was going to ask you, Rex. Please do!'

His listeners enjoyed the quiet, reflective tone of his reading. There was a silence after he finished.

'The mystery, here,' Claire said, ' is not about the wood, but about the promises the rider has to keep, and the miles he has to travel.'

'Yes. I think it's the repetition of that last line that makes the poem so haunting,' said Hugh.

Rhoda said, 'I like the way he describes the horse's puzzlement at stopping in the wood, miles away from anywhere, with the snow falling and night coming on. It's such a vivid picture - I can almost see that horse!'

'Thanks for reading it, Rex. It was good to hear it spoken with an authentic American voice,' said Claire.

'And thank you, ma'am, for askin' me!' he replied, exaggerating his accent, to everyone's amusement.

'Now for a passage from a novel by Thomas Hardy, *Under the Greenwood Tree*,' Claire announced. 'Page four in the handouts. Hardy knew the countryside so well and he describes it with the intimate knowledge of a true countryman. I'll read this one,' she said, when everyone had found the place.

'*To dwellers in a wood almost every species of tree has its voice as well as its feature. At the passing of the breeze the fir trees sob and moan no less distinctly than they rock; the ash hisses amid its quiverings; the beech rustles while its flat boughs rise and fall. And winter, which modifies the note of such trees as shed their leaves, does not destroy its individuality. On a cold and starry Christmas Eve within living memory, a man was passing up a lane near Mellstock Cross, in the darkness of a plantation that whispered thus distinctively to his intelligence ....and to his eyes, casually glancing upward, the silver and black-stemmed birches with their characteristic tufts, the pale grey boughs of beech, the dark-creviced elm, all appeared now as black and flat outlines upon the sky, wherein the white stars twinkled so vehemently that their flickering seemed like the flapping of wings.*'

'I'd have known that was by Hardy if you hadn't told us!' said Hugh, and several others agreed.

'Rather melancholy,' Tony said. 'I've not read anything by Hardy, but he doesn't seem a very cheerful character. Trees sobbing and moaning seem a bit over the top to me!'

Claire smiled. 'Maybe, but those words really do evoke the sounds their leaves make in the wind. Hardy knew from long experience of country life what each variety of tree sounded like when breezes blew through their foliage.

'Now, we'll omit the second Hardy passage in the handouts. It's from *The Woodlanders*, a wonderful novel about people whose lives and occupations are all bound up with trees. I hope you'll read it sometime, but I don't want to overrun my time, and delay the start of your various outings this afternoon. So we'll go straight on now to something else.

'Tolstoy probably isn't the first novelist who springs to mind when we think about trees, but there's an episode in *War and Peace* that impressed me very much when I first read it, and it still does. Prince Andrei is travelling through the Russian countryside in spring. Birches, wild cherry trees and alders are all coming into life. But then, in total contrast, he sees a huge ancient oak tree, gnarled and ungainly, resisting the cheerful springtime mood around it. Andrei is at a low point, unable to see any joy in life, and he equates himself with this oak tree. A few weeks later, he is returning home from a visit to Count Rostov and his family, and has been captivated by the youthful joyousness of Natasha. When he passes that oak tree again, at first he doesn't recognise it, for it is covered with green foliage. Now, his mood is in harmony with the optimism that the tree's spring foliage seems to proclaim, and his life now appears to him in a new light, full of possibilities for joy and fulfilment.'

'But it wasn't the oak tree's doing, was it? The tree only reflected the change of heart he'd had at the Rostov's house. It was all due to Natasha!' Sandy said.

'Not quite,' said Jessica, who had read *War and Peace* recently, 'The oak tree acted as a sort of catalyst, making Andrei realise that his life was still worth living. It wasn't only the beginning of his love for Natasha. His whole attitude to life was transformed.'

'Well,' Claire said, noticing the puzzled expressions of those who didn't know the book, 'I think we'll move on now, to a poem by John Clare. He is one of our best nature poets, writing in the first half of the nineteenth century. He had very little education, and spent part of his life in what was, in his time, known as a lunatic asylum. The poem I've chosen is called *In Hilly Wood*.

> 'How sweet to be thus nestling in deep boughs,
> Upon an ashen stoven pillowing me;
> Faintly are heard the ploughmen at their ploughs,
> But not an eye can find its way to see.
> The sunbeams scarce molest me with a smile,
> So thick the leafy armies gather round;
> And where they do, the breeze blows cool the while,

Their leafy shadows dancing on the ground.
Full many a flower, too, wishing to be seen,
Perks up its head the hiding grass between.
In mid-wood silence, thus, how sweet to be;
Where all the noises that on peace intrude,
Come from the chittering cricket, bird and bee,
Whose songs have charms to sweeten solitude.'

'Had anyone read that before?' Claire asked, after a pause from her reading. No one had.

'He gives a lovely impression of enjoying his solitude, yet at the same time being acutely aware of what's going on around him,' said Sandy.

Jessica agreed. 'And I specially like the description of the flower, perking up its head to be seen above the grass. That's just how I've seen flowers peeping through grass and twigs in woodland, as if they're reaching up to get noticed.'

As quite a lot of interest was shown in this poet, who was less well-known to the group than the others Claire had mentioned, she read a few more of John Clare's verses.

'Now, let's have a look at something by Wordsworth, as he's considered to be one of our greatest nature poets. He believed that nature has a moral influence on us:

'One impulse from a vernal wood
May teach you more of man,
Of moral evil and of good
Than all the sages can.

'We'll now read part of his poem *Yew Trees*. It begins with a description of an exceptionally old tree at Lorton, in the Lake District. It still exists! Would you read it for us, Hugh?' He nodded.

'There is a Yew-tree, pride of Lorton Vale,
Which to this day stands single, in the midst
Of its own darkness, as it stood of yore:
Not loth to furnish weapons for the bands
Of Umfraville or Percy ere they marched
To Scotland's heaths; or those that crossed the sea

And drew their sounding bows at Azincour,
Perhaps at earlier Crecy or Poictiers,
Of vast circumference and gloom profound
This solitary Tree! a living thing
Produced too slowly ever to decay;
Of form and aspect too magnificent
To be destroyed...'

'Wow! That certainly gives a sense of history,' said Ted. 'It makes us humans seem a bit feeble and short-lived!'

'I feel a bit overloaded with poetry,' said Les. 'Great stuff, but I'm not used to such big doses of it!'

'Well,' Claire replied, 'I've come to the end of my material, but Hugh has even more to tell us about the Lorton Yew Tree. Hugh?'

'Yes,' he answered, ' that tree has even more historical associations than Wordsworth's poem mentions! Both John Wesley and George Fox preached there. The tree must have been a good focal-point to attract people. When Wordsworth wrote this poem, the tree was reduced by almost half its size during a storm, but it's still alive! The Mayor of Cockermouth's official chair is made of wood from the part that broke off. The tree is believed to be at least a thousand years old.!'

'Worth a visit next time we're in the Lake District,' said Rhoda.

'Indeed,' Claire said. 'Well, that concludes the *Trees in Literature* session. Thank you for listening to my choices. I'm sure you'll think of lots more that I haven't mentioned. I would like to finish with an old Chinese proverb:

'Keep a tree in your heart, and perhaps a singing bird will come.'

****

The afternoon, free of organised activities, was an opportunity to follow up other interests for a while. Rex and Sandy went to see the strangely eroded millstone grit pillars, known as Brimham Rocks. Jessica went to Richmond to visit the recently-restored Georgian Theatre. Les and Tony headed off in seach of photographic inspiration. At Rhoda's insistence, she and Ted went to a craft centre in Hawes. Hugh, anxious about his teenaged son, telephoned his ex-wife in Sheffield.

Chapter 19

At mid-morning on Wednesday the Dales Bus dropped them in Buckden, a picturesque stone-built village near the head of the Dale and they began the steady climb which, according to Hugh, who led the way, had been originally built by the Romans, and which wound round the flank of Buckden Pike. The view to their left was intensely green as they rose above Rake's Wood and saw the River Wharfe meandering between meadows. Maria, walking with Claire, experienced sheer delight, gazing over those landscapes she had seen only in pictures which had impelled her to come to Wharfedale. She had not said a word after getting off the bus. Most of the others were silent too, few being regular walkers, needing all their breath for the steady, though not steep, climb, until their route diverged leftwards, levelling off before descending to the hamlet of Cray, reached by stepping stones across the lively Cray Gill. Passing the White Lion Inn, they began the most delightful part of this classic walk, which took them across the top of the Dale with wonderful views to their left down the valley, its glaciated origins clearly visible in the wide flat valley floor.

'Time for lunch?' Hugh asked.

'I was hoping someone would say that!' said Sandy, 'That was quite a long stretch!'

'These rocks look just right for sitting on,' Rex said, as they approached outcrops of the limestone pavement.

'Generations of walkers must have chosen this spot for picnics. It's so inviting,' Jessica enthused, as she and the others shrugged off their backpacks and began investigating their packed lunch. Silence reigned for a while.

'These rocks aren't as comfortable as they looked!' Rhoda observed after munching a sandwich.

'No,' Ted agreed, 'It's best to concentrate on the view.'

'And the food!' Les added, 'This is a jolly sight better than the picnics we used to get in the old days from youth hostels and b&bs!'

'Oh, I expect they've improved by now,' said Claire, 'But Pam, in our kitchen, is a walker herself, so she knows what sort of food we want - tasty and filling, but not too dry, and light to carry. Fruit drinks, too.'

Uncomfortable as the rocks were, Rex, Sandy and Les were now using them for sunbathing. Others contemplated the scenery. Rhoda took out a small sketchbook and a soft pencil and began unobtrusively to draw Hugh in profile. He was sitting very still, and Rhoda realised, after a few minutes, that he was gazing at Maria as she leaned on an old dry-stone wall, looking down the valley as if trying to commit the scene to memory. Rhoda felt a bit sorry for her. The course members had been requested not to ask her any questions because she'd had a bad time and it might upset her to talk about it. This had made Rhoda reluctant to speak to the girl, except to say hello when she met her in the garden, where she always seemed to be working. If everyone was doing the same, Maria must feel very isolated. Rhoda thought she might get up and walk over there and have a little chat with her, when she'd finished her sketch of Hugh.

Abruptly, Rhoda's pencil skidded across the page, making a jagged mark from Hugh's ear to his chin; Maria's head spun round to look at Hugh and their eyes met; Tony's camera, waiting for the sun to light a particular group of trees, jolted out of control. Heads hit limestone, or jerked up in shock, as the world was engulfed in the screaming roar of a fighter plane which was then seen, skimming the short, scrubby trees nearby, followed by two more aircraft. As fast as they came, they were gone. Silence fell. A bird squawked.

'That was a near miss!' Claire said.

'Probably not,' said Les, who had been in the RAF, 'Aircraft are never as low as they look from the ground.'

'I'll try to remember that the next time I'm scared out of my wits!' Sandy said.

'It's the suddenness that's so scary,' Rhoda said. 'There isn't time to reason that out when it's actually happening. My hand's still shaking. And this drawing's ruined. Those planes have spoilt my day!'

'No, only a few minutes of it.' Hugh said quietly to her, with a smile, which made her feel better.

'We just have to remember,' Ted said, a bit sententiously, 'that the RAF need to practise - so they'll be able to defend us, when necessary.'

'I used to think that,' said Claire, 'But those planes may be ones they are testing before exporting them. I was a bit shocked to hear on the radio the other day, that Britain is now the leading supplier of armaments and military aircraft to other countries.'

'Nothing wrong with that, is there?' Ted queried.

'Yes!' retorted Sandy, 'The arms trade encourages war. It's irresponsible to supply weapons to other countries.'

'That depends which countries we're selling them to,' Tony said.

'Well, this report I was telling you about went on to say that the countries we're supplying include nineteen of the twenty that the Foreign Office has listed as ones that abuse human rights! That really horrified me,' said Claire.

'Well,' Tony reasoned, ' if we didn't supply them, other countries would.'

'That argument wouldn't be accepted if it was drugs that we were selling,' Hugh said. 'And aren't arms worse than drugs?'

'Well, there's nothing we can do about it,' said Rhoda.

'There must be something we can do about it,' said Jessica. 'We could write to our MPs. If enough people protest, they're bound to take notice. They need our votes! I can't remember who said this, but I've always remembered it: All it takes for evil to triumph is for good men to do nothing.'

There was a silence, then Sandy said decisively, 'Well, I'll write a letter to my MP. I'm beginning to feel ashamed of my country.'

Maria had been listening attentively, though with difficulty, to this conversation. But in the silence that followed Sandy's declaration, she said, quietly but with passion: 'If you lived in my country, you would not dare to say such things! You are so lucky in Britain - especially your newspapers. My father died in prison for writing about the abuse of human rights in my country.'

She stopped and looked away, suddenly embarrassed, with everyone looking at her, and there was an uncomfortable silence.

'Thank you, Maria,' Jessica said. 'I think we needed reminding how lucky we are.'

Several of the others murmured agreement, and subdued conversation resumed. Rhoda got up and went over to Maria and squeezed her hand, giving what she hoped was an encouraging smile. She knew little of international politics, or the rights and wrongs of the arms trade. She had tended to accept Ted's views on such topics. But she responded to this young foreigner and her need for simple human warmth.

Maria smiled back. 'Thank you, thank you,' she said.

Clouds had moved up the valley and the air was turning chilly. It was time to move on, keeping the steep woodland below on their left. A few cows grazed on the short grass below the high moors to the right, while the haunting call of the curlew and the plaintive whistling cry of the golden plover claimed as theirs the lonely uplands beyond.

'Could you identify some of these flowers for us, Hugh?' Sandy asked. She and Rhoda had been conferring for a few minutes about plants. 'The ones that are growing between the cracks in these rocks. I don't think I know any of them.'

'That's not surprising,' he answered. 'This is a very unusual habitat. Some plants that thrive here aren't found elsewhere. These cracks that we find in limestone scenery - they're called *grykes*, by the way - are caused by weak parts of the rock wearing away, over thousands of years, to form this *pavement,* as it's called. They make marvellous habitats for plants that like moist or shady conditions, because it's damp and protected down there. So even plants like that leafy one there - D'you see it? - hart's tongue fern, that loves shade, can grow there amongst these rocks.'

'And what's this little pinky-lilac flower?' Rhoda asked.

'That's birdseye primrose. We're lucky to see it. It's quite rare, except in limestone scenery in the North of England - here, in fact! - and only now in June or July!'

'Is that one a yellow rattle?' asked Sandy, pointing to a plant with spiky narrow-toothed leaves and bright yellow flowers at the top.

'That's right,' Hugh answered. 'And besides flowers, all sorts of ferns can grow in the *grykes* - as you can see here and there.'

'It's a fascinating habitat,' Jessica said.

'Yes. It's not surprising that most of Upper Wharfedale has been recognised as a Site of Special Scientific Interest. Another habitat is the hay meadows that you've seen down in the Dales valleys. Farmers have agreed to wait until a bit later in the summer before cutting the hay, to give time for the wild flowers to set seed. That's why they're so rich in flowers now.'

'They must give joy to everyone who sees them,' Jessica said.

'And what about your own specialism, Hugh, and mine too, trees?' said Rex.

'Well, some of these woods that grow on steep hillsides - like this one we've been following - may have been unchanged for centuries. They're too awkwardly positioned for anyone to want to use the land for farming or anything else. So we have areas of untouched ancient woodland - worth preserving for its own sake. Another interesting point is the prevalence of ash trees in the area. They can grow in extraordinary places, where other trees couldn't get established, like steep hillsides. It's because they have very flexible wood. That's why they've been used for making tools, for centuries. But you know all this, Rex, I'm sure! How about you giving a talk to the group about trees of America - giant redwoods etc.?'

'I'm thoroughly enjoying listening to other people for a change! Do, please, continue.'

'I'm surprised to see ash looking so misshapen and stunted up here,' Jessica said. 'I've always thought of them as very graceful trees.'

'Yes,' said Hugh. 'It just goes to show how adaptable they are. Another benefit ash trees have is that the shade they give is quite light; so flowers can grow profusely below them - snowdrops, wood anemones, ramsons, bluebells...'

'We're getting near to Scar House, Hugh,' said Claire who had gone on ahead with Maria, Tony and Les, while Hugh and the others had lingered. They had been waiting for them to catch up.

'Right,' Hugh said, stopping and waiting till everyone had arrived. Then he explained that George Fox, founder of the Society of Friends, had visited Scar House in 1652 and it became a Quaker Meeting House. It now belonged to the National Trust, who let it out as a holiday cottage.

'Just right for anyone who wants peace and quiet,' said Jessica.

'So long as they don't mind those jets flying over!' Ted added.

'Now,' Hugh said, 'when we get to Scar House, we take a path that leads right down to Hubberholme - unless you want to go on to the next village, Yockenthwaite, in Langstrothdale?'

'Right,' he continued, nobody having made that choice, 'Hubberholme has an ancient church with several interesting features, and a pub that's very popular with walkers - so most tastes will be catered for! Some of us may want to spend longer here than others, and there's no need for us all to keep together on the way back to Buckden. The route is clearly signposted. I suggest you allow a good forty minutes for the walk. The bus times are in those leaflets I gave you this morning. I've a few spare copies here, if needed. Is that OK to everyone?'

There were murmurs of assent, then they headed downhill towards Hubberholme.

'Oh, look!' Sandy exclaimed, as the church tower suddenly appeared below them and quite close.

The beautiful location and the tranquility of the churchyard, with just two people looking at the graves, imposed an involuntary silence as several of Hugh's party approached the porch and went in. The bare, unplastered walls, built of local stone, imparted a feeling of great age and endurance. Claire pointed out the rood loft, made in 1558, its oak structure bare, except for a simple design of trailing leaves painted in black along its base and underlined by a continuous strip of red paint. The simplicity of the design made the loft's survival, one of only two in Yorkshire, seem especially moving.

Oblivious of the contemplative mood of the church, two children, a boy and a girl, were darting from pew to pew, peering at the woodwork. In a triumphant loud whisper, the girl said, 'I've found one! Look!' The boy hurried over to see where she was pointing, at the end of a pew which was lit by a beam of sunlight. They both seemed to stroke the woodwork, then scampered off to search elsewhere.

'What are those kids up to?' Rex asked.

'They're looking for carvings of mice,' Claire explained quietly. 'The man who made these pews, in the 1930s, Robert Thompson of Kilburn, carved a mouse on everything he made. He's known as the Mouse Man. The fun is to try and find them all!'

Soon most ot the group succumbed to this unusual church activity for a while, then, after looking at a wall plaque commemorating J.B. Priestley, a Yorkshire writer who loved the Dales, drifted over to the George Inn for convivial refreshments.

Lingering in the church, Jessica saw Maria sitting very still at the end of a pew, next to the wall. She wondered whether to wait for her, but, noticing Hugh studying one of the stained-glass windows nearby, she too went out.

****

'Oh, Hugh!' Maria said, when they were sitting on the bench beside the church path, watching chaffinches hopping and fluttering nearby, 'I agree with that writer. This is a very beautiful place. I can't remember his words that were on that stone, about Hubberholme...'

' "One of the smallest and pleasantest places in the world," ' Hugh quoted.

'Yes, and in the church I felt so safe and peaceful. I was thinking about the people who lived here centuries ago, sitting in this church, praying, or thinking about their troubles. And now, I have come here with my troubles - from a place so far away that those early people here would never have heard of it - and yet I share something with them.'

'Yes, I think very old churches seem to link us with past generations,' Hugh said. 'I'm not a churchgoer any more, though. I used to be a choirboy when I was in my teens, and I still love a lot of the old hymn tunes and anthems we used to sing.'

'I think your music is very different from what we have in the Orthodox Church,' she said, smiling, 'Our priests sing with very deep voices! Very beautiful, very spiritual. And usually there are no seats like in this church. Everybody stands!'

They were silent for a few minutes, listening to the birds and the gentle babble of the river nearby.

'This is a very special day for me, Hugh, walking simply for pleasure. The first time I can walk freely and not be afraid something bad will happen. But I think I was not wise to tell everyone about my country and about my father, when we were having the picnic. Somebody may think I am an illegal immigrant, and tell other people. I have been so careful what I say, but that was a big mistake.'

Hugh noticed an anxious frown on her forehead. 'I'm sure you can trust the people on the course,' he said reassuringly.

'I think that is true. But someone else may hear them talking about me. Perhaps in the pub it is happening now. Hugh, I want to start walking back to Buckden now, not wait longer here. I will go alone, if you want to go in there for a drink.'

She stood up, gathering her belongings.

'I don't want to be late back today,' Hugh answered, and stood up promptly. 'I'll walk back with you, if you don't mind.'

'Of course I do not mind!'

They crossed the bridge over the Wharfe, walked past the whitewashed Inn and on towards Buckden along the narrow winding road. They paused to watch a pied wagtail which landed on the drystone wall ahead of them, flew a short distance, to alight further along the wall, repeating the same sequence a number of times, wagging its tail up and down at each landing. Soon, they left the road to follow a riverside path beside a meadow, full of wild flowers.

'This river, the Wharfe, where does it begin?' Maria asked.

'Not very many miles from here,' Hugh answered. 'If we'd turned right when we joined the road, instead of coming into Hubberholme, and kept walking, we'd have followed the river through Langstrothdale - getting more and more remote, passing a few tiny hamlets. - Very small villages,' he explained, seeing her puzzled expression at the unfamiliar word. 'The road eventually rises, and the scenery gets wilder and looks more bare. The source of the Wharfe is up there - a spring that forms a tiny stream.'

'I would love to see that,' Maria said. 'But where does it go to later?'

'It flows eastwards and joins up with several other Yorkshire rivers, which form the River Ouse. By the time the Ouse reaches York, it's quite a wide river. Finally it flows into the great Humber estuary, together with the River Trent, and finally into the North Sea.'

'I must look at a map to understand all this! The Wharfe is so beautiful here. It seems friendly, the way it flows. Do you think so, Hugh? I am too sentimental, perhaps?'

'I know what you mean. I think it's partly the effect of the scenery - this field full of flowers, the trees by the water, the birds. - Look at that dipper, bobbing its head into the water! And the swallows, swooping about to catch insects in the air. And with the sunshine making the water sparkle, we're seeing the Wharfe at its most appealing. Yes, I agree, "friendly" describes it well today!'

They sat for a while, gazing simply at the river and its surroundings. The afternoon was hot, with very little breeze. The meadow drowsed in the warm stillness.

'Tell me what these flowers are, Hugh. Some I know, but not their English names.'

He pointed out the white and the red clovers, buttercup, hawkbit and yellow rattle, the thistle-like knapweed, the twisting stems of tufted vetch trailing their bright purple flower clusters modestly among the grasses, and the large blue meadow cranesbill flowers at the field's edge.

'I feel as if I could stay here for ever,' Maria murmured drowsily.

'Well, there's no hurry. We can catch a later bus from Buckden.'

'But you said you needed to get back early. You must not be late because of me!'

Hugh laughed gently.

'What is funny?' she asked, puzzled.

'Oh, Maria, you're so trusting! I wanted your company for a bit longer - to be on our own for a while. And you were anxious to go back straight away, so I said I was, too! Are you cross with me?'

'No,' she answered, smiling, but then she looked at him so searchingly that he felt as if she were trying to peer into his soul, and he had to look away.

'Well, I suppose we'd better be getting along now,' he said, half-heartedly.

He stood up and offered a hand to help Maria.

'Anyway, there's no need to rush, is there?' he asked.

She nodded and they continued their walk at a leisurely, almost languid pace. They noticed young saplings that had been planted recently close to the river, to prevent the bank from erosion by animals, Hugh explained.

'Hawthorn, ash, sycamore, I think,' Maria murmured, 'like those we saw higher up the valley,'

They each felt both relieved and disappointed that their conversation had become impersonal again. Suddenly, Maria stopped to gaze at the grey trunk and jaggedly broken-off branches of a lifeless old sycamore.

'I am sad to see such a dead tree,' she said with a shudder. 'It looks as if it is turned to stone - so grey, with those strange holes in the bark.'

'Yes, it does look grim,' Hugh agreed. 'All part of nature's cycle, though,' he added with a shrug and began to walk on.

'Oh, but look!' Maria exclaimed. 'I think it is still alive!'

She pointed to a slender stem growing straight up from the hollow between two dead branches, fragile and delicate amid the surrounding decay. Hugh turned back and looked up again at the tree.

'Yes,' he said, 'But that isn't a new shoot of the sycamore, is it? Look at those pairs of tiny pointed leaves - That's an ash tree starting to grow!'

Maria opened her bag and fished from it the notebook she normally used for writing newly-encountered English words. Without a word, she began to sketch the tiny tree growing among the surrounding dead branches.

'I didn't know you were an artist!' Hugh said.

'I am not, but I wish to remember this.'

'Take your time; there's no need to hurry. It must be awkward drawing it from below, like that. I wish I could find a rock or something for you to stand on...'

He waited while she made her sketch, with little cries of exasperation at her own clumsiness.

'A very bad drawing!' she said at length, showing it to Hugh, 'But it will remind me.'

'And now, I'll tell you what it symbolises,' he said. 'That tiny ash sapling is like a young refugee who has arrived from a distant country and has found somewhere to settle and flourish. And not only that. The little tree will bring something good and lovely to its new surroundings, reviving the old place with its originality and beauty.'

Maria listened intently, her face serious. When he finished, she said nothing. She seemed to be waiting. Hugh wondered whether she had understood his metaphor.

'All this came to me while you were making your drawing,' he continued. 'I thought of the many people who have had to leave their own countries and seek safety abroad. It's been going on throughout history in different parts of the world. People tend to have a negative view of immigrants, but many of them have enhanced the countries where they settled, bringing new skills and enriching the local culture. They are like that young tree which is going to bring new life and beauty to its aged host.'

He paused for breath. Maria smiled. Again, she waited.

'What I'm trying to say, in fact,' he said, taking her left hand - the one that was not holding the notebook, still open at the page with the sketch, 'is that, for me, that beautiful little tree represents you.'

In an almost choking voice, she said: 'You say such a beautiful thing to me, Hugh. But I cannot do what you say. I may be sent back to Alborus, but even if I stay in England, without permission, I am not allowed to earn money. I will be dependent on other people while I am here. So how can I give anything to this country?'

'Don't think about that,' he said. 'You are giving pleasure to everyone at Wildwood House by making the garden look so good, and we all enjoy your company. As for me, I'm happier with you than with anyone else!'

Chapter 20

When she arrived back at Wildwood House with Jessica, Rhoda and Ted late that afternoon, Claire was astonished by the sight of an enormous rucksack in the hall, near the door to the office. It took only a few moments to realise whose it was. Rory must be back from Guatemala! Typically, he'd been vague about when he would return. Dropping her diminutive backpack next to his, she hurried outside again and found him sitting on one of the garden benches at the far side of the lawn, facing towards the river.

'Rory! Oh, Rory!' she called.

He sprang to his feet, ran to meet her, and threw his arms round her in an exuberant hug.

'You're back!' Claire cried.

'Well, it would appear so,' he said, his tone humorously apologetic.

'Let me look at you,' she said. 'You're so brown, and I'm sure you've grown taller!'

Her gangly youth had returned a man. His voice seemed deeper and she recognised a new confidence in his face and demeanour.

'And you look well, Mum. College doing well? It looks great. Quite a lot's been happening here, according to Jonquil! I've just been talking to her on my mobile, and texting some of the old sixth-form crew - Mark, Des, Andy. Remember them?'

'I should think I do! They've been ringing up, asking if you were here, saying they were back from wherever they've been, almost since the College opened'.

'When was that?' He sounded puzzled. 'Only recently, surely?'

'Last Friday. It seems ages ago to me, though. I've been so busy all the time!'

'Can I stay the night here, Mum? I told Jonquil and Dad I'd go on to York tomorrow. I wanted to see you first, though, and have a look at this place.'

Claire thought for a moment.

'Yes. One of the cottages is unoccupied. Maybe you noticed the pair of them on the way up the drive?'

He nodded.

'It's the one on the left, *Curlews*, that's vacant. You'll see a picture of a curlew on the door.'

'Great! Actually, I could do with an early night,' he said, trying to suppress a yawn, 'Quite a journey, that was! - Guatemala City to Mexico City, so far so good. Mexico to Heathrow flight was the eventful bit! Suspected bomb on board! Emergency landing at a US airforce base in the Azores! Don't look so worried: I survived! It'll probably be on the telly tonight. I'll give you my version of the events tomorrow. Heathrow to Manchester, no problems. It was the last stage, train then bus to here, that really knocked me out. I slept most of the way.'

'I'd have been frantic if I'd known what was going on!' his mother said. 'And *was* there a bomb?'

'No, but it took hours and hours to make certain, and not much in the way of tourist facilities at the American air force base to keep us happy!'

'Thank goodness you're OK!' said Claire. 'Well, I expect you're hungry. One or two people on the course are going out for dinner this evening, so, if you like, you can eat in the dining room with the others. Or we can both eat privately in the flat. Which d'you prefer?'

'The flat, please, Mum. I won't be at my sociable best till the jet-lag has worn off, and I'd be embarrassed yawning through the meal. Not a pretty sight!'

Claire laughed, glad to have her son to herself for a while.

****

Sandy and Rex were in the dining room of *the Racehorses* in Kettlewell, their huge appetites from the day's walking in the fresh air being satisfied with lamb shanks in tasty gravy with generous portions of vegetables. A glass of red wine before, and another with, the meal made Sandy feel increasingly relaxed and carefree, as she listened to Rex's tales of life in Connecticut. The warmth of the room was making her feel slightly drowsy.

Glancing casually around, she could see several people at the bar, waiting to order meals or buy drinks. She looked again at one man standing there. It was Peter! Peter Holmes! She'd hardly thought about him since he left on Saturday morning, after bringing her forgotten tablets on Friday night. Why was he here? Most likely he just wanted to see her again. But why come to Kettlewell, several miles further up the Dale than Wildwood House? Maybe he was here for reasons quite unconnected with her, but that seemed unlikely. Anyway, it was inevitable they would meet now, and she would have to introduce him to

Rex. She looked again towards the bar. He was still there, waiting. Had he seen her already? Would he come over and speak to her? Or should she make the first move? And what would he think about Rex? And Rex about him? Guilt assailed her. She hadn't missed Peter at all, but he would certainly have missed her. But they'd been together for two years, on and off, and had planned to marry - no, to be accurate, Peter had wanted them to marry. And he was a good, kind, loyal friend. She thought gratefully of his sensitive kindness to her in the long aftermath of Val's death in the car crash. He'd put up with her crying fits, her outbursts of temper when he'd tried to persuade her that she wasn't to blame.

'Are you all right, Sandy?'

She gave a slight start, and turned towards Rex. He looked puzzled.

'Yes,' she said, expressionlessly.

'You looked - kind of absent - just then. You've gone a bit pale, too. Are you sure you're all right?'

'Oh, I'm sorry, Rex. I'm quite OK.'

She pulled herself together. 'You were saying...?'

'Nothing very important. How d'you like the food?'

'Delicious!' she said, a bit too emphatically, 'Just what we needed after all that fresh air and exercise!'

Rex smiled.

'I suppose walkers are their main clientèle here?'

She nodded.

Peter was still there, chatting with the barman now. Why did she feel so guilty at the prospect of coming face to face with Peter? All she needed to do was to introduce them to each other - Rex as a fellow-student on the course. But how could she describe Peter to Rex? An 'old friend'? Peter would be affronted. As her boyfriend? Her partner? No, she didn't want to say that. She realised, as if only vaguely aware of it before, that Rex was rather more to her than a 'fellow-student'. In fact, Rex had achieved, quite effortlessly, in just a few days, what Peter had tried so long and so devotedly to do - alleviate her obsessive guilt about Val's death.

Rex broke in startlingly on her thoughts: 'I expect you've got a boyfriend, haven't you?'

'Well, yes. But it isn't really a serious relationship.'

What a liar she was! And Peter standing just a few yards away! She despised herself.

'Not now, anyway,' she added, more accurately, though she still felt wretched.

But something was happening. He was walking towards her, mug of beer in hand and a copy of the dinner menu under his arm. She looked down, tried to concentrate on putting a piece of potato onto her fork. What on earth would happen now! She looked up furtively, without raising her head, watched him sit down at the nearest table. And it wasn't Peter! In fact, seen this close, the man bore no resemblance at all to Peter. Relief surged through her, and in a completely spontaneous action, she reached both her hands across the table towards Rex. Baffled, but pleased, he grasped them warmly, as Sandy gazed joyfully into his eyes.

Chapter 21

Maria switched on the radio in the cottage, and the little room was flooded with the serene music of a piano concerto. She lay down on the sofa and let the lovely melodies wash over her as she relaxed and thought over the pleasures of the day - the walk through such beautiful countryside, with people who were friendly in an easy, uninquisitive way; the flowers and trees whose names she'd learnt; and the long conversation with Hugh in the churchyard and beside the river. Again, she thought about that tiny ash tree he'd compared to her, that had taken root on an old, dead sycamore - the most original and extraordinary compliment she had ever received! She smiled to herself, as the music flowed through her mind, reflecting the day's enjoyment.

Then she heard a light tap on the front door. She got up, reluctant to change her position or her mood. Opening the door, she spotted something loosely wrapped in brown paper, on the doorstep. Then she saw Hugh, walking slowly away.

'Hugh!' she called softly.

He turned, smiled and walked back.

'Sorry if I've disturbed you. I just remembered the tree book I promised to lend you. And I've brought one on birds as well.'

She picked up the parcel and unwrapped the books. Hugh waited awkwardly.

'Thank you, Hugh. I shall enjoy looking up the birds we saw today. First, the wagtail on the wall, taking little short flights in front of us. Do you remember him, Hugh?'

'I remember everything that happened today, especially our walk back from Hubberholme.'

'Why are you laughing, Hugh?' she asked, perplexed.

'Ever since I taught you how to pronounce my name - out here in the dark - you've said it almost every time you've spoken to me!'

'It is a good name. I like to say it,' she said simply. 'Come in, Hugh. I will make some coffee, if you like.'

'Thanks. That'd be great,' he said stepping inside, ducking to avoid banging his head on the low lintel.

'People must have been shorter when these cottages were built!' he said, as she showed him into the sitting room. 'I like your choice of music. Mozart, isn't it?'

'I don't know. I just switched on this radio to a programme with classical music. This music was already playing. I think it is Mozart. I like very much his music. Perhaps they will say what it is at the end. I will make our coffee now.'

She disappeared into the kitchen. Hugh gazed around him. He was immediately struck by the fewness of personal possessions in the room. Apart from a tiny posy of buttercups on the window-sill, it looked as if no one was in residence. He was reminded sharply of the harshness of Maria's journey from Alborus, the necessity of travelling extremely light. She might have been forced to trade some of her possessions as well as money - and God knows what else, he wondered with dread - to be brought to Britain. He shuddered, but felt an increased respect for her courage.

He wandered over to the bookshelf at the other side of the room. The books looked quite old. No doubt they belonged to the main house, to Claire probably. He noticed *Jane Eyre* on the table, a slip of paper marking the place where Maria had stopped reading. Out of idle curiosity, he opened the book at the place. It was a part of the story that he had no recollection of, where Jane, having fled from Mr Rochester's house on discovering at their wedding that he was already married, wanders, hungry and destitute through the countryside, fruitlessly seeking work, and trying to barter small possessions in exchange for food. Certain passages had been lightly marked with pencil in the margin.

What was I to do? Where to go? Oh, intolerable question, when I could do nothing, and go nowhere! when a long way must yet be measured by my weary, trembling limbs before I could reach human habitation - when cold charity must be entreated before I could get a lodging; reluctant sympathy importuned, almost certain repulse incurred, before my tale could be listened to, or one of my wants relieved!

This must have been similar to Maria's experience before she finally arrived at Wildwood House, when she'd walked up the Dale, stopping at guest houses and pubs asking for work, always being rejected. At that moment, Maria came in with a tray of coffee and biscuits. He closed the book and put it down quickly, embarrassed, as if he'd been reading her private diary.

'Sorry! I was having a look at *Jane Eyre*. It's years since I read it.'

She smiled but made no comment, put the tray down on the coffee table, poured coffee from the jug, offered milk and sugar.

'How long will you be teaching at Wildwood House?' she asked.

'Just until the present course ends on Friday. Then I'll be giving lectures and courses at other centres in North Yorkshire.'

'So, we will not see you after this week?'

She looked anxious.

'Not much. But I live in Grassington, so I'll be based just a few miles from here most of the time. Most of the places are in easy travelling distance.'

'And you always talk about trees?'

He smiled and nodded.

'You must love them very much!'

'Yes. Ever since I was a young boy, when I found a hollow tree where I used to hide. I told the group about this on the first day of the course. They were quite amused that I used the tree as a hiding place from my parents! I got to know all the insects and birds that lived there, and of course climbing trees was a big attraction too! When I went to University, I studied biology, then later I did an MSc in dendrology - the science of trees.'

The music ended and they listened for the announcement. 'Mozart's Piano Concerto, number 23 in A major, was played by Vladimir Ashkenazy with the Philharmonia Orchestra.'

'We were right!' Maria said, as she switched the radio off. 'I cannot understand the advertisements between the music. The speech is too rapid, or too colloquial, for me! Now I will look at this beautiful bird book you brought me. First, the wagtail.'

Several were listed in the index, but she quickly recognised the pied wagtail, by its black and white colouring.

'What is the meaning of *pied*?'

'Having two colours, or sometimes more than two, I think. Most English children know the word from a poem called *The Pied Piper of Hamelin*. His clothes were "half of yellow, half of red!" '

Maria laughed. 'I was thinking, when I made our coffee, about those children in the church. They looked so serious, searching for the mouse carvings, then their faces changed to delight when they found one.'

'Yes. They certainly livened up the old church,' Hugh said.

'They reminded me a little of my brother's children - similar ages, I think,' Maria said.

'I expect you'll miss them.'

'A little, yes. But they live a long way from my home. We rarely saw them, but they used to send us photographs sometimes. Have you a family, Hugh?'

'I have a son, Giles. He's thirteen. I don't see him very often though. His mother, Vera, and I are divorced. Giles lives with her, in Sheffield.'

Maria was very still. Hugh felt that she was waiting for him to say more.

'Vera and I married very young, just after I got my degree. I'd intended to continue at University, doing research, but it soon became apparent that a baby was on the way, so instead I got a job, at a garden centre. I quite liked the work, though I hadn't expected to. I learned a lot about plants; and that stood me in good stead later, when I was able to go back to University. Anyway, I don't want to bore you with my troubles, so I'll summarise what happened. Vera and I should never have got married. We were quite unsuited to each other, and this became more apparent after Giles was born. We quarrelled over just about everything, including Giles's upbringing. I worried that our constant rows would have a bad effect on him. In the end we divorced, by mutual consent. Naturally, Vera got custody - horrible word - of Giles, and I was on my own again and able to go back to studying; and trees became my life. Not a very impressive biography, I'm afraid!'

'Do you see Giles sometimes?' Maria asked.

'Yes, but it's always difficult. Vera isn't very cooperative when I go to their house. I take him out, try to interest him in things I think are worthwhile. Sheffield is on the edge of the Peak District - marvellous countryside. But Vera's a real townie - never ventures into the wilds! It was easier when Giles was younger. He loved coming for walks with me, bird-watching and so forth. Vera used to make up a picnic lunch for us and we'd eat it at the top of a hill we'd climbed. I think she was glad to be rid of us - or me anyway! But he's thirteen now, a teenager, and we're not the same together as we used to be. I can tell, sometimes, that he's bored with my company and he'd rather be with his mates, playing computer games, or watching violent films. I've met some of his friends and I'm a bit uneasy about the crowd he's with. Vera lets him do more or less as he likes. That's the impression I get.'

'Has Vera a job?'

'Yes. She's a hairdresser. She's got her own salon now and employs several people. She's done quite well.'

'Is she at home when Giles returns from school?'

'Not now, and this is one of the things that worry me. When he was little, Vera worked part-time and was always home when he got back. But now that she's got her own business to run, and Giles is older, I suppose she thinks a bit of independence is good for him. Maybe she's right. He's got to learn to stand on his feet and be streetwise, as they say.'

'Is he working well at school?'

'Not as well as I'd expected, I must admit. He was a bright little boy at primary school. He could read before he went to school. I must give Vera the credit for that. She taught him to read. But he doesn't seem interested in his schoolwork now.'

'Perhaps you worry too much, Hugh. I think teenagers are not so keen to study as when they were little. There are other things that interest them at that age.'

'Yes. Well, some of those things aren't very good for them! Anyway, I expect you're right.'

He pondered for a while, then he said, 'Tell me more about yourself now.'

She told him about her upbringing in Alborus, emphasising her father's influence, especially after her mother's death when she was fourteen, his insistence that Maria learn English in addition to Russian, her first foreign language which she was taught at school. English was not on the school syllabus, so she'd had to study privately with a tutor, a woman who taught linguistics in the college where Maria's father lectured on engineering. At the same time, she'd had to look after her mentally handicapped sister, Elizaveta, helped, while Maria was at school, by her brother's wife.

'It was quite hard, fitting in all my home responsibilities and my education! I think you already know about my father's journalism which got him into trouble with the authorities. They would not tolerate any criticism. But my father insisted on writing about the abuse of human rights, and the result was imprisonment, then death in prison.'

She paused, in an effort to control her emotions.

'And that is why I wanted to come to England, where people can express themselves without fear. I tried at first to write newspaper articles, continuing my father's work, but I was stopped, and I was not allowed to go back to school teaching. There was no future for me in Alborus, and when I realised that I was being followed, and received death threats, I was very frightened. I had to get away. But I was advised not to become a refugee.'

There was a long pause. She wondered whether to tell Hugh about Pavel.

'What did your friends think of the idea?'

'It was difficult. I tried to persuade my friend Pavel to come with me. I was so disappointed when he refused. He had good reasons, as I have realised since. So I had to make a difficult choice. I chose England.'

They were silent for a while, then Hugh asked, 'Was Pavel very important in your life?'

She did not answer immediately and her facial expression was difficult to interpret.

'I thought so. We shared many interests,' she said after a few moments. 'But in those last few weeks before I left home, I think I gradually realised that we were not really suited to each other. Sometimes I think about him, but not in an emotional way any more.'

'I think you've been very brave,' Hugh said.

'I think we need some more coffee!' Maria said, standing up and collecting the cups and saucers. This time, he followed her into the little kitchen and insisted on making the coffee himself.

'We shall have cake also!' Maria said, as if announcing a celebration. She opened a cupboard and took a tin from a shelf. 'I think it is very good cake - date and walnut! Claire made it. She is a very talented lady.'

'Yes, she is. But so are you! Your English is almost perfect - now that you've mastered the pronunciation of my name! Whoo! indeed! As if I was one of those owls we heard out there!'

The kettle came to the boil, and Maria reached to pick it up, but Hugh took it from her, put it down and switched it off.

'The coffee can wait a few moments,' he said, putting his arms round her and looking tenderly at the face which had become more beautiful to him each time he saw her. He kissed her. He need not worry about Pavel, nor she about Vera. They were free to love each other.

The kettle needed to be boiled again when they were ready for more coffee and Claire's cake.

'I would have thought your English would have helped your application for asylum,' Hugh said while they finished the refreshments.

'I hoped so also,' Maria sighed, 'but it did not. It helped me with living in England. I do not think I would have survived here if I did not know the language. Even so, it was not easy. I had not much practice with speaking English. Few people in my country know the language. My learning was mostly from books, but I had tapes to listen to for pronunciation, besides my teacher. She was very good. But when I arrived in England, I was so confused - such strange accents! The driver who brought us to the North of England from London - He was impossible to understand!'

'His accent was probably cockney, the London accent,' Hugh explained.

'And then, the speech of the northern people - quite different again! I could not understand the landlord and his wife at the guest house where I worked in Skipton! They thought I was very stupid, because I could speak English but did not know what they said.'

Hugh laughed. 'No wonder you had problems!'

'But here at Wildwood House, I can understand most of what people say, and most of them live in the North, I think?'

'Yes, but most of us speak fairly standard English - just a few differences with some of the vowel sounds. If you were to talk to some of the farmers round here, people who've spent their whole lives in these Dales, you wouldn't understand them very easily.'

'The one I find hardest to understand here is the caretaker.'

Hugh laughed again. 'Oh yes, Geoff! He was born and bred in this area and he's proud of his speech. He doesn't make any concessions to people from further away! Between you and me, I think he exaggerates his accent to make it harder for them! Puts in a few dialect words deliberately that he knows they won't understand!'

They both laughed. Maria felt more relaxed than she had for many months. Hugh moved over from the armchair to sit beside Maria on the sofa. Her hair smelt nice, as if freshly washed, and the soft light of the table lamp gave a gentle lustre to its dark abundance falling loosely to her shoulders. He put an arm round her and she snuggled closer to him. He looked earnestly into her eyes for a few moments.

Then he said, 'I love you, Maria. And if it weren't so ridiculously early in our acquaintance, I'd ask you to marry me! It *is* ridiculous, isn't it?'

For a moment, she didn't speak or move. Then, with a warm, welcoming embrace, she answered his question.

It was very late when Hugh left the cottage.

Chapter 22

In the darkened lecture room, the picture projected onto the screen glowed with rich colour.

'This is called *The Magic Apple Tree*. It's one of Samuel Palmer's best-known paintings. Have a good look at the picture, then we'll discuss it.'

Claire sighed with relief. Although she was embarking on a task for which she was unqualified, she now felt quite relaxed. Two hours earlier she had almost panicked, when one of the things she most dreaded had happened - a tutor cancelling a class at short notice! Rachel Williams, a noted art historian, booked to talk to the group today, Thursday, on the subject of *Trees in Art*, had telephoned two hours ago. She was, she'd said, virtually stranded, somewhere in the Midlands. Setting out early from her home in Hertfordshire, she had encountered torrential rain after about an hour's driving, 'bouncing like pound coins', she'd said, on the road ahead. The situation had worsened in the Midlands, and the police had directed north-bound traffic off the motorway, owing to severe flooding ahead. Apparently, a large swathe of central England was affected, and the only route to the North was via a big detour eastwards, indicated by the police. Not surprisingly, the traffic on this route was extremely heavy and progress was painfully slow. When her car had been stationary for half an hour, Rachel had realised the hopelessness of her journey and phoned Claire on her mobile, with profuse apologies for being unable to give her lecture.

'Don't bother about my fee,' she'd said, and when Claire protested, she'd conceded, 'Well, a few pounds for petrol, if you like!'

Claire wondered briefly where Rachel was now, trying to get home after a totally wasted journey. She'd probably spent ages preparing her talk. Claire decided she would send her the lecture fee after all. Rachel deserved it, though, at the back of her mind, was a recent reminder from her accountant brother, Charles, that she should not be spending too freely. The first year of the College must show a decent profit, or she would have to cut back drastically on expenses. 'Not just a matter of omitting those chocolate biscuits from the students' welcome trays!' he'd warned.

Claire's mind had raced to solve the problem of the cancelled lecture. She'd telephoned a local retired art lecturer who had said he might be able to substitute if she ever needed a tutor at short notice, but his daughter, who answered the phone, said that he was away on holiday. Claire would have to improvise, using her collection of slides and reference books which she'd brought to Wildwood House in case of such an eventuality.

She announced her talk rather apologetically. She couldn't, she said, give them a scholarly account of the development of *trees in art*, and the social and historical changes which had influenced this. Instead, she would 'enthuse', as she put it, and encourage discussion about her favourite artist, Samuel Palmer, whose landscapes featured a great many trees. Later, they would discuss a few works by one or two others. To Claire's surprise, a spontaneous round of applause had followed her introduction.

'It's very good of you, Claire,' said Rhoda. 'And I'm sure I'll understand it better than a talk by an art expert.'

Murmurs of agreement followed.

'Well, thanks for the encouragement,' Claire answered. 'I hope you'll enjoy the session.' After a short pause, she asked, 'Do you like this picture?'

'Gorgeous colours!' Sandy enthused.

'Not very realistic!' Tony said. 'You'd never get a tree with as many apples as that - and all of them bright red! They look more like tomatoes!'

'It seems very idealised,' Hugh observed. 'That golden hill at the back, and the sheep and the shepherd-boy dozing there, without a care in the world.'

'Anything else?' Claire asked.

'I don't think it's idealised,' said Ted. 'That dark sky in the background looks ominous to me. If there's a storm coming on, the corn, if that's what it is, might be ruined!'

Jessica admired the picture's composition: 'The trees, leaning towards each other, give a sheltering effect, as if they're protecting the boy and his sheep, and the apple tree, and the church - if that's a steeple, Claire, right in the middle?'

Claire nodded.

'Do we get any impression of the artist's character or outlook on life?' she asked.

'I think he was happy and loved nature,' was Rhoda's view.

'A bit fanciful, I'd say,' said Les. 'You'd never see all that richness and brightness in the English countryside. I've spent a lot of time photographing the English landscape, and I've never seen such intense colours as those.'

'When was it painted?' Hugh asked.

Claire referred to her notes. 'About 1830. Palmer would be about twenty-five.'

'Well, Claire, what *was* his outlook on life?' Rex asked. 'You asked us, but I imagine you can enlighten us, now!'

'Palmer was a Christian mystic. He was very influenced by William Blake. They met when Palmer was nineteen. He loved nature as an expression of the love of God.'

'In that case,' Jessica said, 'the title is surprising, *The Magic Apple Tree*.'

'I wondered about that, too,' said Claire. 'Apparently, it was his son who gave it that title later, because he thought the enormous apple crop implied magic. But later writers about Palmer's work say the name is misleading, because it detracts from Palmer's known belief in God's bounty towards man. That's what inspired him to paint those fat woolly sheep, that ripe golden corn, and the heavily laden apple tree. The church is there, too, and look how those trees meet in the shape of a Gothic arch, again suggesting a mingling of nature and religion.'

Jessica said, 'It's very reminiscent of Psalm 65. May I recite?'

Claire nodded.

'*Thou crownest the year with thy goodness and thy paths drop fatness. They drop upon the pastures of the wilderness: and the little hills rejoice on every side. The pastures are clothed with flocks; the valleys also are covered over with corn; they shout for joy; they also sing.*'

'Not many people can quote chunks of the Bible nowadays,' Rex said admiringly.

'Well, it's part of my job!' Jessica said, smiling.

Claire changed the slide. The next one showed a large number of people *Coming from Evening Church*.

'Don't they look solemn and serious!' Rhoda exclaimed.

'Very dignified, too - even the children!' added Rex.

'I like the full moon,' Sandy said. 'Doesn't it glow?'

'The painting seems very serious,' said Hugh, 'but the houses look a bit comical, don't they? Those tall pointed roofs, a bit like the Gothic style of the church, but to me they look rather like an illustration in a children's book. And those high mountains at the back! Surely the setting is quite fanciful?'

'Well,' Claire answered, 'Palmer painted this when he lived at Shoreham, in Kent. The church there was important to him. But Shoreham Church had no spire, and this obviously isn't Kentish scenery!'

After they had looked at several more of Samuel Palmer's landscapes, Claire said, 'Now we'll go over to France, for a change!'

The colours which now filled the screen could hardly have been more different than Palmer's glowing jewel colours, reminiscent of stained-glass windows. The light and airy blues, yellows and greens of Monet's *Poplars on the Epte* now claimed everyone's attention.

'We're into Impressionism now, are we?' Ted asked.

'Yes,' Claire replied, 'and you can almost smell the fresh air in this picture, can't you? This is one of a series of paintings Monet made of the poplars that lined the river near his house at Giverny, trying to capture them at different times of day and in different weather conditions.'

'It looks as if it was painted from an extremely low viewpoint,' Les commented. 'The sky comes down almost to the bottom of the picture.'

'Yes. In fact, Monet painted it from a boat which he used as a studio. That's why it feels as if we're looking up from the river,' Claire explained.

The next slide showed a painting Manet made, many years earlier, of Monet on his studio-boat working on a picture, with his first wife, Camille, watching him from inside the cabin.

'By the time Monet came to live at Giverny, though,' Claire added, 'his life had changed a lot. Camille had died, and he was quite wealthy by then.'

A discussion about the mixed fortunes of painters took up several minutes.

'Back to our theme of trees now!' Claire said. 'Here is *Le Moulin de la Galette*, by Renoir. The trees themselves aren't very noticeable, but it's the effect of sunlight, dappled by their leaves, on the people and the tables in the outdoor café that makes this picture so special, I think.'

'And now for what I think must be two of the most dramatic tree paintings ever made!' she announced. 'I'd like to know what you think of them.'

Van Gogh's *Wheatfield with Cypresses* now appeared.

'This was painted in the year before Van Gogh died, soon after he entered the asylum at St Rémy de Provence.'

'You can tell he was very disturbed when he painted that!' said Rex. 'The whole landscape is moving - the wheat, those foreground trees or bushes, and that amazing cypress tree, swirling upwards like black flames.'

'And aren't those clouds strange?' said Rhoda. 'They're swirling about, not going in any definite direction, quite threatening, I think. And look how thickly he's put the paint on there!'

'Even those mountains at the back look as if they're moving!' Sandy added.

'Was he really mad?' Ted asked.

'I think it's really beyond our scope to discuss that here,' Claire replied. 'But I feel that the composition of this, and the next picture, are so strong and so controlled, that they suggest remarkable mental power. As regards that extraordinary tree, Van Gogh mentioned, in a letter to his brother, a cypress tree that was always occupying his thoughts. He described it as "a splash of black on a sunny landscape." Here's the other picture, *Starry Night*.'

'The tree looks more frightening here than in the other picture,' Rhoda said, 'probably because it looks so big. I wouldn't want that on my bedroom wall!'

'But the village below looks quite safe and serene, doesn't it?' said Jessica, 'with the little lights in the houses reflecting the yellow of the stars.'

'Those huge stars and moons whirling around are marvellous!' Tony enthused.

'I think,' said Sandy, 'that the picture is disturbing, but inspiring too. The tree looks ominous, but it seems to be striving, heroically, towards those glorious lights.'

Claire smiled. 'Well,' she said, 'the Van Goghs have provoked more excitement than all the other paintings, which isn't surprising. Now, to finish this session on a calmer note, we'll look at a couple of paintings that evoke, very beautifully, in my opinion, two different times of the year. This one, painted in 1855 by John William Inchbold, is called *Study in March*.'

No one in the group had seen this before, and there was a silence before anyone spoke.

'The light is wonderful,' said Les. 'That cold, clear sunshine of early spring is perfect. It's easier to capture it in photographs, but I've rarely seen a painting that shows it so well.'

'The sunlight picks out every detail of that big tree and its strangely shaped branches,' said Hugh.

'I like the way the light colours of the sky are balanced by the reddish brown earth and the trees in the distance,' Sandy added.

'What I like is that the artist hasn't sentimentalised the spring, as some do,' said Jessica. 'I think he deliberately chose a slightly misshapen tree. And the flowers look so fragile and delicate - slightly understated.'

'Yes,' Sandy agreed, 'That sheep and the two lambs haven't been sentimentalised either. I think that was done mainly by not putting them in the foreground, where they would have been sure to steal the show!'

'Finally,' said Claire, 'here's John Everett Millais's *Autumn Leaves*, dated 1855-6. I hadn't noticed till now the coincidence with the date of the previous picture. Perhaps we're seeing the spring and autumn of the same year!'

'The paintings couldn't be more different,' Hugh said, 'especially as this has four young girls and the other had no humans at all!'

'It isn't a straightforward representation of nature, is it?' said Sandy. 'I think it's awfully sad,' she added. 'It's about mortality.'

'How can we know that?' Claire prompted, then wished she hadn't asked, remembering Sandy's distress about her friend's death.

'Those two girls in black, and their sad expressions, the time of day - twilight.' said Rhoda.

'And the burning of the leaves - the end of the year's cycle.' Jessica added.

'Yes,' Claire said. 'I'm sorry to end with a melancholy painting, but what I love about it is the beauty of those colours - the golden sky, the colours of the younger girls' clothes and hair, and those beautiful leaves, so wonderfully painted!'

Chapter 23

Several decades ago, when the British Government was trying to gain support from the landowning community, Edward Ploughdon, who farmed a substantial acreage in the Vale of York, was, to his great surprise, offered a life peerage, and became Lord Ploughdon of Appletreewick. His choice of title reflected his attachment to the village in Wharfedale where his wife had grown up, not far from an area where the Ploughdons had owned a tract of land farmed by one of Edward's ancestors. In the course of time, the family had sold this land as a number of separate plots, on one of which Wildwood House had been built in the late eighteenth century. The terms of purchase for these plots were unusual, not to say eccentric, for the Ploughdons, though no longer farming in that part of Yorkshire, nominally retained ancient grazing rights there, although none of them had ever asserted the privilege - or certainly not in Edward's or his parents' lifetime. However, to retain the right, which, inexplicably was considered a matter of family honour by all its previous generations, the act conveying the right stipulated that the senior member of the family must visit these places every three years, to confirm the ongoing privilege to graze sheep on that land.

And that is why Lord Ploughdon was now driving his Range Rover from York to Wharfedale, to call on the Principal of the College which now occupied Wildwood House. Turning off the busy A59 onto a quiet B-road near Skipton, he wondered what kind of reception he would receive from this woman. A modern teacher would probably be scornful of ancient rights and have little patience with the perpetuation of such nonsense, as he assumed she would consider it. For his part, Edward regarded it as one of those comical eccentricities which endeared the English to their heritage in an entirely unpompous way, and were therefore worth preserving.

Edward had little interest in party politics and, when appointed to the House of Lords, he had chosen to sit on the cross benches. He had occasionally spoken in debates concerning agriculture - the only subject on which he considered himself competent to advise. Because his speeches were rare and based on sound judgement, he always received an attentive and respectful hearing.

It was three o'clock when he turned into the drive of Wildwood

House. He parked in front of the building. All was quiet. No doubt the students were out on some field trip. The only person in sight was a young woman who was tending some potted plants at one side of the front porch. As he alighted from his vehicle, she looked towards him, her expression somewhat wary of this stranger, with his ruddy complexion, thick and silvery hair, and wearing tweeds despite the warm June weather.

'Good afternoon,' he said.

'Good afternoon,' she replied, in an unusual accent.

'I've an appointment to see Mrs Martindale.'

She looked puzzled.

'The College Principal,' he added. 'Claire Martindale.'

'Oh yes! Of course, Claire!'

Maria had hardly, if ever, heard Claire's surname.

'Would you tell her I'm here, please, and give her my card?'

Maria looked in some confusion at the name - impossible to pronounce, but she had a try: 'Mr Ploogdon?' she asked tentatively.

'Plowdun,' he answered phonetically.

'Oh, I see, yes. I will tell Claire. Please wait a few minutes, Mr Ploughdon,' she said carefully.

'Just say Ploughdon of Appletreewick,' he said, a slight twinkle in his eye. 'Can you manage that? No, you can't! Just give her that card.'

'Please come in. I will find Claire for you.'

Maria hurried to the office and was relieved to find Claire there. She was glad to get back to the pot plants.

'Call me Edward, please,' were his first words to Claire, before she had time to greet him. They shook hands.

'The title's still a bit of an embarrassment - after all these years!' he said. 'You should have seen that young woman's face when I asked her to tell you that Ploughdon of Appletreewick had arrived! What a strange accent she has! Sounded a bit Slavic to me. Where's she from?'

'Alborus, in Eastern Europe. It's a very small country - one of those that used to be part of the Soviet Union. It's independent now; but apparently it's more or less a dictatorship.'

'Sounds grim.'

Eager to change the subject, Claire said, 'Come into the sitting room. I've ordered some tea and cakes.'

She gestured to a pair of armchairs and a coffee table, near the large window.

'Fine view you have,' he said, gazing across the lawn to the river and the hillside beyond. 'I remember it well from visits to the previous owners.'

'Yes, we're very lucky.'

After a pause, Claire said, 'Now you can tell me why you're here. I didn't really understand when you telephoned yesterday. You said something about having to call at the house, or walk through the grounds - to keep up an ancient tradition?'

'Yes, that's it in a nutshell. It probably seems ridiculous to you - one of those finicky legal details, almost meaningless. Rest assured, I've absolutely no intention of bringing a lorry-load of sheep here to graze on your lawn - though that's what the law stipulates! Between you and me, it's nonsense. But I do like these funny old traditions! And it's good to visit these places where some of my ancestors lived and farmed, and to meet the current occupiers. Of course, I'd be appalled if some ghastly superstore was built in the area, but with neighbouring landowners like the Duke of Devonshire and the National Trust, I can't see that ever being allowed, can you?'

'No, indeed,' said Claire. 'Oh, here's Linda with our tea.'

'Tell me about the College,' he asked, after tea had been poured and cakes selected.

Claire was glad to have a chance to speak. She was warming to Edward's personality, after her initial distaste for his amusement at Maria's embarrassment over the pronunciation of his name, and with her concern to protect Maria from idle curiosity. She talked non-stop for ten minutes about the College, from her lottery win to yesterday's walk in Upper Wharfedale. Edward was clearly impressed by her achievement, and pleased to find her very different from his expectation of a humourless person, intolerant of quirky hereditary rights. For her part, Claire found him sympathetic with her aims for the College, as a place where subjects were studied for their intrinsic interest and where life could be enhanced by studying with like-minded people in an encouraging and friendly atmosphere. Thinking especially of Sandy, she told him that she'd noticed how several students already seemed more relaxed and cheerful than when they'd arrived.

'I'm convinced that being here is a really positive experience for people,' she said. 'I can't think of anything I'd rather be doing than this. And yet it all came about by chance. I won a lot of money on the National Lottery! The first time I'd ever bought a ticket! So I was able to do something I'd vaguely dreamed about since I began teaching adults.'

'You've obviously worked extremely hard, getting the place organised,' he said, 'I'm glad you've had such a good start. What would you do if a tutor cancelled a talk at short notice?'

'It's already happened, just this morning! I gave my first-ever session on paintings featuring trees!'

'You must be very versatile and competent; and I get the impression that you're very caring, too, for the people who come here.'

For a moment, Claire hesitated, but she had gradually warmed to this man and, on an impulse, wanted to confide in him.

'The biggest problem I've had to deal with was something I'd never have imagined. I found an asylum seeker in the garden shed, early on Sunday morning!'

'No!' he said, 'The cheek of these people!'

'No, please! Wait till I tell you more. You've met her yourself!'

After a moment's thought, he said, 'The girl who showed me in?'

Claire nodded.

'She seemed quite harmless. She's from somewhere in Eastern Europe, you said, didn't you? Alborus, is that it?'

Claire told him as briefly as she could about Maria's background, her escape from her native country, her harrowing journey, her experience after she arrived in England, and her predicament now that her asylum application had been refused, and what she, Claire, had learned about the asylum process in Britain.

After she had finished, he was silent, at a loss. Then he said: 'I had no idea about all this - refugees from brutality in their own countries being refused asylum here, held in detention centres, then sent back to the countries they've fled from, or living rough here, barred from employment, yet denied financial support, left destitute unless they're lucky enough to be helped by people like you.'

He pondered for some time.

'I've just remembered,' he said eventually, 'There's going to be a debate in the Lords some time in the next few weeks, about asylum seekers. It's not something I've ever taken any interest in, I'm ashamed to tell you. But I think I'll attend that debate, and possibly bring up Maria's case, if it seems appropriate. D'you think that would be all right?'

'I'm fairly sure it would,' she said after a moment's thought, 'My husband, Aidan, who researched the subject not long ago, noticed that when cases have received a lot of media attention, the people concerned have sometimes been allowed to stay in Britain. It might be worth a try. Thank you so much, Edward.'

'Well,' he said, 'I'd better be getting back to the farm now. But I'll definitely be in touch with you about this and I'll see what I can do.'

Before he left, Claire gave him a copy of Aidan's article on asylum seekers and the websites of organisations involved.

'It's a complicated topic,' she said, 'as I discovered myself!'

'Thanks for the tea and cakes!'

With a cheery wave, he was gone.

Chapter 24

'Another knife attack by teenage boys!' Vera Armstrong said in a shocked tone, after switching off the television news. 'They nearly killed a man who was trying to stop them vandalising his car. He's in hospital, seriously injured. And it happened in broad daylight!'

Giles looked up briefly from his computer game, but showed no interest.

'I don't know where they get their knives from. Do you know anyone who carries a knife?'

Giles shrugged.

'What sort of an answer is that?'

'Some kids do, I suppose.'

'Why do they?'

'Self-defence, I reckon.'

'Against who?'

'Boys in other gangs, maybe. I dunno.'

Again, that shrug, dismissing the topic. He wasn't in a communicative mood. He never was, these days. Vera never knew what he did in his spare time when he went out with his friends. They used to come round to the house, but nowadays he went to their houses instead, when they weren't hanging around the shopping centre, that is. She supposed that was what you had to expect. As soon as a boy got into his teens, there was no keeping him at home. She just hoped he wouldn't get into drugs. There'd been quite a scandal at his school last term - two boys expelled. She'd read it in the local paper - Giles hadn't even mentioned it to her. He seemed to go around with his eyes shut - didn't know what was going on half the time! He'd need to be aware of the undesirable elements in society and keep clear of getting mixed up in anything suspicious.

'Have you done your homework?'

'I haven't got any tonight.'

'You usually have a lot on Thursdays, don't you?'

'Well, I haven't, see!' His voice rose defiantly.

'How's that?' she persisted.

'They're not setting homework now the exams are over.'

Vera doubted the truth of this - His tone was over-emphatic. But she didn't press the point further. She'd been feeling uneasy for some time about Giles. He was often evasive, and prone to flare up if she questioned him about anything. She felt inadequate to cope alone with an adolescent boy. She wished now that Hugh visited more often, but he hadn't been round for nearly two months and she resented his freedom. He ought to take more responsibility for Giles, now that he was a teenager. A boy needed a role model, and Hugh, she had to admit to herself, would have been a much better influence on him than any of the rock stars and footballers Giles idolised nowadays.

Giles had been going to go on a school camping holiday next month, but he'd suddenly decided he didn't want to go. He'd persuaded her to write to the teacher who was organising it and make some excuse for him. She'd felt ashamed. It seemed so ungrateful when teachers were giving up a week of their holidays to take the kids away. It turned out that Giles had been ridiculed by his friends, Des and Rick, who thought camping was 'uncool' and childish - like the Scouts, they'd said - and he'd weakly accepted their opinion and given in to it. She wasn't at all happy about these two boys, especially Rick. He was older than Giles, nearly fifteen. She felt that he was not to be trusted and that he was a bad influence.

Chapter 25

Friday dawned, the last day of the *Trees in Britain* course, and Sandy found a letter addressed to her in the rack in the hall. Peter's handwriting! She took it up to her bedroom to read in private, her thoughts in a whirl of uncertainty. The feelings produced by her imagined sighting of Peter in *the Racehorses* on Wednesday evening had shown her the true state of her emotions. She could not marry Peter, but she would always feel guilty at rejecting so kind and considerate a man. She had had a wonderful week at Wildwood House, mainly because of Rex and their increasing rapport. But the departure of his wife six months ago to live with another man had astonished Rex, and he had believed that she was merely infatuated and would want to return to him eventually. So Sandy had determined to regard her friendship with Rex as a light-hearted holiday acquaintance, and she was trying not to let herself become too involved with him.

It was several minutes before she could bring herself to open the envelope. The letter was not long - just a single page.

Dear Sandy,
While you've been away, I have been thinking about our relationship and I now realise that you and I are probably not right for each other. For one thing, I'm too old for you! When I saw you last Friday at Wildwood House, just before you noticed me there, I couldn't help seeing how happily you were chatting with new acquaintances. It made me realise that you never showed such spontaneity and enjoyment when you were with me - at least, not in recent months. After your accident, I wanted to look after you and help you to cope. I would never have left you then, even though I think - looking back - that I already knew, subconsciously, that you didn't love me.

Anyway, when you come home from the course, we can talk things over, if you like. And you mustn't feel guilty about us breaking up. I recently met a nice lady the same age as myself, at the bridge club. We get on quite well. I won't be lonely!

I feel almost sure that you will be relieved to read this letter. I will always remember the happiness we shared in the early days of our relationship, and I'm sure we will always be friends.
Yours ever,
Peter

Sandy sat down after reading this. Then she read it again more slowly. Peter was a straightforward man, so she believed his letter was sincere - although she did just wonder whether the lady at the bridge club really existed. Was he trying to make it easier for Sandy to reject him? She felt gratitude for his thoughtfulness, and it was with a light heart that she went back downstairs.

Rex was already at the breakfast bar, selecting a copious cooked meal. Sandy joined him at a table near a window, when she'd collected her muesli with lots of fresh fruits on top.

'Last day here!' Rex said. 'Are you pleased to be going home soon?'

'No - not very. I've enjoyed this week so much - the course, the gorgeous countryside, the people here. It's taken me right out of myself!'

'Yes, I can see it's done you good, having new scenery, new interests,' he said. 'And it's done *me* good meeting you, Sandy. I hope we can keep in touch.'

'Yes, I'd like that,' she answered, smiling.

'Judy called me last night, from Hartford, Connecticut.'

Sandy felt - and looked - apprehensive.

'She's still with that man I told you about. - Having quite a fling, apparently! It begins to look as if it's going to be a permanent arrangement. I must say, I'd already begun rethinking my life this week.'

He paused for a moment, then went on: 'Becky, my daughter, seems to be adjusting easily to her mother's new man. That hurts me a bit, you know.'

Sandy nodded.

'Anyway, I'm staying in Britain for a year. I'd have flown to the States for a visit if she'd sounded encouraging. But, as things are, I might as well go up to St Andrews early and get settled in well before the academic year starts.'

Sandy felt bleak.

In a sudden desire to confide in him, she told him about Peter and how their relationship was at an end.

'So, where will you live now?' he asked.

'My flat in Southport,'

'Alone?'

'Yes, alone.'

'D'you think we could meet up, now and again?'

'Where? Somewhere between Southport and St Andrews? - Hadrian's Wall, perhaps?' she said, keeping the conversation light.

They laughed.

'Well, I certainly want to see Hadrian's Wall while I'm over here! But seriously, Sandy...?'

She concentrated on her muesli and fruit, and he on his bacon, eggs, sausage and tomatoes. Then she said, 'I've just thought of something. I don't need to go back to Southport yet. There's a new course starting here tomorrow evening, *Historic Houses of Yorkshire*. I wonder if there are any places left. I'd like to stay on. I love it here.'

'Excuse me,' Rex said, standing up. 'I'll be back.'

He returned soon, looking delighted.

'They've still got places on that course. Shall we enrol now? When we've finished eating?'

****

'Anyone else for Hackfall?' Hugh called. 'The minibus leaves in five minutes!'

To avoid possible long waits for public transport connections if he decided to extend the tour after the Hackfall visit, Hugh had hired a local minibus and driver for this expedition.

'Yes, us!' said Rex, slightly breathless as he and Sandy hurried to join the group that had gathered in front of Wildwood House.

'Sorry, if we're late!' Sandy said, 'We've just been signing on for *Historic Houses*.'

'What is Hackfall?' Les asked.

'A grade one listed garden,' Hugh enthused, 'painted by Turner, praised by Wordsworth, recommended by Thomas Pennant...'

'Who he?'

'A Welsh naturalist. He called it "one of the most picturesque scenes in the North of England." '

'Why haven't we heard of it before, then?'

'Because it fell into neglect in the twentieth century. But it's been brilliantly restored to its former splendour. Anyway, let's get started. I'll tell you more about the place as we go along - better than giving you a lecture when we arrive. Then you can wander round as you like, and absorb the atmosphere.'

Half an hour later, well on their way, Hugh said: 'Hackfall was bought in 1731 by John Aislabie, but it was mainly designed by his son, William. He aimed to create what would look like a wild landscape, with trees, waterfalls, and surprise viewpoints cleverly contrived, plus rustic follies here and there. He even made an 18th-century replacement for a ruined medieval tower. The place was hugely popular until, as I said, it was allowed to get overgrown and neglected.'

'Why would that be?' Rex asked.

'Just a change in popular taste, I suppose.'

'It sounds quite romantic, bringing the garden back to life,' Sandy said.

'Yes,' Rhoda agreed, ' a bit like the Lost Garden of Heligan in Cornwall.'

'Hackfall is now an SSSI - a Site of Special Scientific Interest,' Hugh added, 'because of its ancient woodland. That, of course, is why it interests me specially.'

Hackfall did not disappoint. Its dramatic setting, in a rocky gorge of the River Ure, inspired Rhoda to make a sketch. Others took photographs, botanised, or learned about the recently-discovered elm-wood pipes which had fed a forty-foot high fountain, but whose good state of preservation would only survive if they remained submerged.

When they returned to the minibus, Rex said, 'I noticed a sign to Fountains Abbey on the way here. Would that be worth a visit?'

'It certainly would,' said Hugh.

'Could we get some lunch there?' Ted asked.

'Yes, there's a big café. These couldn't be hints, could they, by any chance?'

They all denied collusion.

'Well, I expected some interest might be shown in Fountains Abbey. It's a World Heritage Site, after all, and that includes the Water Garden at Studley Royal - more of the Aislabies' work for you - quite different from Hackfall, though.'

Jessica, Rex and Sandy joined a guided tour of the Abbey in its beautiful setting beside the River Skell. They were especially moved by the voluntary austerity of the 12th-century monks - their habits of coarse sheep's wool, their diet barely above subsistence level, their long periods of silence, their humility and reverence.

'What a hard life!' Sandy said. 'They must have been so cold in the winters, getting up in the night to attend services!'

'Yes,' Jessica said, ' but they had a sense of purpose, didn't they?

We have so much materially, but I think those monks were more at peace with themselves.'

'And having the day portioned out for different activities, alternating with their services, meant that their life had a definite structure,' said Rex.

'They wouldn't have much time to brood and get depressed - as I have done, since my friend Val died in a crash,' said Sandy. 'I've got things more into proportion while I've been on this course and I'm sure it's partly due to the structured, purposeful week we've had,' Then, more quietly, she said to Rex, 'But it's not only due to that,' and squeezed his hand. Suddenly, she remembered that she hadn't taken any of her tablets since last weekend. She wondered where she had put them, but felt confident of not needing them now.

****

'Best thing to do with them,' said Geoff, 'is to grow 'em up pyramids.'

'Pyramids?' Maria looked puzzled, momentarily thinking of ancient Egypt.

'You know - stick some bamboo canes into the ground, in a circle, tie them together at t'top and plant the seeds in the ground. Then the plants'll climb up the canes, twisting round 'em.'

'Oh yes, of course,' Maria said, 'but where...?'

'Here! These canes have been in here since last year.'

He pointed to a pile of bamboo canes lying along one side of the shed.

'They seem very long,' Maria said doubtfully.

'Eight foot, they are. You need to press them right down into the earth. Then tie them together about six inches from the top. They'll grow lovely - First you get the bright red flowers, then the beans. They'll keep on producing for weeks.'

'How many pyramids will fit in that space?'

'You'll probably get six in there, I should think. I'll do t' first one for you, if you like?'

'No - thank you, Geoff. I like to do them all myself, but can you show me how far apart to put the canes?'

'No problem,' he said, and made holes to indicate the best spacing.

Geoff had become much friendlier than when she'd first met him - or maybe she'd just got used to his rather blunt manner, she wondered.

Perhaps it was because she was working so conscientiously in the garden. It was her increasing sense of guilt at being a burden to Claire that drove her to make every effort to justify Claire's generosity. So she was thrilled when anyone admired the flowers she'd planted, the shrubs she tended, the lawn she kept so well-trimmed.

While she worked, Maria was looking forward to a walk she and Hugh planned to do tomorrow, in Langstrothdale. Alternately with worrying about her future, she delighted in the beauty of the Dales, which was bound up with her growing love for Hugh. Through him, she was getting to know those places whose photos had made such a strong impression on her in the library at Bradford. She smiled to herself as, perched on an upturned wooden box from the shed, she tied together six of the bamboo canes and tested the structure for firmness. Claire had invited Maria to attend a party she had arranged this evening for the last night of Hugh's course, and she was looking forward to that too.

****

When the Hackfall and Fountains Abbey party returned in the late afternoon - usually the quietest part of the day - they found a flurry of activity in progress. Claire, assisted by Jonquil, who was staying at Wildwood for the weekend, was putting up display screens and tables in the Lecture Room, to receive the art and craft work made by course members during the week. Two hours later, the exhibition was open for viewing.

Sandy and Rex laughed at their own efforts at painting, then moved on to look at Les's black and white photographs, clearly the work of a professional.

'I never knew stone walls could be so interesting!' said Sandy. 'Look at all the detail there - the rough texture of the stone, then those soft mossy bits. It's almost as if you could reach out and feel the different surfaces on the photo!'

Rex nodded. 'And even feel the chilly wind blowing through that gap!'

'So much atmosphere shown in a photograph of about two feet of wall!' Sandy added. 'I feel inspired to try that sort of work. Maybe Les will give a course on it here!'

'Look here, Ted!' Rhoda exclaimed. 'Here are those snaps I took on Monday, on that walk to Starbotton! They look a bit amateurish, compared with some of the photos here, though.'

'Don't worry!' said Tony, who was standing behind her, 'You're talking about two different categories of photography. No one would try to judge between detailed studies of textures and holiday photos. They do quite different jobs. That one of yours,' he added, pointing to a shot of Ted climbing over a stile while the others stood around watching, 'is jolly good. It immediately reminds me of the fun we were all having at that moment.'

'Thank you,' said Rhoda, looking more closely at the photo. 'Yes,' she said, 'I see what you mean now.'

She and Ted moved on to look at the paintings.

'These are a mixed bunch, aren't they?' Ted said.

'Yes. You could even have put *your* paintings on show among these!' Rhoda chuckled. 'But seriously, some of these are lovely, aren't they? Those vivid colours... Oh, look - Rex did that one!'

'The colours are ridiculous!' Ted laughed.

'Well, maybe Rex was trying for a more abstract interpretation!'

'Thank you, Ma'am, for taking my work seriously!'

Rhoda was covered with confusion.

'But your comment has made my day!' Rex protested. 'After all that's the first picture I've painted since Miss Dauber banned me from doing art at school - a good few years ago! Maybe I've got a latent talent, after all!'

'Here's something unusual,' Sandy said, when she and Rex had moved on to a group of sketches. 'Look at this tree study.'

She pointed to a small inconspicuous pencil drawing.

'Unusual to choose a dead tree to paint, at this time of year,' Rex said.

'Yes, but it isn't completely dead, is it? Look at that thin stem, growing up out of the gap between those two branches. It's strange, though. The tree looks like a sycamore, but the leaves on that stem are ash leaves, aren't they?'

'I think they are. But maybe it's growing independently - out of some earth between those two branches,' Rex suggested. 'Who drew this one?' he said, peering at the tiny label below. 'It just says M - the initial.'

'That must be Maria,' said Sandy. 'And there's a title - "*New Life*". I think it's lovely.'

Hugh and Maria, seated nearby in a window recess, looked at each other and smiled.

****

After dinner, everyone moved into the lounge, where Claire had also invited the main staff of the College.

'I'm not going to inflict a speech on you!' she said, when everyone had arrived. 'I just want to give my heartfelt thanks to everyone who has been involved with Wildwood House this week: Diane, who runs the office with quiet efficiency and whose warm smile greets everyone who arrives here; Geoff's unobtrusive care of the building and its security; Linda and Pam who have kept us so deliciously fed. You have all played a big part in launching the College....'

A burst of applause interrupted Claire for a few moments.

'And the garden is now looking absolutely lovely, thanks to Maria's devoted work out there...'

Again, spontaneous applause broke in. For the first time, Maria was the focus of everyone's attention. She gazed at Claire, trying to convey by her smile the gratitude she felt for her kindness.

'And, most importantly, I want to thank Hugh, for being the tutor of our first course here...' She waited until the clapping subsided. Then she said, 'Finally, very many thanks to you, our students, for spending the week with us at Wildwood House. I will always remember this particular group because, as you all know, this has been the very first course here so you are really special. I hope you have enjoyed this course and that we'll see you here again soon.'

Claire sat down. Immediately, a voice from the back of the room called for 'Three cheers for Claire!'

'And now,' she said, when quietness fell again, 'we have some entertainment for you! I'm delighted to introduce my daughter Jonquil and two of her friends, Katy and Sue, who will give us some music.'

When two music stands had been set up and the piano stool adjusted, the girls, wearing dresses of the same simple style, but different colours - green, blue and red - played a sequence of short pieces, some light, some serious, for viola, flute and piano.

'What a delightful surprise!' Rhoda said, expressing everyone's reaction.

When the applause for the young musicians had subsided, Claire announced:

'And now for our quiz! Thank you those of you who provided a question about trees, after I waylaid each of you this morning! You made my job much easier! This is very informal,' she added hastily. 'I see a few people who look as if they're trying to escape! You just have to catch my eye, if you know the answer. This isn't *Mastermind!* There are very few rules. If necessary I'll make them up as we go along. Anyone who answers their own question will be disqualified! Ready?'

The audience nodded, some eagerly, some tolerantly, but all in good humour.

'First question: What's the national tree of Canada?'

'Maple,' said Jessica promptly.

'Correct. Now a literary one - We've got quite a few of those, actually. Which tree did the poet A.E. Housman recall "in a western brookland"?'

'Christmas tree!' said Tony, who had had a few more drinks than most of them.

'Any other offers?'

'Poplars,' said Sandy, and grinned at Rex.

'Correct. Next question: Where would you find the Major Oak?'

'Sherwood Forest,' Ted answered.

'Yes. What shall I do if everyone scores one point?'

'Split the prize between us,' Tony suggested, confidently.

'If it was chocolates, that would be easy, but it isn't something that can be split.'

'Have a tie-breaker - or a sudden-death play-off,' said Hugh, who was keeping the score.

'Well, we'll see what happens,' Claire said. 'Next question: Name a country in the Middle East that has a tree on its flag.'

'Lebanon, and it's a cedar,' said Jessica.

'Correct, and a bonus point for the cedar,' said Claire. 'Next one: Which English king hid in an oak tree?'

Les said the first thing that came into his head: 'King Alfred.'

'Any other ideas?'

'Wasn't it Charles the Second?' Ted asked, 'in the Civil War?'

'Yes, but what about the other details?'

'Wasn't it after the battle of Worcester?' Sandy said. 'He was hiding from the Parliamentarians.'

'Good. One point for Ted, and one for Sandy. Now here's another one: Under which tree did the Buddha receive enlightenment?'

'The banyan tree?' said Sandy. Claire shook her head.

'The bo tree,' Les said, surprisingly.

'Correct. Name a character in a Thomas Hardy novel whose surname is the name of a tree.'

'Gabriel Oak,' Rhoda said promptly.

'That's right. Now, which tree is the title of a novel by H.E. Bates?'

Several facetious answers were offered, then Sandy asked, 'Is it *The Jacaranda Tree?*'

'Yes, it is indeed. Who wrote the line *Under the spreading chestnut tree, the village smithy stands?*'

No one knew. There were a few wild guesses.

'It was Longfellow. No mark for anyone there.'

'What's the origin of Hardy's novel title *Under the Greenwood Tree?*'

Silence. Then Sandy said, 'Oh!' as if suddenly enlightened, 'It's a song in "*As You Like It*" '

'Good, and a bonus point for knowing the play!' Claire said. 'And now, the last question: What is the national tree of Alborus?'

'Never heard of it,' said Ted.

Before any discussion could develop, an unfamiliar male voice from the back said, 'The silver birch.'

Several people turned to see who had spoken.

'It's the man in the grey suit,' Sandy whispered to Rex. 'It's the first time I've heard him say a word, all this week!'

Then Sandy noticed Maria. Her face had turned very pale, as she turned anxiously and whispered something to Hugh at her side, as soon as he'd totted up the score and passed a note of the winner's name to Claire.

'You won't be surprised to learn that the clear winner of the quiz is Sandy! Here is her prize, made by a local craftsman.'

It was a small carved model of a chestnut tree, made of chestnut wood. Sandy held it up for all to see.

'How lovely!' she exclaimed. 'I'll always treasure this. Thank you so much.'

When she sat down, she noticed that Maria and Hugh had slipped unobtrusively out of the room.

Chapter 26

Wildwood House suddenly seemed very quiet and empty on Saturday morning, as Claire and Hugh talked over the success of the course. The students had now departed, after a flurry of thanks, exchanges of addresses, goodbyes and promises to return soon.

'Such a relief!' Claire said. 'Everything went well, despite the two crises - Maria's arrival and Rachel's last-minute cancellation!'

'You've done brilliantly, Claire. Maria couldn't have landed in a better place,' Hugh said warmly.

'Well, she certainly looks a lot better now; but I think much of that is due to you, isn't it?'

'I love her, Claire,' he said quietly, and she realised, from his understated manner, that he was serious. 'We're going for another walk today. Maria just loves the countryside here. When I asked her where she'd like to go - a film, concert, meal out, she said she'd prefer a walk. She wants to continue up the Dale from Hubberholme and into Langstrothdale.'

'Well, have a good day. It looks as if there'll be plenty of sunshine for you.'

'Cheers, Claire. Good luck with the next course.'

****

An hour later, Hugh parked his car beside the Wharfe at Hubberholme.

'Look!' Maria exclaimed, noticing a small beach of light-coloured, rounded stones beside the river which bubbled and murmured on its way. They spent a few minutes stepping on the pebbles and watching a few ducks and moorhens swimming busily about, until their eyes were distracted by the brilliant blue of a kingfisher as it darted across the river and disappeared rapidly into the overhanging branches.

Soon they were on their way, striding along the narrow hilly road with gently rolling green hills to left and right, the varying gradient and curves of the road presenting subtly changing views of the way ahead. Cattle and sheep grazed in the fields. Few vehicles passed them, and they walked hand-in-hand, finding a pace that suited them both. Although they had known each other less than a week, they felt comfortable enough walking together for some distance without feeling constrained to keep up a conversation. After a while, they stopped for a rest and sat on a low wall at the roadside, listening to a lark as it rose from the grass, singing itself into invisibility.

'Hugh,' Maria said quietly, 'were you really serious on Wednesday night, when you said that you wanted to marry me?'

'Of course I was! I've thought of little else since Wednesday - our conversation walking back from Buckden, and our evening together in the cottage. How can you doubt me after that, Maria?'

She blushed slightly, remembering their lovemaking, so spontaneous and joyful. Hugh took both her hands in his and looked at her face, trying to read her thoughts, and seeing still the uncertainty and vulnerability of her life as a refugee. But he also thought he saw a tremulous joy, as if she were beginning to believe in the possibility of happiness.

'Let's get married as soon as we can!' he said suddenly. 'If you were the wife of a British citizen, I'm sure you'd stand a better chance of being allowed to stay in this country. I think you might automatically get British citizenship. They couldn't send you back to Alborus then!'

'Hugh!' she said, almost angrily, 'Is it to help me get asylum here that you want to marry me? You must not do that! You might always regret it. There is only one good reason to marry.'

'I fully agree,' he answered, 'and you know I love you. But if we are going to get married, we should do it soon - to prevent us being separated. It might be possible to get a special licence, so we wouldn't have to wait as long as usual. Now, shall we walk on?' he asked, looking again intently at her face to discern her true feelings, and seeing certainty and happiness as she nodded and stood up.

After a while, they walked across a cattle grid, and the road was now unfenced as they approached the hamlet of Yockenthwaite, with its farm across the river, and its ancient stone circle in a nearby field. The country was changing subtly as they left Yockenthwaite. There was now a wide grassy bank between the road and the river. A few cars were parked on the grass and a family were picnicking, small children running about, fascinated to be so near the water.

'That farm!' Maria exclaimed, after they'd been walking in silence for a while. She pointed to a group of old stone buildings, with several leafy trees behind them. 'I saw a photograph of it in the magazine I told you about, in the library in Bradford. It was one of the pictures that made me want to come to these dales!'

'Yes, I remember,' Hugh said. 'They made a big impression on you, didn't they?'

'I love the way the trees seem to be protecting the farmhouse,' Maria went on.

'It looks sad, though,' she added after a few moments, 'as if everyone has deserted it.' As they walked on, an extensive conifer plantation came into view, darkening the hillside ahead, while to their right rose the austere beauty of the high moors. Just ahead lay the small community of Beckermonds.

'D'you see that stream flowing into the Wharfe?' Hugh asked, pointing ahead of them.

She nodded.

'Upstream from here, the Wharfe is much smaller - just a stream.'

'Are we near its source?'

'No. That's a good few miles further on, and the country's rougher up there.'

'I wish I had enough energy to walk there!' Maria said with feeling. 'I think there is something special about the beginning of a river.'

Hugh nodded. 'Well, let's have our picnic here, where we're in sight and sound of those two streams,' he said, shrugging off his backpack more carefully than usual, then producing a pork pie, sandwiches, salad, a cake, and some fresh fruit, and setting them all out, with surprising formality on a small tablecloth, each item on a paper plate. He had even brought paper napkins which matched the plates, with a design of yellow and white daisies on a blue background. He was smiling broadly.

'Very pretty!' Maria exclaimed.

She took out a flask she'd brought in her bag, and was about to start pouring coffee into plastic mugs when Hugh said, 'Keep the coffee till later. This is a special day!' and produced a bottle of wine wrapped in a pullover from his pack, then two wine glasses, carefully wrapped in a pair of socks.

'I even remembered the corkscrew!' he said, flourishing the tool before opening the bottle and pouring sparkling wine into the glasses.

'To us!' he said, clinking his glass to Maria's.

The wine was cool, delicious, and seemed like the best thing either of them had ever tasted.

'And to our future!' he added. 'Our future together!'

'Our future together!' she echoed, smiling, and savouring each word thoughtfully - only the merest hint of doubt in her tone.

'Well,' said Hugh, after their second glass, 'we'd better start eating or we'll be really tipsy - drinking on an empty stomach!'

'Tipsy!' she repeated, laughing. 'I have not heard this word before, but I learn, from the context, what it means!'

'From the context, of course!' he agreed, laughing at her mock formality.

'I'll put the bottle between those rocks in the river, to keep it cool for later,' he said, standing up. 'Chilled in the Wharfe - It'll taste better than ever!'

Their picnic was serenaded by the lonely cries of lapwings and curlews, and for a while they watched the alternately flapping and gliding flight of a sparrowhawk.

Chapter 27

The clientèle for the course on *Historic Houses of Yorkshire* were rather older than the previous week's students, but no less enthusiastic and energetic. Rex and Sandy were impressed by the prodigious amount of knowledge most of them could already display at mealtimes, about the castles, great houses and smaller stately homes they were to visit, and the families who had owned and cared for them over the centuries - the Howards, the Lascelles, the Sykes, the Worsleys, the Cliffords, an especial favourite being the formidable Lady Anne Clifford in the seventeenth century, who had devoted much of her life to the restoration of churches and castles, including her birthplace, Skipton Castle.

The course tutor, Dr Antonia Fielding, took the party out each day to visit one or two houses. They began with the nearest, Skipton Castle, already familiar to Rex and Sandy, then the elegant Newby Hall near Ripon. Whole days were spent at the great treasure-houses of Castle Howard and Harewood House. Sandy's favourites were the smaller houses they explored, including Burton Agnes Hall with tall Elizabethan chimneys, and Sledmere House in its peaceful setting on the Wolds, and its serenely landscaped grounds. She was amazed to learn, after touring the house, that it had been destroyed in a fire in 1911 but rebuilt exactly as before, including its long library, one of the most beautiful rooms in England.

During this week, Hugh was out lecturing on trees and environmental issues at colleges, schools, and meetings of various societies. His working hours were irregular and involved much travelling, so Maria saw less of him than she had recently, and realised how much she missed him. Her acquaintance with Sandy developed at this time and the two would occasionally stroll round the College grounds together.

'You are the first person that I met here,' Maria said, one afternoon. 'That seems so long ago to me, now.'

Sandy was embarrassed to recall how she had tried to avoid speaking to the unkempt stranger in the lane.

'You gave me something to eat,' said Maria. 'That was the beginning of things getting better for me.'

She was silent for a few moments, as if pondering something. Eventually she said, ' I think, perhaps, you know a little about me. Hugh told me that Claire had explained to a few people why I came her.'

'Yes,' Sandy answered. 'She told us you came to England to seek asylum, but your application was refused. Claire advised us not to ask you questions about it. She thought it would worry you.'

'Yes. It is illegal for me to be in Britain now, so I am afraid of being found by the police. The more people who know about me, the greater risk I take. It is a horrible situation to be in!'

'I'm sure it is,' Sandy said, 'But you've made a good friend, haven't you? Hugh? Maybe you feel safer with him to help you?'

Maria smiled. 'Yes, I do. But all I am doing is troubling other people with my problems.' She wondered whether to mention Hugh's marriage proposal, but decided not to.

'You also have found a new friend here, I think? The American?'

'Yes, Rex. We get on very well. That's why we both decided to stay here another week. When I first arrived here, I was a nervous wreck. I couldn't stop blaming myself for a friend's death in an accident. Since I came here I've managed to calm down - In fact, I've stopped taking my sleeping pills. I'd been on them for months, but I don't need them any more!'

'I think perhaps Rex has helped, too?'

'Yes, he certainly has! Goodness! I've overrun the break-time by ten minutes. The old ladies will look very disapproving when I go in late! See you soon!'

****

For Claire, the second week of Wildwood House's existence as a college was much easier than the first. Everything was running smoothly and she was able to relax more. With Jonquil and Rory dividing their time between the family home at York with Aidan, and Wildwood House to which both had taken a great liking, Claire felt happier. The children's return had had a beneficial effect on Aidan, too. He and his son were on far better terms than before Rory went to Guatemala, and Claire hoped that his dependency on alcohol was subsiding now that he was in better spirits. She was still concerned about Maria, hoping that her growing involvement with Hugh would not end in disappointment, but she was constantly anxious lest Maria's presence here would become known to the immigration authorities, with potentially disastrous consequences.

A recent incident had disturbed her peace of mind a little. On Thursday a police car drew up in front of the house and a young policewoman walked in through the open door. Claire almost laughed when, after a brief greeting, she said: 'Farmers in this area have reported a stray dog that has been worrying sheep for some time.'

She showed Claire a photograph of the breed.

'If you see one of these around here, would you please phone us at once?'

'Yes, of course.'

The woman looked around her, then said, 'This College opened about a week ago, I think?'

Claire nodded, wondering what was coming next.

'Everything OK here?'

'Fine, thank you.'

'Good.'

She turned to go, then paused again.

'Oh, by the way, see that all your doors are locked securely at night. There are some people around that we're keeping an eye on.'

Chapter 28

The *Historic Houses* course ended on Thursday night, so the next morning Maria said goodbye to Sandy, who gave her her telephone number and encouraged her to phone whenever she liked. Maria would certainly miss her; she had enjoyed their chats, and it was good to have a woman friend nearer her own age than Claire, and Jessica who had returned last weekend to her church on the Wolds.

Heavy rain on Friday restricted Maria's gardening to tending and watering the houseplants. She decided to use the extra free time to give the cottage a thorough clean. Whilst sorting out a kitchen cupboard, she took from it a pile of old newspapers and put them on the table. Sitting down later with a mug of coffee, she glanced idly at a copy of the Sheffield Star at the top of the pile. There was a photo of a black family - a man, a woman and three small children, and above it the headline *Refugee fears for kids*. The father was a teacher from Cameroon. He had fled to Britain six years ago, because he had been imprisoned and tortured for protesting against the illegal executions of nine schoolboys. The family were now threatened with deportation, and the parents were desperately worried that two of their children might not survive the journey, without the regular treatment they needed for a serious health condition. A hospital doctor had confirmed the risk involved. The father had appealed twice, unsuccessfully, against the rejection of their asylum application. There was another newspaper, more recently dated, with an article stating that the family were now in Yarl's Wood detention centre, awaiting deportation. They were being held in a small room, the children had been denied their essential medicine, and the family had no change of clothes, as they had been given no time to pack anything when they were arrested at 6.30 in the morning.

Maria looked back at the first report to check something she'd noticed, and on which she'd at first pinned some hope. - Yes, a spokeswoman for the Home Office's Border and Immigration Agency had indeed said, *'Removals are carried out in the most sensitive way possible, treating those in question with courtesy and dignity'*. Immigration officials were also quoted as insisting that the area where the Cameroon family was to be sent was safe, while, at the same time, the Foreign Office was advising people not to travel there because of risks posed by *'civil unrest.'*

Maria felt as if a huge lump had formed in her throat. Dumb with outrage and grief, she could not have spoken if there had been anyone nearby to hear her. She put her head down on her folded arms on the table, and wept long and hard. If that family, with such desperate need for refuge in a safe country, was being treated so harshly, there was surely no hope at all that she herself might eventually be allowed to stay in Britain. She had been wondering if it would be of any use for her to make a further appeal against her refused claim for asylum. Now, she lost all hope of that.

Three recent events made her fear that she would soon be taken to a Removal Centre. When she saw a police car arrive at Wildwood House yesterday, she'd been terrified. It had taken Claire a long time to convince her that the police were simply trying to track down a troublesome stray dog. But Maria wondered why Claire had urged her so insistently to make sure the cottage door was locked at night. As she sat alone, this preyed on her mind. Also, there was that Lord who came to see Claire a few days ago. She hadn't liked him and the way he'd seemed to be laughing at her. And earlier, at the party on the last night of Hugh's course, the man in the grey suit - who Hugh and Sandy had told her never said a word to anyone - had answered her own quiz question. He knew the national tree of Alborus! She'd been alarmed at the time, wondering if he was a spy of some kind, but had put him out of her mind, until now.

When she was with Hugh, such fears loomed much less vividly in her thoughts. He always made her feel secure. Where was he now? He'd gone to give a lecture at Scarborough, but he was coming to see her this evening. He expected to be at Wildwood House by seven o'clock. The hours were passing so slowly. She went back to cleaning the kitchen, and when that was finished she dusted and tidied the sitting-room. She didn't feel at all hungry and gazed out of the window, at the rain-drenched prospect.

Some time in the early evening, a knock at the door startled her. She opened it with trepidation. It was Claire.

'Are you all right?' she asked, puzzled by Maria's worried look. 'I expect you're wondering where Hugh has got to? Well, I can tell you! He's just phoned me with a message for you. He's on his way home, but he's stuck in an awful traffic jam. A lorry has grounded on Sutton Bank - that's a very steep hill somewhere between Scarborough and Grassington - and it's holding up all the traffic coming in this direction. Lorries often get stuck there. Hugh sends his love, but he says he's very sorry he won't be able to see you this evening.' Seeing the disappointment on Maria's face, she went on hastily: 'But he asked me to tell you that he's taking you out for a special dinner in a restaurant tomorrow evening!'

Maria smiled, but Claire noticed the redness round her eyes.

'You're a bit lonely here now. Do come up to the house and have supper with me and Rory. I'm not so involved with this week's course as I was with Hugh's, so I'm eating in the flat rather than with the students'

'But, your son, Rory. He won't want me there, will he?'

'Oh, don't worry about him! He just loves relating his adventures to anyone who'll listen! He's been excavating ruins in Guatemala. He's got some amazing photos. Do come, won't you?'

After a few moments' hesitation, Maria accepted.

'Remember to lock the door, won't you?' Claire said.

'Of course.'

Maria smiled, but wondered again, why such insistence on locking up, just now?

'You'll be all right walking back later. It'll still be daylight. And Rory's staying in *Curlews* cottage, so he'll walk back with you. Just in case you were worried at all,' Claire added.

Chapter 29

Hugh was browsing cheerfully through the advertisements for restaurants in the local newspaper, as he ate a very late sandwich lunch in his house in Grassington on Saturday morning. He was just about to pick up the phone and book a table when it rang.

'Hugh?'

Vera. She sounded anxious.

'Yes. Hallo, Vera,' he said in a neutral tone, half-way between friendly and guarded.

'Hugh!' Her voice was urgent. 'You've got to come here! Giles...'

What followed was inaudible, choked by tears. He felt a chill of dread.

'What about Giles? I couldn't hear what you said.'

It seemed like minutes before Vera spoke again.

'He's in hospital - the Hallamshire. That's where I'm phoning from.'

Horrific scenarios flashed through Hugh's mind.

'What happened? Has he been run over?'

'No - He's been stabbed!'

'My God! Is he going to be all right?'

'How should I know? He's in surgery now. But Hugh, I can't cope with all this...'

'Hold on, Vera. I'll come over right now. I'll be there...' He checked his watch, 'about four o'clock. I'll go straight to the hospital. I'll see you there - OK?'

'Yes. Oh, thank God I got through to you! He was in a fight! But I'd better not delay you with the details - not that I know much yet...'

Her voice tailed off.

'Are you all right, Vera? Is there someone with you?'

'No. I'll be OK now I know you're coming.'

'Well, get yourself a hot sweet drink or something. I'll be on my way very soon.'

They exchanged shaky goodbyes.

Fifteen minutes later, Hugh was in his car, driving as fast as the traffic allowed, his mind in tumult. How serious were Giles's injuries? He hadn't asked Vera which part of his body was wounded, and he shuddered at the possibilities. Suddenly, his son seemed very young and vulnerable. He wished he could hold him in his arms and imbue him with his own strength. As he drove, through heavy rain, he clung to this idea, as if, by some kind of telepathy, he could fortify Giles across the too-slowly decreasing miles. Sometimes he muttered encouragements:

'Hang on there, Giles!....You'll be OK...I'll be with you soon.... Keep your spirits up!...'

The journey to Sheffield seemed far longer than it ever had before. He started wondering about the incident itself. What kind of person had stabbed his son? Fury against Giles's assailant replaced for a while his anxiety. Some psychopath roaming the streets, looking for a stranger to attack? Or someone Giles knew? A number of knife incidents in schools had been reported in the news recently. Surely not one of Giles's friends? He realised he didn't even know their names. He pulled up sharply to avoid a car that slowed down ahead of him, and realised he'd been exceeding the speed limit.

He'd expected to make better progress once he was on the M1, but soon after he joined the motorway two lanes were closed and the traffic slowed to a crawl. Later, he passed the wreckage of a car and a van slewed across two lanes. The revolving lights of police vehicles and two ambulances illuminated the grim scene, while medics attended to the casualties. Rain fell relentlessly.

****

Arriving at the ward he'd been directed to, Hugh noticed a policeman talking quietly to one of the hospital staff. He heard the phrase *'inadequate parental supervision'* and felt both shame for what he now regarded as neglect of his son, and indignation at the glib expression. Seeing Hugh, they stopped talking. The police officer spoke to him. Hugh hardly absorbed his words of introduction.

'Mr Armstrong?'

'Yes.'

'I'm here to ask your son some questions when he wakes up.'

'How is he?'

The policeman turned to the nurse.

'Giles came out of surgery an hour ago. He's asleep now, here in the ward. His mother's with him.'

'Can I see him?'

'Of course - second bed on the left.'

They both looked disturbingly pale - Giles's face still and expressionless, Vera's creased with lines he hadn't seen before. She looked up, smiled faintly, murmured, 'Thank God you've come!'

Hugh sat down on the chair at the other side of the bed. Unaccustomed to hospitals, he glanced nervously at an instrument he took to be monitoring his son's heartbeat. It bleeped quietly at intervals.

'The surgeon was here a few minutes ago. He told me everything's satisfactory,' Vera said, but she didn't sound convinced.

'What injuries has he got?'

'He was stabbed in the chest - just missed his lung, the surgeon said.'

Hugh winced and looked grave. Vera's voice quavered as she went on:

'The police came to the house - It was an awful shock - A man and a woman. They said he'd been in a fight. I couldn't believe it. But then the policewoman asked me if I'd missed any of my knives from the kitchen! I went to look in the tool drawer, and the knife I use for cutting up meat wasn't there! I searched everywhere, desperate to find it. I even went through the rubbish in the kitchen bin - but in the end I had to admit that it had gone. It was awful, having to tell them - like betraying him.'

Hugh nodded.

'But what actually happened? And where was this?'

'In the shopping centre. He was with those two friends of his - Rick and Des - you know?'

Hugh looked blank.

'They met up with two other boys, and a fight broke out. That copper out there told me they won't be able to tell us anything till all the boys have been interviewed, and a couple of witnesses, too. He's waiting to talk to Giles when he's fully awake.'

'I expect it'll be ages before we know what really happened. The police won't give us much information and their names won't be released to the media - protection of minors, you know?'

'Thank goodness for that! I couldn't bear everyone knowing that Giles was involved - the school! the neighbours! Oh Hugh, this is all so horrible!'

'Why don't you go home now? Try to get some sleep?' he said. 'You look tired out. I'm not surprised after what's happened. I can stay here overnight.'

'I think I will. Thanks, Hugh. You'll phone me if anything...?'
'Of course I will. I'm sure he'll be OK,' he said trying to sound confident.

He listened to Vera's footsteps receding bleakly out of the ward and down the corridor. With Giles deeply asleep, he had ample time for reflection. What a mess he and Vera had made of their son's upbringing! At the time of their divorce, the boy was so young that Hugh had not thought ahead to his adolescent years, and how his own absence then might affect the boy's development. But if they'd stayed together for his sake, Giles would have been increasingly aware of the disharmony between his parents. Maybe, he now wondered, that would have been better than an absent father. Impossible to know, really, and nothing could be done about the past. What mattered now was to do whatever he could for Giles - at least, to keep him on the right side of the law!

A slight movement made him look eagerly at Giles's face. His eyes were half-open. He seemed to be trying to say something. Hugh took hold of the hand that lay above the blanket and gave it an encouraging squeeze.

'Dad,' Giles whispered hoarsely. It seemed a big effort for him to speak.

'Yes, I'm here. You're going to be all right.'

'I didn't...'

He seemed about to doze off again, but he was still trying to speak. It was painful to watch the effort he was making, Hugh squeezed his hand again, trying to encourage him.

'I....I didn't....'

'What didn't you do, son?'

'I didn't ... stab anyone.'

Relief surged through Hugh. The possibility that Giles himself had attacked one of the other boys had been disturbing him ever since Vera's phone call.

'I'm sure you didn't. Now, how about going back to sleep for a bit?'

But Giles's eyes were already closed. Hugh leaned over and kissed him on the forehead. It was the first time he'd done that since Giles was a toddler, he reflected, but now it happened entirely by instinct. He looked at his son, now sleeping peacefully - as if he'd woken specially to give his dad that vital message - and hastily brushed a tear from the corner of his eye, though no one was looking.

Now that he had what little information was available about the fight, and with Giles fast asleep, Hugh contemplated the long night's vigil ahead of him. It was then that he remembered Maria! She would be expecting him to call for her at the cottage to take her out to dinner in Skipton! He took his mobile phone out of his pocket, then remembered the notice in the entrance hall saying that mobile phones must be switched off in the hospital. He stood up, told the nurse at the desk that he'd be back shortly, and hurried to the exit.

The rain that had fallen steadily during his drive had now stopped, and the air outside felt warm and humid. As there was no telephone in Maria's cottage, he dialled the number of Wildwood House. It rang and rang. Clearly, there was no one there. Of course, he remembered, the secretary, Diane, finished work at lunchtime on Saturdays, but surely the office wouldn't be unattended for very long. He could try again. He looked at his watch - five thirty. He felt wretched about having to cancel the meal out, especially after last night's meeting had been impossible too. Maria would surely understand that nothing less serious than this crisis with Giles would have made him cancel tonight's meeting. She wouldn't start worrying before seven o'clock, the time he'd promised to call for her. It was to have been more special than Maria realised. In his pocket was a sapphire ring he had bought her, to allay the doubts she still seemed to have about the seriousness of his marriage proposal. He'd been looking forward to seeing her sweet face when she opened the tiny box.

Half an hour later, he tried to phone again. Still there was no reply. In case there was something wrong with his mobile, he tried a public phone box near the entrance hall. Again, the office phone rang continuously. He tried the number of Claire's flat. Something was wrong; instead of the ringing tone, there was silence. He waited, in case there was an invitation to leave a message, then switched off.

What now? - email! Yes, computer facilities were indeed available and, yes, he had the email address of Wildwood House. He typed a brief explanation, with the request that the message be given to Maria without delay. Then he wrote another email, more informative, to Claire's own email address. Feeling a little more confident, he returned to the dimly-lighted ward, nodded to the patient policeman and the nurse, and hurried to Giles's bed. The boy looked exactly as Hugh had left him, as if he'd only been away a few minutes. He sat down, relieved to have sent the emails, but he wondered - Would there be anyone in the office in the evening? Would Claire look at her own emails and find his, before Maria began worrying about his non-arrival? He would continue trying to phone, but it looked as if that line was out of order. And if so, he wondered, maybe the email system would be, too.

Chapter 30

The church clock had just struck midnight. All was quiet now that the rain had finally stopped, but when Maria looked through the window, few stars were visible, much of the sky being still obscured by clouds.

How could Hugh have deserted her, after all that had passed between them? She had been pacing restlessly around the cottage for hours, wondering why he had not come. Surely, he would have sent her a message if he'd been delayed, as he had done on Friday night? But had that traffic jam been simply an excuse for not coming to see her then? He must have changed his mind about her. Perhaps on reflection he thought it would be unwise to marry a failed asylum seeker, living in Britain illegally. Maybe he'd learnt that someone in her situation wouldn't be allowed to marry in this country? But it was so cruel of him not to have contacted her! She couldn't believe he would be so heartless. Had he had an accident? The heavy rain might have made driving conditions dangerous, especially on those sharp bends on the route from his house at Grassington to Wildwood. He might be injured - or even dead! This idea reminded her how much she loved him, and depended on him for her happiness. Everything else in her life was wrong. Her fears of being denounced as an illegal immigrant had been intensified by recent incidents, which preyed on her mind - the policewoman who came to Wildwood House, the man in the grey suit who, in her disturbed state, now seemed to have been a sinister figure lurking there, waiting to denounce her. After all, he knew the national tree of Alborus! And there was that Lord somebody... Any of those people, or anyone who had heard any talk about her locally, could have reported her presence to the authorities.

With no one to talk to, her fears grew and seemed to loom over her. She had been fortunate for two weeks, but her luck couldn't last. Soon, she would find herself in one of those Removal Centres. Then she would be sent back to Alborus to face grim consequences. Or, if Alborus refused to have her back, she would probably be confined indefinitely in the Removal Centre, with no hope of improving her life, unless she managed to escape, a fugitive, always on the run, dependent, again, on people's charity for her survival. And even if none of this happened, she hated the thought that other people, especially Claire, were probably acting illegally by sheltering her, taking risks for her sake. She could not let this go on. She had to get away. She knew where she would go.

The brief summer night seemed endless. She began to pack some basic essentials in her bag but, once the decision was made, her mind relaxed a little, and she lay down on the sofa and dozed off.

****

Waking to see the greyness outside beginning to change into faint colours as the mist lifted slowly from the fields, Maria stretched her limbs, stiff from the awkward posture in which she'd been lying, and stood up. She went upstairs for a brief wash. Through the open door of the bedroom, she saw hanging there the dress Jonquil had lent her, that she'd put on last night, in such a happy mood, for the evening with Hugh, and she felt as if she would choke with disappointment. She hurried downstairs, picked up her bag, quietly opened the door, closing it after her, and stepped the short distance to the door of the adjacent cottage. Here, she paused for several moments, as if trying to make a decision, then she tapped lightly on the door. When nothing happened, she tried the knocker, below a small picture of a curlew in its lonely moorland habitat. In the early-morning silence, the sound seemed violently loud. Then she heard someone coming down the stairs. The door opened and Rory stood there in his pyjamas, amazement on his face.

'Maria!' he exclaimed, 'What's the matter?'

'I have to go away from here! Please help me!'

Immediately she felt embarrassed, ashamed. On the strength of a couple of hours in Rory's company in his mother's flat on Thursday night, hearing about his year in Guatemala, she had woken him up in the small hours to help her to run away.

Rory looked very puzzled. He wondered if he were dreaming. This beautiful woman, whom he'd often seen around the garden but had hardly spoken to until Thursday, now wanted his help.

'Rory - could you take me to Buckden, please?'

As he seemed to hesitate, she added, 'It is important for me to go now. I need to see a friend there.'

'It's very early,' he said. 'Will your friend be up when we get there?'

She nodded, but he was unconvinced. There was something wrong about this.

'It is very important for me to go now,' she said, her face betraying her distraught state of mind.

'Well,' he said, feeling very doubtful about the situation, 'if you're sure that's what you want to do, I'll take you in my mother's car.'

'Please - I do not want anyone else to know.'

'OK. I don't suppose anyone else is up and about yet. I'll just be a few minutes. I'll see you in front of the main house.'

She nodded, and turned away.

As he dressed hurriedly and splashed water on his face to make himself feel more awake, he was torn between a desire to help Maria and a conviction, growing with almost everything she had said, that there was something desperate - maybe irrational, in her plan. Was he right to do as she asked? She looked so helpless and unhappy. He couldn't refuse to help her, could he? He would drive her to Buckden. After all, it wasn't an outlandish request - except for its timing. What would he say to his mother? At the very least, she'd wonder why her car was missing if she looked out in an hour's time.

Like conspirators, they got quietly into the car, holding the doors until they reached the end of the drive, so that no one would hear them slammed. Not a word passed between them until they were well on their way, but he sensed that Maria was unwell. She seemed to be shivering, though she'd put on a fleece jacket; and crying too, he noticed when he took a sidelong glance at her.

'D'you want me to say anything to my mum?' he asked after a while.

'I don't know,' she answered, in a tone of such bleak hopelessness that it chilled him, making him feel responsible for her. For all his experience of travel, of strange situations and unpredictable people, he felt at a loss with this woman, only a few years older than himself, and he felt responsible for her. He knew about Maria's circumstances and wondered whether she was trying to escape from the immigration authorities.

They travelled in silence and the journey was slow because yesterday's heavy rain had produced a thick mist, slow to clear in places. He wanted to speak, to lighten the atmosphere, but ordinary conversation seemed impossible.

Eventually he asked, 'Have you got some definite place to go to? I mean, somewhere to stay?'

She didn't answer at once, and when she did, her words were ambiguous.

'I know where I'm going,' she said.

'Is there a phone number I could give my mum - I mean, in case she wanted to contact you?'

'No.'

A few moments later, he tried again.

'If you're scared of being caught, I'm sure you'd be much safer back at Wildwood than on your own, or with strangers.'

She didn't answer.

'We can turn round now and go back. No one need ever know about this trip.'

Again, she said nothing, until after they'd gone through Kettlewell.

'Starbotton is the next village, then Buckden. Please take me straight there,' she said, adding in a tearful voice, 'And don't ask me any more questions.'

The Dale looked beautiful in its early-morning freshness, dew sparkling on the grass as the sun rose and the mist gradually receded up the hillsides.

'You've got a nice day, anyway,' Rory said in a deliberately cheerful tone, as Maria stepped out of the car, near the old post office at Buckden, where the road divides, on the right climbing towards Bishopdale, and leftwards continuing by the Wharfe, towards Langstrothdale.

She smiled faintly, said, 'Goodbye, Rory, and thank you,' Then she waited while he turned the car round, waved, and headed back down the Dale, full of misgivings.

Chapter 31

Claire had been trying to phone Aidan, but found that her telephone was out of order. It was eight-thirty in the morning. She'd better go down to the office and notify BT at once. She hadn't tried to ring anyone since yesterday morning. It might have been out of order since then. It occurred to her also that there might be some new emails for her and, as she was going to the office anyway, she might as well check them at the same time. She disconnected her laptop and took it with her, not yet having got to grips with the office computer. After calling BT to request attention to the fault on her own telephone line, she postponed her call to Aidan while she checked her emails. There was only one, from Hugh, sent yesterday evening. She hadn't expected to hear from him. She clicked up the message and was dismayed to read:

Hello Claire, Could you please give Maria a message and my apologies for not being able to take her out to dinner tonight? I think your phone is out of order; I've been trying repeatedly to get through. I'm at Sheffield. My son Giles is in hospital - a stab wound in his chest. I'm staying here at least until his mother comes tomorrow morning. Please tell Maria I'll see her as soon as I possibly can, and give her my love. Thanks very much, Hugh.

Claire printed out a copy of the message to give to Maria, and went outside to deliver the note without delay, imagining how distressed the girl must have been by Hugh's unexplained non-arrival. She tapped on the door of *Swifts* cottage. No answer. She tried the handle and was surprised to find that the door was not locked, despite her repeated advice.

'Maria?' she called gently up the stairs, but almost at once she sensed that the cottage was empty, and a quick run upstairs proved this true. Had Maria gone out for an early-morning walk? It was a lovely morning. Or maybe she'd gone to the main house for something? But Claire felt that something was wrong. Had the police come in the night and taken her to a Removal Centre, as Maria so dreaded? There was no sign of a sudden departure. The cottage was reasonably tidy. Her canvas bag was not visible, but she didn't seem to have taken much with her in the way of clothes, Claire noticed when she looked round the bedroom. The simple blue dress that Jonquil had lent Maria hung from a hanger on the wardrobe door.

How long had she waited, wearing it, expecting Hugh to arrive, before giving up hope that he was on his way, and changing back into her everyday clothes and hanging the dress there? What must her feelings have been at that moment? It seemed worryingly possible that Maria's disappearance was connected with Hugh's non-arrival last night. And Maria had been on her own quite a lot last week, with Hugh travelling to give talks in distant parts of the county and then the traffic jam that prevented him seeing her on Friday too. Claire began to be seriously concerned for Maria's state of mind.

As she stepped out of the cottage, it occurred to her to ask Rory if he'd noticed anything happening next door, but even as the thought struck her, Rory himself stepped out.

'Mum!' he said, 'I'm worried about Maria!'

'Where is she?'

'I don't know exactly. But she knocked on my door - must have been about five o'clock - and she asked me to take her to Buckden.'

'You didn't...?'

'She was very insistent - said she had a friend there she wanted to see. I advised against going. I suppose it was the time of day that made me think there was something odd about it, and she looked so worried. But in the end, I took her there, in your car.'

'You did what?' Claire exclaimed. 'You took my car, without asking me! You drove her to Buckden without any good reason?'

'Yes. I'm sorry. She was in such a state - I couldn't refuse. Tried to persuade her against it, though. I hope I haven't blundered...!'

'I hope so, too! Oh, Rory, I wish you hadn't done that! She never mentioned a friend at Buckden - or any friends at all in this area . I think she'd have told me...'

'I wish I hadn't taken her,' said Rory, 'But it would have been cruel to refuse - she looked so miserable... '

'I think you're getting a bit fond of Maria, aren't you?' Claire asked.

'Dunno, maybe. Is there anything we can do now?'

'I'll phone Hugh. But he's in Sheffield. His son's in hospital there. He couldn't get here for ages even if he set out right now! I came down here to give Maria an email that Hugh sent last night, explaining why he couldn't take her out as planned. Have you got your mobile phone? I doubt if BT will have corrected the fault on my line yet,'

He handed her his phone. 'I'll do anything to help,' Rory said, feeling useless.

Claire nodded, then dialled the hospital number, which Hugh had included in his email. At last, Hugh was located for her. It was a relief to hear his voice. She briefly told him the facts - Maria hadn't received his message and had now disappeared after being taken to Buckden at her own request.

'Oh, my God!' Hugh exclaimed, after taking in what Claire had said.

Remembering the startling news about Giles, she added, 'I'm very sorry about your son, Hugh. How is he?'

'Stable - so they tell me. They think he'll be OK.'

'Good.'

'Anyway, he's being cared for here. But, Maria....' His voice tailed away.

'Rory and I could try to find her,' Claire said, 'Any idea where she might have gone?'

'Search me! I only wish I knew!'

Claire waited. Then Hugh said: 'Listen, Claire. Giles's mother will be here soon to stay with him. I don't think I need wait till she comes. I've a feeling Maria's need is greater than Giles's just now... I'll be at Wildwood in a couple of hours or so.'

'Can Rory and I do anything in the meantime?'

'You might try that old farmhouse in Langstrothdale, up the hillside, to the left of the river, between Yockenthwaite and Beckermonds.'

'You think she might be there?' Claire was alarmed. 'It's a desolate spot...'

'Just an idea. We walked along that road, and Maria commented on the place. She said it looked so safe, protected by those trees nearby.' Hugh's voice sounded shaky.

'Rory and I can go up there now. We'll keep in touch.'

'Thanks, Claire. You're a real friend.'

'Take care driving, Hugh. See you soon. Bye for now.'

****

Maria was glad to be on her own. She had felt too tired and confused to cope with Rory's efforts to persuade her against going to Buckden, and had feared that he would turn the car round and take her back to Wildwood House. One half of her mind argued that she would be safer there than wandering on her own, but she had made up her mind and would not change it now.

She left Buckden by the riverside path, and stopped to look at the young ash sapling growing out of a dead sycamore. Tears welled up in her eyes as she remembered Hugh's lovely metaphor, comparing her with the new tree. But it was all wrong - she wasn't thriving in the country she'd landed in.

Joining the narrow road to Hubberholme, she turned for a moment to look back at the field, full of wild flowers, committing it to memory, something lovely that she might never see again. There was no one about, though she heard some activity at one of the farms, and once a milk lorry came down the road and slowed down for the driver to ask if she wanted a lift. She shook her head and raised a hand to wave him on. It occurred to her that, despite the scarcity of vehicles - indeed, because of it - she must be very conspicuous to anyone who did drive along here. A quarter of an hour later, she saw a police car approaching. As it slowed down, she felt despair. This was what she'd been dreading for so long. The car stopped, the policeman lowered his window.

'Have you seen a stray dog in any of these fields?' he asked.

The relief was almost as overpowering as the fear had been, and for a moment she couldn't find her voice.

'No,' she said, 'I haven't seen any dog.'

'It's been playing havoc round here. But it's a crafty animal! Keeps itself well hidden in the daytime. Well, I'll be on my way. Enjoy your walk. It'll be a grand day when all the mist's gone.'

Every step Maria took along this road, she had taken just a few days ago with Hugh. She'd been so happy then. But everything had changed and she'd lost faith in him. The countryside comforted her, though - the gently rolling hills, the river, the little clumps of trees, and then the change of scenery after the cattle grid, and Yockenthwaite with its farm, loud with bleating as sheep were collected in a pen, then into Langstrothdale, lovely and remote.

By the time she reached the old farm, after a steep walk up from the riverside, Maria realised that she was very tired after the long walk. The almost sleepless night had taken its toll, and although the sun now gave a little warmth as it rose higher, she felt stiff and cold. The farmhouse seemed less welcoming than it had from the road below. Its windows were boarded up and bars had been fixed across the doors. She walked right round the house, trying to find a way in, but, although derelict, the place had been well secured. The trees were lovely, though, their lush foliage rustling gently in the light wind. She was too tired to try to break into the house. She had to rest for a while.

She sank down onto a stone slab - perhaps an old gatepost that had fallen or been knocked down years ago. Its coldness startled her. She shivered, wondering what to do next, and - with increasing unease - what she was going to do later today, tonight, and in the coming days, which now seemed to yawn ahead dauntingly, with no prospect in view? Why had she wanted to come here? This farm must have been abandoned decades ago. But if she was going to spend the night here, she must find a way into the building soon. She stood up and began trying to move a few of the boards nailed across the windows. They had been firmly fixed. If only she'd brought a few tools - even a garden trowel might have enabled her to shift one of these planks. Eventually, she found a board that seemed thinner than the others, rotten and loose at one corner. With great effort, she managed to break the piece of wood, but only enough to show a little of the interior, through the small broken pane of a window behind it. What she saw gave her no encouragement. Though so firmly shut up, the interior looked as weatherbeaten and neglected as the outside. There was what looked like an old cooking range. Could she learn how to use it? Not without cleaning all that rubble piled up in and around it, as if part of the roof had caved in. She could hear scuffling noises - animals inside, probably rats! Maria shuddered, and went back to the stone slab. What now?

Idly, whether to pass the time or to seek comfort from familiar things, she opened her canvas bag that she'd brought all the way from Alborus with her meagre possessions inside it. She began taking out a few of her belongings - the little notebook in which she'd written English words that were new to her, a cheap ball-point pen, a small bottle of water, a spare jumper, an apple - but she didn't feel hungry. Then she took out the increasingly shabby envelope that contained the photos of her father. At the sight of these, she broke down uncontrollably, her shoulders shaking, in her grief for his unjust and lonely death in prison and for her loneliness without him. How, she wondered, could she have let new friendships obscure her memory of him?

After a while, she reached inside her bag again. Her hand felt something unfamiliar at the bottom. She pulled it out - a tiny brown bottle. Sandy's sleeping pills. Maria had found them under a bench seat they'd been sitting on during a break on Sandy's last day at Wildwood House. Sandy had told her she no longer needed her pills and hadn't taken any since she came on the course. Maria had intended to return them to Sandy before she left, but had forgotten about them.

If only she could sleep now, and not think about her future at all! That would be wonderful - to sink into oblivion and not worry about anything... She opened the little bottle, took out a pill and swallowed it, then another and another, helping them down with hasty gulps of water from the plastic bottle. The more she swallowed, the sooner sleep would come... Soon, she began to feel drowsy, but she would swallow as many as she could, to make the sleep last longer and longer and longer... She lay down on the fallen gatepost, clutching her father's photograph, and waited....

Chapter 32

'What's this place we're going to?' Rory asked.

Claire had been driving for ten minutes in silence, keeping her thoughts to herself.

'It's a farmhouse - uninhabited for generations.'

'Sounds grim. Why would Maria want to go there?'

'You heard what Hugh said.'

Claire was in no mood for chatting.

'About it looking safe, with trees around it?'

'Mm...'

'Good thing it's Sunday,' Rory said, hearing church bells, after another spell of silence in the car. 'Hugh won't find the traffic so bad getting out of Sheffield.'

'Something to be thankful for,' Claire muttered, then suddenly she exclaimed, 'I forgot to say where we'd meet him!'

'Have you got his mobile number?'

'Yes. Thank goodness!'

The journey seemed frustratingly slow, especially after Buckden, where the road to Hubberholme became narrow and tortuous.

'Damn!' Claire exclaimed.

She'd pulled into a passing place too sharply, to avoid an oncoming tractor, scraping the left wing ominously against the stone wall.

'I'll get out and look at the damage,' Rory said.

'No! We haven't time for that now!' Claire snapped.

'Sorry! Just trying to help.' Rory subsided into tactful silence for some time, as the miles disappeared behind them with exasperating slowness.

When they'd crossed the cattle grid near Raisgill, and were driving along the unfenced road, Rory said, 'By the time we get to the farm, Maria will have been there about an hour, I reckon - assuming that Hugh's idea is right, about her going to that farm. She's a good walker, you said?'

Claire nodded. At Yockenthwaite, with its busy farm, loud with bleating sheep and clucking poultry, ramblers making an early start along the Dales Way gave them a friendly wave. To Claire's agitated mind, the walkers' cheerful normality seemed unnatural, almost bizarre. She stopped the car soon after a much-photographed house at Deepdale, in its lovely riverside setting. As they left the car, crossed the river by the footbridge and began to climb the hillside, both realised more strongly than before, that they might be about to make an appalling discovery.

****

Hugh had left the hospital at Sheffield at 9.30 and was now on the M1 heading north. Low-lying fog had impeded his progress at first, but this had mostly cleared now and he was able to keep his foot down, thankful that this was Sunday, with lighter traffic in the morning. His sleepless night at Giles's bedside was already taking its toll on his alertness. *TIREDNESS KILLS! TAKE A BREAK!* coloured lights warned him at intervals. How could he, with Maria in trouble...? Instead, he reached for a chocolate bar he'd put on the passenger seat, tore it open with his teeth and bit off a big chunk of comforting sweetness. He chewed it ravenously, finishing the bar in two minutes. It was a long time since he'd had a proper meal. To stop his mind wandering, he switched on the radio - a church service, a hymn he remembered from his schooldays, then a sermon that would send him to sleep. Classic FM - the Toreador's Song from Carmen - impossible to fall asleep now! He turned up the volume, even joined in with the words he knew. He would leave the motorway at Leeds, take A-roads to Ilkley, and then the peaceful B-road to Grassington and Upper Wharfedale.

****

With each step she took towards the farm, Claire's misgivings increased. She dreaded what she might find in the next few minutes. Rory went on ahead. Now he had reached the farm buildings and she couldn't see him. She stood still, waiting. Then he appeared. He was coming down to meet her, not calling to her to join him, and she took this as a bad sign.

'She's here, Mum,' he said as he joined her, 'but she seems to be unconscious.'

Claire turned very pale and, fearing that she might faint, Rory put his arm awkwardly round her waist.

'We must get help as soon as possible,' he said gently.

Claire suddenly realised the urgent need for action. She hurried up the remaining slope to where the land flattened in front of the farm, stumbling a few times in her haste. Then she saw Maria, lying, white-faced, on what Claire assumed was an old gatepost, long since fallen. On the ground, just below her right hand, was a small brown pill bottle, which Claire put in her pocket. Nearby was a photograph, yellowed with age, of Maria as a young girl with her father, both smiling happily. Maria had shown it to her just a few days ago. Claire knelt on the hard ground and took Maria's hand, though recoiling at its coldness.

'Maria, dear...I'm Claire. Can you hear me? '

After a few moments, Claire added, 'If you can hear me, can you squeeze my hand?'

No response.

'Is she...?'

'Alive, d'you mean?' said Rory.

Claire nodded. He reached for Maria's wrist, and felt clumsily for the pulse.

'Yes!' he said, 'She's alive, but her pulse seems very weak.'

'And I can just see now that she's breathing. It's very shallow, though,' Claire added. 'We need an ambulance. Can you phone Skipton Hospital?'

'It'd take ages for an ambulance to get up here from Skipton or Grassington! And we haven't got their number! We'll have to take her there ourselves, in the car.'

'How can we get her to the car? Can we carry her, between the two of us?'

Rory looked at Maria, as if assessing her weight.

'I'll carry her - fireman's lift style! You carry her bag.'

Humbled by Rory's enterprise and determination, Claire bent down and collected the various belongings that Maria had left lying around - including the photograph, which she carefully put inside an old envelope containing other photos and newspaper cuttings, and placed them carefully in Maria's canvas bag.

By the time she'd done this, Rory was half-way down the hillside, with Maria over his shoulder, her head and arms dangling down his back, jolting and swinging with each step he took. Claire shuddered. It was hard to believe that Maria was alive, seeing her like that. Much sooner than Claire had thought possible, they were at the car. She unlocked the doors and they managed to lay Maria down gently on the back seat.

'Next,' said Rory, 'we phone a doctor.'

Claire's diary had the number of the local surgery, and she was quickly through to the emergency number for weekend call-outs. An ambulance would be at Wildwood House in twenty minutes.

'The question is, can we be there in twenty minutes?' Claire said.

'You bet!' Rory smiled. 'I'll drive!'

****

When Rory turned the car into the drive of Wildwood House, they saw the anbulance already parked at the front entrance. Two paramedics immediately got out and came to the car.

'I do hope we're in time,' Claire murmured.

With swift expertise, the paramedics transferred Maria onto a stretcher and put her in the ambulance. One of them got into the back with Maria, while the other explained that they would take her straight to Skipton Hospital, but they would need somebody to provide information about the patient. Claire and Rory agreed to follow the ambulance, and the convoy set off.

'What a relief! She's in expert hands now,' said Claire, getting back into the passenger seat.

****

'Now, Mrs Martindale, can you tell me this patient Maria's surname?'

Claire had realised on the way to the hospital that she would need to exercise great discretion to avoid betraying the fact that Maria was now an illegal immigrant, but that it would be very difficult not to arouse suspicion.

'Petrova.'

'Her age?'

'Twenty-three.'

'Her address?'

Claire gave the name and address of Wildwood House.

'Is that her own home?'

'No. Wildwood House is a college. I'm the Principal and I live there. Maria is a friend of mine, and she lives there too.'

The woman made a few notes. So far, so good, thought Claire, but then things became more difficult.

'Who is Maria's doctor?'

'I don't know whether she has registered with a doctor yet...probably not...'

'We'll need to have her NI number as soon as possible.'

Claire's heart sank. Thank goodness she wasn't expected to produce documentation on the spot. She nodded.

'Religion?'

Claire looked surprised.

'It's a routine question.'

'I don't know,' she lied. Best not to draw more attention to Maria by mentioning the Orthodox Church, she thought.

'Thank you,' the woman said briskly, 'That's all we need at present.'

'Could I have a word with the doctor who's looking after Maria, before I leave?'

Ten minutes later, a tired-looking young man in a white coat with a stethoscope round his neck came into the waiting room, and after speaking briefly to the receptionist, walked over to Claire and Rory.

'How is Maria?' Claire asked.

'Impossible to say for some time yet, I'm afraid, but her condition is stable. Her heart rate is very slow. We don't expect her to regain consciousness for some time yet.'

'Should we stay here, do you think?'

'Frankly, I don't think there's any need. There won't be any change in her condition for several hours, and no visitors will be allowed to see her for quite some time anyway.'

He paused, then added, 'You did very well to get her here so promptly.' He smiled, then turned away to deal with a teenaged girl, an accident casualty, who had just been brought in, whimpering with pain.

****

As soon as they were back in the car, Claire's mobile phone bleeped. It was Hugh.

'Claire? - I'm phoning from Ilkley, on my way home. Any news of Maria?'

'Yes,' Claire told him, trying to keep up a cheerful tone.

'So, if I go to Skipton Hospital, you don't think I'd be allowed to see her?'

'No. They said no visitors can see her for "quite some time" -

whatever that means. Hugh, why not come to Wildwood and have lunch with us in the flat? There are no students here today. The next course doesn't start till Tuesday. Better than brooding on your own. d'you think?'

'Very nice of you, Claire. Yes, thanks, I'll do that. I'm going home to have a shower and change my clothes. I might even get an hour's sleep - I was up all night in the Sheffield hospital...'

'Are you OK to do all this driving? You've not had any sleep for ages, have you?'

Rory interrupted Claire with a loud whisper, 'I can go and fetch him from Grassington.'

'Rory's going to Grassington to collect a few items. He says he'll pick you up and bring you here. Then, if the hospital tell us later that Maria's conscious and can be visited, we can all go there together. And don't argue!' she said firmly, as Hugh was beginning to protest. 'Rory will be at your house around one o'clock. That'll give you time for a sleep. OK?'

'Yes. Thanks very much, Claire.'

He sounded weary.

'Do take care driving, Hugh. We don't want anyone else in hospital!'

'I will. See you later, and thanks again.'

When Claire had put the phone down, Rory asked her, grinning, 'What are these "items" I'm going to Grassington for?'

'Just useful items to convince Hugh that you were going there anyway! He wouldn't have wanted you to go there specially to fetch him. Anyway, as it happens, I do need a few things for the lunch, if you don't mind popping into that little supermarket - some broccoli to go with that salmon in the fridge, and some ice cream for pudding.'

****

'*Was* it a suicide attempt?' Hugh asked, not for the first time, unable to associate the word with Maria as he knew her. Again, neither Claire nor Rory offered an opinion.

'I can't accept it. I *won't* accept it!' His tone was defiant, as if challenging the others to contradict.

They were in Claire's flat after lunch. His declaration hung in the air.

'You found her. Tell me exactly what you found at the farm...Claire? ...Rory?'

This time, Rory answered. He gave a clear, factual account, expressing no opinion.

Then Claire said, 'If Maria went there to take refuge, she must have been appalled when she got there. You said, Hugh, that Maria thought the farm looked welcoming. Well, so it does from the road, at a distance. She must have had a horrible shock when she got up there. It's all boarded up. I doubt if she could have got inside. Of course, with Maria as she was, we didn't stay to look around.'

'I'd like to go up there and have a good look at the place,' Hugh said.

'Ever since we were there,' Claire continued, 'I've been trying to imagine how Maria might have felt. She'd placed far too much hope in that farmhouse. When she discovered how derelict it was, she must have got panicky about what to do next - especially if she couldn't get into the house. She wouldn't know where else to go....'

'Unless to come back here,' Rory suggested.

'I expect she was exhausted by then, anyway - couldn't face going back straight away, even if she did consider it,' Claire said. 'Maybe she just took those pills to postpone taking further responsibility for herself. In a way, playing for time.'

Hugh nodded. 'Thinking she'd cope better after she'd had a sleep?' he asked.

'Yes, that's what I thought.'

'That sounds much more like what Maria might do,' Hugh said. He seemed visibly to relax more, settling back in his armchair.

'More coffee?' Claire offered. She poured them all another cup.

'Have a chocolate,' said Rory, producing a box.

'Where are these from?' his mother asked.

'Just an extra I bought with your "items" in Grassington!'

'Thank you, Rory. Just what we all need - something sweet and comforting,' Claire said.

They tried to talk about other topics.

'I wonder if that dog has been found that was playing havoc among the local sheep,' Claire said.

'Visitors think life's all sweetness and light in the Dales,' said Hugh, 'but there's always something for the farmers to worry about.'

'What's your next course about, Mum?' Rory asked.

'Wildlife photography. Quite a lot of people have enrolled.' Claire said.

'It's an attractive subject,' Hugh said. 'I hope they'll have good weather.'

'Will they be out all day, in hides?'

'No; though I daresay a few real devotees will want to spend all their time like that. But quite a lot can be done without leaving our grounds - so the tutor told me when he came to look round. I hope I'll have time to join the group a few times, with my old camera, but I've still got a lot of admin work to catch up with and, well, all that's happened...'

'Hadn't we better phone the hospital now?' Hugh asked.

Claire nodded. She got through quickly to the ward sister. The news was disappointing. Maria had not yet woken up and there was still no change in her condition, and no, they did not encourage visitors in these circumstances. The hospital would notify Claire of any change in Maria's condition.

'There's just one good thing about not being allowed to visit Maria,' Claire said to Hugh, 'When we took her in, I was asked for information about her. I managed to cope mostly, but they needed her National Insurance number. I said I didn't know, but of course, she hasn't got one, and if I tell them that, they'll soon find out that she's a failed asylum seeker!'

'They wouldn't chuck her out of the hospital, would they?' Rory asked.

'No,' Claire answered. 'Aidan gave me a lot of info about asylum seekers, and I remember that emergency treatment was never refused, but long-term medication wouldn't be provided...'

'But,' Hugh interrupted, 'the NHS and the immigration authorities may see things differently. There was a shocking example earlier this year. A Ghanaian woman was having treatment for cancer in a hospital in Cardiff. Her visa had expired, and she was forcibly removed from her bed, put on a plane, and sent back to Ghana, where she died soon afterwards.'

'Oh yes! I remember that now,' Claire said. 'The Archbishop of Wales said her death would be on Britain's conscience. I don't suppose you heard about that in Guatemala, Rory?'

He shook his head. 'That's scandalous,' he said. 'Better invent an NI number for Maria quickly! But be careful - all those numbers and letters mean something. It'd be easy to blunder and give the show away.'

'I think that's too risky,' said Claire. 'It would be almost impossible to invent a viable number, and we'd just be drawing attention to Maria's situation.'

'Play for time then, if you can,' said Hugh. 'Actually,' he went on, in a confidential tone, I'd really like to be her first visitor when she wakes up. They wouldn't expect me to know that number, and you could postpone your visit for a little while.'

Claire looked at him quizzically.

'Well,' Hugh continued, 'I hadn't intended to tell anyone yet, but I've bought Maria an engagement ring. I was going to give it to her at the restaurant yesterday, but of course, that never happened. I think it might cheer her up.'

'I'd say it will!' Claire exclaimed. 'She'll be over the moon!'

Hugh smiled. 'Thank you!' he said. 'But now I want to go and look at that farm.'

'I'll drive you there,' said Rory. 'I'd like to get out of Wildwood House for a bit.'

'Not very complimentary, I must say!' said Claire. 'Anyway, off you go, you two. I've got some phone calls to make. Good thing the fault's been put right.'

****

First, she dialled Jessica's number. They had not spoken to each other since the Trees course ended, but had promised to keep in touch. Never great friends at school, they had become so in just a week, meeting as adults and sharing concern for Maria. Claire poured out the story of Maria's disappearance and its consequences.

'And after all out efforts to keep Maria's presence here secret, what she's done will attract far more attention to her than she'd have got otherwise! I've already had to prevaricate about her National Insurance number. If its non-existence gets known, her illegal status will soon come to light, and then it'll get in the papers...'

'Take it easy, Claire!' Jessica's voice was calm and steadying.

'Sorry! It's just that you're one of very few people I feel I can really pour out my thoughts to. It's a great relief, I can tell you!'

'Well,' said Jessica, slowing the pace in her quiet, thoughtful way, 'the main thing is that you and Rory found Maria and got her to the hospital, and she's now getting the medical care she needs. That's far more important than a missing number, isn't it?....Claire, are you OK?'

'Yes. Sorry - just thinking over what you said, putting things into perspective for me.'

'Good. It looks as if what's called for now is patience. You've just got to wait maybe a day or two, and see how Maria gets on. That gives you a breathing space. You'll be able to concentrate on the College better - catch up on the admin or whatever.'

'Yes, I certainly need to get back to my normal work,' Claire said humbly, 'and to be around more to speak to the students and the tutors - as I was when we first opened with the Trees course.'

'It was a lovely course, Claire. And the atmosphere was perfect. Experiencing it as a student, I can tell you we all loved it, especially the way you and the tutors mixed with us. We learned such a lot, in such an enjoyable and effortless way.'

'This is what I love to hear!' Claire laughed. 'I'm just jotting it down to put in our next prospectus - *We learned such a lot, in such an enjoyable and effortless way!* That should bring the enrolments rolling in! Thanks, Jess.'

'Now,' Jessica said, 'At Evensong today, I'm going to include Maria in the prayers we say for individual people who are ill or in trouble of some kind. I won't give any details about her, of course. And I'll include her in my private prayers over the next week. You may be sceptical, but there's no knowing what prayer can do. Why not try it yourself? I'll let you go now - got to polish up tonight's sermon! Bye, Claire, and good luck!'

'I feel a lot better for our chat, Jess. Thanks so much, Good bye.'

After putting the phone down, Claire realised that she hadn't asked Jessica how she was, or shown any interest in her life. She would ring her again soon. She sat for a few minutes thinking over her friend's calming and encouraging remarks, then she made a few notes for things she would do in preparation for the *Wildlife Photography* course, such as telephone the tutor and explain how to get to Wildwood House, and ask if there was any special equipment required for his talks. Then she picked up the telephone handset again. There was a long time before anyone answered, and she was just about to hang up when a woman's voice said, 'Ploughdon Hall.'

'Hello,' said Claire, 'Would it be possible to speak to Lord Ploughdon, please?'

'Who is calling?'

'Claire Martindale.'

There was no sign of recognition from the woman, so Claire added,

'I'm the principal of Wildwood House College, in Wharfedale. Lord Ploughdon called here quite recently.'

'Oh yes! I know who you are now, of course! My father isn't here just now. I'm sorry. He's gone to London.'

Claire's heart sank.

'But I can give you his phone number there, at his club, if you like.'

'Thank you. I'd be very grateful.'

The woman dictated the number. Then she said, 'My father is usually at home, but he's involved in a debate in the House of Lords this week.'

Claire had just replaced the handset and was wondering if this was the debate on asylum seekers, when it rang.

'Mrs Martindale? Edward Ploughdon here.'

'Hello, Lord Ploughdon. Do call me Claire, by the way.'

'Well, Claire, here I am in London. The debate I told you about takes place on Tuesday. Asylum seekers - remember?'

'Of course. In fact I was just trying to contact you. Your daughter has just given me your number. I wanted to speak to you, because something's happened to Maria , the girl you met here...'

'Yes, Claire. I need more information about her than I've got if I'm to speak effectively on Tuesday.'

Half an hour later, Claire felt much more optimistic. Lord Ploughdon had clearly taken up the cause of Maria and the thousands of people in similar circumstances. She had told him everything she could, about the current asylum process generally, and Maria's personal experience culminating in her overdose and hospitalisation, trusting him to use the information with discretion. Later, she worried. Might Lord Ploughdon inadvertently draw attention to Maria's whereabouts, leading to her deportation? It was a gamble, but one worth taking, she concluded.

After this, Claire telephoned Aidan at York, and told him all that had happened over the last few days.

'I wish I could be there to hear Lord Ploughdon's speech,' she said, 'but I can't possibly leave Wildwood House just now.'

'I'll go,' Aidan said decisively. 'I can get an early train from York and be in London in plenty of time.'

'Would you?' Claire said, delighted at his enthusiasm. 'I'd love to know what he says.'

'I'll try to produce a verbatim report for you, if my old shorthand skills aren't too rusty.'

****

Hugh was silent, wrapped in his own thoughts, as Rory drove him back from the abandoned farmhouse. But they were now approaching Grassington, and he bestirred himself to thank Rory for his help.

'You did well to carry Maria down the hill to the car,' he said. 'It can't have been easy.'

'Oh, it wasn't as difficult as I expected, but if she'd been conscious, she'd have found the ride pretty bumpy!'

'Thanks very much, Rory, for all you've done today. I won't forget that.'

'Well, at least Mum might forgive me now for driving Maria to Buckden to begin her walk. If I'd refused, maybe she wouldn't have found anyone else to take her there, and then the awful consequences wouldn't have happened.'

'Don't blame yourself. She must have been very distressed. She'd probably have hitched a lift on a tractor, or gone somewhere else. I guess she'd have swallowed those pills wherever she went, and it would have taken much longer - probably too long - to find her.'

'Has it helped you at all, going up there?'

'I think so. When we found that piece of wood that had been broken off from the board covering that window, I just *knew* it was Maria who'd done that. And when I peered through the little window-pane and saw that old kitchen range with rubble piled on it and on the floor below, it was as if I was seeing it as she herself had and I was feeling her own emotions at that moment - utter despair.'

For a few moments, Hugh could say no more, as if reliving the experience. Then he said, 'I suppose she'd thought she'd be able to get inside and make herself comfortable for a while, but it was clearly impossible. From that moment, I was sure that she took those pills just to send her to sleep for a while, so she wouldn't have to think what to do next, because she'd run out of ideas.'

Again he paused, absorbed in thought.

'I was surprised, though,' he resumed in a more practical tone, 'that Maria had those sleeping pills with her. She never mentioned to me that she had trouble sleeping.'

'No', Rory said, relieved to be able to say something useful after listening, embarrassed though sympathetic, to what had seemed to him like Hugh's private meditations, 'We - Mum and I, that is, - we forgot to tell you. Those pills weren't Maria's. They had someone else's name on the label - Miss S Marlowe.'

'Sandy Marlowe! She was on my course. I remember her specially because Claire told me she was in a very nervous state, to do with a car accident. But, I remember now. On the first evening of the course, a man friend of Sandy's turned up to give her those pills. She'd left them behind at home. How ironic that they should end up like this! I remember, she seemed much better after a few days. Maybe she didn't bother with the tablets any more.'

'And somehow they got into Maria's bag?'

'Yes - a bit surprising. I don't know what to make of that,' Hugh said, looking troubled.

They were now in Grassington, and stopped outside Hugh's small stone-built house.

'I'd ask you in for coffee or a beer,' Hugh said awkwardly, 'but I'm pretty exhausted. I feel as if I could sleep for a fortnight! But I've got to phone my ex-wife and see how Giles is getting on. It's strange - the two people I care about most being both in hospital at the same time!'

'You're going to be busy, then, for a while?'

'Driving to and fro between Sheffield and Skipton! And giving lectures all over North Yorkshire. My cherished principle of using only public transport has had to be put on hold for a while!'

'I expect they'll be out of hospital soon.'

'I hope so - I really do! Anyway, as I said, thanks for all your help, ferrying me from place to place etc. Don't suppose I'll see you for quite a while. What are your plans for the summer?'

'A long-distance bike ride - London to Paris - to raise money for a charity, next month.'

'Splendid idea. Enjoy yourself! Cheerio!' Hugh said as he got out of Claire's car. It was then that he noticed the long scratch along the left side, between the front light and the passenger door. He was puzzled; Rory's driving, though fast, had been skillful on the narrow winding roads. Rory noticed him looking at it.

'Not guilty!' he called through the open window. 'That was Mum's work, believe it or not!'

Chapter 33

As soon as he had shut the door behind him, Hugh telephoned Vera's home number, but after six rings and an invitation to leave a message after the tone, he clicked off and dialled the number of the hospital at Sheffield. Eventually, Vera spoke to him.

'How could you just go off like that, before I got here this morning?' she stormed. 'You promised to stay with Giles till I came...'

'I'm sorry, Vera, really I am.'

His mind fumbled for words to explain about Maria. Vera waited, her silence full of anger.

'I was called away because a friend had been rushed into hospital in Skipton. With Giles being stable and fast asleep, I thought her need for me was greater than his...'

'Is this friend,' - She uttered the word with contemptuous emphasis, - 'the reason why Giles has hardly seen you in the last few months?'

'No. I've only known Maria a few weeks, and she...'

'A few weeks!' Vera interrupted, enraged. 'A few weeks! - You're putting the whims of some woman you've only known a few weeks, before the needs of your own child! He might have died and neither of us with him!'

Her high-pitched, strangled tone conveyed genuine distress.

'And, if you remember,' she added after taking a breath, 'I told you at the time - I stopped seeing my friend Douglas because Giles hated him. - And you just go on doing whatever you like with whoever you like!'

'I can understand why you're angry and upset,' Hugh said as gently as he could, 'But you and I shouldn't be quarrelling at a time like this.'

'No,' she said more calmly, 'we shouldn't.'

'Anyway, how is Giles now? Any change?'

'Yes.' Her tone brightened. 'He woke up, properly, for the first time, about three hours ago. Said he was hungry!'

'Thank God! A sure sign of recovery! Has he said anything to you about the fight - if that's what it was?'

'Yes. It was a bit strange. He said, "Dad knows I didn't stab anyone."'

'That's right. He told me. During the night, he suddenly seemed distressed - moving about a bit. He opened his eyes and turned his head a bit to look at me. I realised he was trying to say something. He seemed to be making a mighty effort, and eventually that's what he said, "I didn't stab anyone." Then he closed his eyes and went straight back to sleep. At first, I was just so glad that he could speak. Then I felt a huge surge of relief at what he'd told me.'

'Me too,' said Vera. 'Oh, by the way, a policewoman took over from the man who was waiting when you were here. She asked Giles some questions, quite gently, not like those police interrogations on the telly'.

'What did she ask him?'

'Who he'd been with in the shopping centre. - That lout, Rick it was. I might have guessed, and another boy they go around with called Des. Then she asked Giles what happened. He said they'd met up with two lads Rick had had some quarrel with last week, and Rick taunted them. The language they used! Words I'd never heard when I was their age. It was awful to hear Giles talking like that, but he was only quoting what Rick and the boys he'd quarrelled with said - as the policewoman told him to. Anyway, one of the other youths pulled out a knife, but Rick dodged out of the way, so the knife went into Giles instead.'

'He must have had the shock of his life,' said Hugh. 'I don't suppose he thought he'd really get involved in violence. I think it was just a fantasy to him.'

'Yes,' Vera said, without conviction, 'But he's not that innocent. He had a knife on him, remember? One of my kitchen knives! I expect it made him feel important and dangerous just carrying it around. Whether he'd ever stab anyone with it - well, it's something I can't imagine.'

'Nor I,' said Hugh. 'Anyway, I think this incident will bring him to his senses. He's had an almighty shock. He'll realise, now, that he's been on the fringe of serious crime. This'll probably set him back on the straight and narrow.'

'Oh, I do hope so,' said Vera.

Hugh yawned uncontrollably.

'I'm sorry, Vera. I'm dog-tired. No sleep at all last night. I'm going to bed now for a few hours. Then I'll come over to Sheffield again, for the night shift, if you like.'

'Well, you can leave it till tomorrow, if you like. The doctor told me Giles is out of danger now. He'll probably sleep right through the night.'

'Thanks, Vera. I do realise you've had a difficult time with Giles lately. I'm going to take more responsibility for him now. I'll see what I can do.'

'I hope you will, Hugh. I hope you will. Good night.'
'Good night, Vera. Look after yourself.'
Did she believe him? he wondered.

****

Waking several hours later, Hugh telephoned the hospital at Skipton and enquired about Maria. Her condition was, like Giles's, stable. Did hospitals always say that? But her progress had to be closely monitored in case there was any liver damage from the overdose. No, they did not think visiting was a good idea. Maria needed as much rest as she could get.

Frustrated, he said, 'Well, could you at least give her a message, please? It's very simple - "Hugh sends his love." '

'We'll see that she is told,' the voice replied after a pause, during which Hugh presumed his words were being written down.

Ten minutes later, a nurse coming on duty on Maria's ward found several notes that had been left for her. She was puzzled by the last one on the list: 'Message for Maria Petrova - Who sends his love?' She looked at Maria who was sleeping serenely, and smiled. It was like one of those tantalizing anonymous Valentine's Day greetings, from a boyfriend, she supposed.

Hugh consulted his diary for the week ahead. Tomorrow he was giving a lecture at Ilkley in the morning. Fortunately, nothing was booked for the afternoon, and Ilkley was on his route to Sheffield, so he would go straight from there to see Giles. He got out the notes and slides for the lecture and put them in his briefcase, ready for tomorrow.

****

'Dad!'

Hugh heard his son's greeting as soon as he entered the ward and his heart lifted. He hurried to Giles's bedside, ruffled his hair playfully, and sat down on the nearby chair.

'You look much better than when I last saw you! How d'you feel?'

' Very sore. It's awful when I move. But OK otherwise.'

Giles seemed slightly apprehensive. He'd been wondering all day what his father thought of his involvement with what had nearly been a serious incident.

'I'm sorry, Dad - about what happened. I'm not going to go around with Rick and Des any more,' he said.

'I should hope not!' his father said. 'If you want to stay alive, you'd better keep well clear of them.'

Giles nodded, contrite and, Hugh hoped, prudent now.

'What happened to that friend of yours - David, wasn't he called?'

'He lives in California now. His family emigrated ages ago.'

'D'you hear from him at all?'

'Only cards at Christmas and birthdays.'

'That reminds me - your birthday's coming up next month, isn't it?'

Giles nodded but showed little interest.

'What happened to your old bike?' Hugh asked, after a pause. An idea had just occurred to him.

'I sold it to a kid down our road - last year.'

'Why did you do that? A bike gives you a bit of independence.'

'The tyres kept getting slashed.'

'Who by?'

'Dunno. I used to ride to school, and twice they were slashed by the time school finished. So it must have been one of the kids there.'

'Didn't you tell your form teacher?'

'Yeah. Nothing happened though. I just stopped biking to school. I go on the bus now.'

'Seems a shame.'

'Yeah.'

Hugh was saddened by the dull monotone of Giles's voice.

'A young chap I know is going on one of those charity cycle rides next month,' Hugh said, 'London to Paris! How'd you fancy doing that?'

'Well I can't can I? No bike!'

'Would it interest you, if you had?'

'It might,' he said cautiously. 'Yeah - it would!'

'Would you like a new bike for your birthday?'

'Yeah - That'd be really cool, Dad. Yes please!'

Giles had regretted the over-hasty sale of his old bicycle. He seemed a bit suspicious about the cycle ride though.

'What charity is it in aid of?' he asked.

'People choose any charity they want to support, like they do in Marathons. You've seen them on TV, haven't you?' Giles nodded. 'You get people to agree to give a certain amount, and you collect it from them afterwards. I went on one myself a few years ago, for the Lifeboats.'

'Oh yeah! I remember now. But...'

'What's worrying you now?'

'I couldn't go on my own, could I?'

'No. You'd have to be with an adult. I'll go with you - if that doesn't put you off the whole idea! But you'd get on well with Rory - the chap I mentioned. He's just come back from excavating ancient temples in Guatemala. That was his gap year, before he starts University in the autumn.'

The more Hugh talked, the more interested Giles became.

'Has your mum made any plans for your summer holiday? I'd better check the dates of the bike run, just in case they clash with anything.'

'No, she hasn't.'

He sounded sheepish, as if he was covering up something. Hugh waited.

'Well,' Giles began, reluctantly, 'I was going to go camping with school, but I pulled out. Mum was furious - having to tell the teacher who was organising it.'

'Why did you pull out?'

Giles looked down and muttered: 'Rick said camping was childish.'

'And you just swallowed that, did you?'

Giles nodded miserably.

'Well,' Hugh said, 'nearly all the major expeditions ever made on land have involved camping - including the ascent of Everest, and treks to the North Pole. Just mention that, if Rick says camping's childish again!'

****

Hugh returned to the hospital car park, relieved by Giles's recovery and pleased at the interest he'd shown in the cycle run. He hoped this event would help to distance his son from the trauma of the knifing incident, although of course, he would have to give evidence later at the trial of the boy who had stabbed him. And how would he cope, back at school in September with Rick and Des? Would it be possible for him to change schools? He would talk these things over with Vera, and with Giles himself. There must be, from now on, a continuous dialogue between the three of them, so that Giles would feel more confident, and Vera too. He now understood her resentment at the infrequency of his visits to Giles, and her anxiety about Rick's influence, her sense of powerlessness to intervene. Hugh had been shaken, more than he realised, by what had happened. That expression that had so angered him when he heard the policeman and the nurse talking about Giles - *inadequate parental supervision* - kept recurring in his mind as a justifiable rebuke.

Before setting off to drive home, Hugh phoned the hospital at Skipton. The news that Maria was still not to be disturbed alarmed him.

'Is she all right?' he asked anxiously.

'She is still in a stable condition.'

'I've been told that several times before,' he said, irritated by the overused word, 'But what does it mean?'

'Maria's progress is steady. We would not expect a rapid recovery from the overdose she took. I don't think you need to worry too much, Mr Armstrong, but she has to be carefully monitored, to check if any permanent damage has been done - to her liver, for instance. If you were thinking of visiting her, I'm sorry to say this again, but it's best if she isn't disturbed at present.'

Hugh began his long drive home to Grassington. It was only yesterday that Maria had swallowed those tablets, but it seemed like an eternity to him.

Chapter 34

Aidan Martindale sat in the public gallery of the House of Lords. It was many years since he had been here, but nothing had changed, so far as he remembered, in this bastion of tradition. The heavy ornate red and gold decoration, the Throne, the walls painted with heraldic designs and coats of arms, the predominance of red also in the leather benches and the Woolsack - seat of the Lord Chancellor, (or, as today, his deputy) - all these gave Aidan a feeling of mild claustrophobia. He recognised a number of leading political figures, including two former Prime Ministers, and was pleased to note that the Chamber was fairly full.

Lord Ploughdon was already seated in the area reserved for cross-benchers. Aidan had never met him, but he recognised him easily from Claire's description. He looked grave, except when someone he knew came to speak to him. When this happened, his face, tanned from a life spent mainly out of doors, would soften into a smile as he exchanged a warm handshake with a friend.

Aidan cast an eye over the programme he'd been handed on entering - a printed schedule, listing the main speakers. Lord Ploughdon's name appeared towards the end.

While waiting for the debate to start, Aidan reflected on the events of the last few weeks - how Claire's life had been almost dominated by concern for Maria since the girl had turned up at Wildwood House. Although he'd been at home in York most of the time, he'd been affected too, re-reading that article he'd written previously about asylum seekers. That had been not much more than a year ago, but it had been a brief revival of his passionate feeling against injustice, reminding him of an earlier time, when his journalism had the power to move readers. The shock of Maria's disappearance, her overdose and hospitalisation, seemed to be stirring his campaigning spirit, as if after a long sleep. He felt the way he had as a young man, grabbing a pen whenever he heard of injustice of any kind, giving a voice to the indignant but usually speechless thousands whose causes he espoused. Perhaps the novel he'd laboured over for so long without success had been a mistake - its plot contrived, its characters unrealistic. It had taken up so much of his time, had eventually soured his outlook. He and Claire had drifted apart...

The House had fallen silent. A junior minister from the Home Office rose as the Government's spokesperson. Firstly, she said, she had been asked by several of the noble lords if she would give a summary of the process by which asylum seekers are dealt with when they arrive in Britain. She was happy to do this.

'Firstly,' she said, 'an asylum seeker is required to make application as soon as possible on arrival in this country. This would normally be at the port or airport of entry. If this was not possible, they must report without delay to one of the two asylum screening units, at Croydon or Liverpool. Within a few days the applicant meets their Case Owner, who explains what will happen at the Asylum Interview they must attend when notified. They are told how they can get legal representation, and are normally given a subsistence allowance or provided with accommodation. They are offered the services of an interpreter at the asylum interview, provided that they request this in advance They are told where they must report regularly, for example, at a police station, in the time before their interview. They are told to bring proof of their identity and that they will be required to explain why they fear returning to their own country. It is their Case Owner who decides, at the asylum interview, whether or not asylum can be granted. If asylum is refused, the applicant is told whether he or she is entitled to appeal against the decision. If the application is finally refused, they are free to leave this country voluntarily. If they refuse to leave, they are deported. They may be detained until this can be done, in one of our Removal Centres. Their subsistence allowance is stopped twenty-one days after asylum has been refused. They are not allowed to take paid employment. I hope this has clarified the matter,' the Minister said.

There were murmurs of thanks. She then said that she would finish with a brief overview of recent progress. She was pleased to announce that the number of applicants for asylum had gone down, partly because of the deterrent effects of heavier penalties against people-traffickers, and the larger fines or prison sentences imposed on people who employed failed asylum seekers illegally. A points system was to be introduced, she said, to simplify and speed up the process of dealing with asylum seekers.

As she sat down, there were a few murmured comments, mostly to the effect that it all sounded very reasonable.

An opposition spokesman stood up. He first thanked the Home Office minister for her clear account of the asylum process. Then he congratulated her on the progress she had reported, saying that he broadly agreed with the policies outlined. Nevertheless, there were still many thousands of refused asylum seekers roaming the streets, sleeping rough, and possibly resorting to petty crime. Surely, more might be done, he said, to prevent this situation deteriorating still further. Prevention was probably easier than cure, and he asked the minister to consider urgently how the smuggling of people into Britain might be more effectively prevented.

The next speaker was a Liberal Democrat. He asked the minister to consider the possibility of allowing refused asylum seekers to take paid employment - especially those who had been here for some time after their application was refused. It was shameful, he said, that people were being forced into destitution when they could be earning their living and contributing to the life and economy of this country. Some of these people could not return to their countries of origin, even if they wanted to, because they no longer had identity documents and their countries wouldn't accept them as genuine nationals.

At last! They were getting nearer to thinking about the plight of individuals caught up in this system, after all the generalisations. Aidan listened to several short speeches, mostly about minor points. He looked at his watch. By now, more than forty minutes into the debate, he noticed that two of the older noble lords and one noble lady had dozed off. He hoped they would wake up in time to hear Lord Ploughdon.

Eventually his turn came.

'My Lords and Ladies,' he began, an agreeable hint of the northern shires in his voice, 'Some of you are no doubt surprised to see me here today. I rarely attend debates that are not connected with agriculture in some way, but I am making an exception today.'

He paused. All eyes were on him.

'Two weeks ago, I met a young asylum seeker. She was looking after the garden of a friend of mine in the Yorkshire Dales, in exchange for board and lodging. She is the daughter of a well-known dissident writer in Alborus - a country I hardly knew existed - who had protested against the tyrannical régime there, and had died in suspicious circumstances in prison. Maria's career prospects as a teacher and writer had been blocked because of this, and she was reduced to very poorly paid menial work Then she began to receive threats against her own life. Not surprisingly, she decided to escape to another country. Her father's last advice had been to go to England, where she would be free to write, so this was where she planned to go. The only way she could do this was to contact an illegal organisation which took people to countries of the European Union, including Britain. Maria paid a large sum for this, and, with great reluctance, she handed over her passport, as was demanded.

'Her journey was horrendous - very few stops on the way, sitting cramped in darkness, among total strangers, for many hours at a stretch. But, eventually, she arrived in England and went to Bradford to stay with some distant relatives of her family. She immediately applied for asylum, but, after several months, and despite the help of a solicitor who believed she had an excellent case, she was refused. Maria was in fact lucky to get a solicitor; few of them will take on asylum cases, as the work is very badly paid.

'I have recently spoken to this solicitor. He described to me the unsettling tone of Maria's asylum interview. She was not given enough time to answer the questions put to her, even though she has a good understanding of English and speaks it well. Her Case Owner hardly looked at the photographs Maria showed, which proved her identity, and brushed aside Maria's fears of persecution in Alborus, saying that she had not heard of any trouble in that country. This solicitor told me that there seems to be a "culture of disbelief " among the authorities towards asylum seekers. He encouraged Maria to appeal at a tribunal against the refusal. An independent Judge would see that a fair decision was reached. But there, again, she was refused asylum.

'Maria was now terrified that she would be taken to a Removal Centre and eventually deported to Alborus, so she left the people she was staying with in Bradford and began a journey - mostly on foot - to the Yorkshire Dales. She seems to have been captivated by photos of that beautiful area. Eventually, after a very brief spell of employment in a bed and breakfast place, she arrived, exhausted and undernourished, at my friend's house in Wharfedale which is run as a residential college for adults.

'This was probably the happiest time of her life, but it was very brief. She loved the Dales, and she fell in love with a tutor at the college, and he with her. But suddenly everything went wrong. She ran away again, apparently because she feared that she would be caught and deported to Alborus, and hated to be a burden to people who had been kind to her. Fortunately, she was found by the college principal and her son, lying unconscious in the yard of a derelict farm.

'This young woman is now in a hospital in Yorkshire, fighting for her life, after an overdose of sleeping pills.'

Here, Lord Ploughdon paused, for the first time. The stillness in the Chamber was almost palpable.

'I will leave you with a quotation,' he added. 'It is from the United Nations Convention on the Status of Refugees, 1951, to which Great Britain is a signatory:

"No Contracting State shall expel or return a refugee in any manner whatsoever to the frontiers of territories where his life or freedom would be threatened on account of his race, religion, nationality, membership of a particular social group or political opinion." '

He paused again. Then, in a quieter tone, he said, 'My Lords and Ladies, what is happening to our country?'

He sat down, amid a deep and respectful silence.

Chapter 35

Maria opened her eyes and immediately she was fully conscious. This had only happened once before, this morning when the doctor had talked to her about her recovery. Until then, she'd been only partly aware of her surroundings and the hospital staff attending to her.

'Hugh!' she said, her voice rather weak and slightly rough, as if she hadn't used it lately, and her face - expressionless ever since she was found by Claire and Rory - now took on the beginning of a smile.

'Maria!' Hugh said, 'Oh, Maria!'

He picked up the slender hand which she'd moved slightly towards him and squeezed it. Then he leant closer to kiss her, and her tremulous response answered a question he now knew he need not ask.

'Lovely roses!' she said, as Hugh looked for somewhere to put his bouquet, and deposited it at the end of the bed.

'I'm so sorry,' he said, 'about Friday night,' and he began explaining about Giles's injury in Sheffield, But Maria interrupted him:

'You don't need to explain,' she said gently, stroking the golden hairs on the back of his hand and wrist. 'But how is Giles now? Is he getting better?'

'Yes. He's going to be all right.'

'Good.'

'Did the staff give you my message yesterday?' he asked.

'Oh yes! "Who sends his love?" I was puzzled at first, but then I realised you were making a joke about my saying your name wrongly at first!'

He was baffled for a moment, then he realised that the staff must have mis-heard him on the phone. He let it go.

'Do you remember? - that night with the owls?' she said.

'Of course I remember! It was only a few weeks ago!' he answered. 'Seems ages, though. It does to me, anyway. So much has happened...'

'Hugh,' she said, suddenly very serious, 'You must be wondering why I swallowed those tablets.'

'No need to talk about it now,' he said. 'There's plenty of time.'

He was almost afraid of learning her reason.

'I will tell you everything later. But I want you to know that I was not trying to kill myself. I went to that farm - You know the one?'

'Yes, I know.'

'I thought I could stay there, to avoid being captured, but I could not even get inside! I was afraid, and so terribly tired. I just wanted to sleep, and forget my problems for a while. So I swallowed those tablets. They belonged to Sandy, who was on your course. I found them, and I was going to give her them before she left, but I forgot. But I could not stop swallowing them!'

She seemed to be getting agitated.

'Yes, I understand, darling. You needn't think about it now. I'll look after you.'

She relaxed, smiled, then she said, 'Something puzzles me. How did people find me, at the farm?'

Hugh answered: 'Claire asked me if I'd any idea where you might have gone, and it occurred to me straight away - that was the only place I could think of. So she and Rory went straight there and found you!'

'So it was you, Hugh, who saved my life!'

'Well, partly, but they were the ones who actually rescued you.'

'You all three saved me.'

Both were silent for a few moments. Then Hugh spoke, in a serious tone.

'Have you really forgiven me for not contacting you on Friday about cancelling our meal out?'

'Of course I have!'

'But you must have doubted me. You must have thought I'd changed my mind about you. Wasn't that the reason why you ran away?'

She was silent for a while, then she said: 'It was partly that, but only partly. I was becoming more and more afraid that I would be taken to a Removal Centre and then sent back to Alborus. Things happened which made me afraid. I saw a police car outside Wildwood House one day. Claire told me they were only asking about a stray dog - but, well, I doubted her a bit. Perhaps she didn't want me to be alarmed. There were other things too. A Lord came to Wildwood one afternoon, to speak with Claire, when I was working in the garden. He spoke to me and he laughed because I could not say his name.'

Hugh looked puzzled, then he smiled.

'Well, I laughed when you couldn't pronounce my name, and I've not done you any harm, have I?'

'No, I don't think you have,' she said rather gravely, but with a hint of a smile. 'Anyway, I was becoming so frightened and that is what made me despair when you did not come. Oh, Hugh, I am so cowardly!'

'Nonsense! It wasn't cowardly to make that terrible journey from Alborus to Britain. You were brave and strong to do that. And you've been so courageous, coping with difficulties since you came to this country. You're the bravest person I know.'

He kissed her again, then he said, in a softer tone, 'And you're the dearest girl I've ever known.'

Then, to her utter amazement, he got off his chair and knelt down on one knee, and said, 'Maria, will you please marry me?'

'Yes! Oh, yes!' she said, tears flowing down her cheeks.

'Here's something for you,' he said, presenting a small package. She opened it with trembling fingers. Inside was a tiny box, which she opened, and found the sapphire ring.

'How beautiful it is!' she said. 'Thank you so much, Hugh.'

'Let me put it on you,' he said, taking her left hand and slipping the ring onto her third finger, 'I was going to give it to you on Friday, at our special dinner.'

'Congratulations!'

They both looked up, mildly startled to realise they were not alone. An old lady in the opposite bed was smiling and waving to them. 'And you did it the proper old-fashioned way!' she added, 'Like my husband in 1950! I hope you'll be as happy as we still are!'

Chapter 36

Returning home from the hospital, Hugh switched on his television for the news, before going into the kitchen to make a cup of coffee and get a pork pie out of the fridge. Before the kettle had boiled, he caught the words *'daughter of a dissident writer in Alborus'* and rushed back to the television, where, to his utter astonishment, he saw a member of the House of Lords speaking about Maria - her background, her escape from Alborus, and her experience as an asylum seeker in Britain, culminating in her overdose and hospitalisation. And this was Lord Ploughdon, the man Maria was afraid might betray her, making an impassioned plea for the rights of asylum seekers!

****

'Jason!' Caroline Entwistle called up the stairs, 'There's something on the news that will interest you!'

He emerged promptly from the study and hurried down. Caroline would only call him for something she knew was important to him.

'It's Lord Ploughdon!' she said, 'speaking about Maria!'

She scooped up Benjie from his blanket on the floor, where he was making resonant utterances comprehensible only to himself, and carried him out of the sitting-room, closing the door quietly behind her.

****

'Lord Ploughdon champions Asylum Seekers' Cause' was the front-page headline of one of the more liberal-minded newspapers the next morning. Hugh seized his copy anxiously when it landed on his doormat, skimming through the summary of the Lords' debate to study carefully the speech he'd heard on television last night. His most immediate concern was to protect Maria from the publicity which seemed likely to ensue, and which he knew she would wish to avoid. Had the hospital staff realised that she was the Maria some of them had heard or read about on television or in the papers? Were local photographers even now arriving at the hospital? He telephoned the hospital and enquired how soon Maria would be allowed to go home. To his relief, she could be discharged later today, so long as there was someone who could look

after her until she'd fully recovered her strength. Hugh had a three-day course to teach in Leeds, starting tomorrow, so he telephoned Claire. She had just been reading the same article, and she offered to let Maria stay in the flat at Wildwood House until she could cope on her own. She would be relatively safe there from intrusion by reporters.

****

Lord Ploughdon's speech was widely reported and generally press reaction was sympathetic to his appeal, though several papers warned their readers against letting sentiment override the fact that asylum seekers were costing this country an inordinate amount of money, and that, in view of the current financial crisis, it was unrealistic to devote any additional resources to helping them.

Aidan Martindale studied the style and viewpoints of the articles in the batch he bought the morning after the speech. After spending the morning thus occupied, he knew where his real vocation lay. He could write as well as most of these journalists, better, in fact, than some; and he had the right combination of objectivity and conviction to take up again his role as a campaigning journalist. As a symbolic gesture, he took from the shelf above his desk both the computer disc and the printed manuscript of his unsuccessful novel, put them right at the back of the deep bottom drawer of his desk, then closed the drawer and locked it. That episode, which had so frustrated him, made him lose control of his alcohol consumption, and nearly wrecked his marriage, was over, for good.

****

'It's all over the papers this morning! Front page on some of them! Look at this!' the Home Secretary said, prodding with an angry finger a photograph of Lord Ploughdon in a newspaper on the desk, and adding, 'He shouldn't have been allowed to go on like that!'

'An intervention was impossible,' said the junior minister, 'You could have heard a pin drop in the chamber. It would have been too obviously a cover-up.'

'Anyway, the cat's out of the bag now,' said the Home Secretary. 'Best thing to do - Grant Maria Petrova a two months' residence permit. Then we'll see.'

****

Dear Maria,

I do hope this letter will reach you somehow. I will send it to the address you gave me when we parted company in London. I f you have moved on, I hope your Bradford relatives will be able to forward it to you.

It was a great surprise to read about you in a newspaper - in a speech by a member of the House of Lords! I was shocked to read that you took an overdose. It made me think how desperately unhappy you must have been. I hope you are now recovering well.

In London, where I am living, there are very many people like us - seeking asylum. Many of the ones I have met seem to be waiting interminably for their applications to be considered. But the saddest of all are those who have been refused asylum and are now living destitute, some of them on the streets, dependent on people's charity for survival. They are too afraid of what would happen if they went back to the countries they fled from. Others have been refused entry to their countries of origin, because they cannot prove their identity or nationality.

Some of the women have resorted to prostitution, in order to stay alive. It is not surprising, either, that some people steal, for the same reason. It is tragic that people of otherwise good character are being driven to such extremes. I know that we are a burden to the British Government, but if we were allowed to have jobs and earn a bit of money, our pitiful condition would be relieved, and we would regain our self-respect.

As for me, I too am still waiting for the result of my asylum application. Perhaps the fact that my daughter lives here will make it easier - Yes, to my great joy, I found her! - after much anxious searching and enquiries. It turns out that she is one of the lucky ones and is now a British citizen. She had a terrible time when she first came to England. That is why she never wrote to me. She and I live in a tiny flat above a fast-food shop, where she now works, so we are coping as well as we could have expected. I am glad, now, that I made that journey. It was worth all that danger and discomfort to be with my daughter again, though at the time, I thought I'd made a dreadful mistake. I was so glad when you and I got to know each other. It was a great comfort to have a friend in that horrible container, wasn't it? I will always remember you, Maria. I do hope you feel better now, and that your life will be happier soon. Please write to me. It would be lovely to receive a letter in our own language. I have enjoyed writing this in Alboruvian!

Ever your friend,
Nina

Chapter 37

The ambulance stopped in front of Wildwood House, and Claire hurried to greet Maria as she stepped out, pale but smiling.

'How good it is to see you again!' Claire said, giving Maria a hug.

'I must have caused you so much trouble,' Maria said. 'Thank you for all you have done for me. You saved my life! You and Rory. I want to thank him too. Is he here?'

'No. He's back in York now, with his father, and so is Jonquil,' Claire answered. 'Now come in. We don't want you catching cold after all you've been through. You can stay in my flat here for the time being. I don't want you to be lonely when Hugh is out lecturing in Leeds for the next few days.'

When they were in the spare bedroom of the flat, Maria said: 'I had such a shock when I was coming out of the hospital! There were two photographers waiting to take pictures of me! I thought they had mistaken me for somebody else. I said to them, "I am not a famous person!" But one of them said, "You are now!" Then a reporter came, with a recording machine. She said, "What are your plans now, Maria?" I did not know what to say. But one of the hospital people came up and said to her, quite sternly, that I was ill and could not answer questions yet.'

'I'm not surprised that you were bewildered!' Claire said.

The look of dismay, which Claire had seen so often on Maria's face, had returned suddenly.

'I suppose everyone will think I wanted to kill myself. I feel ashamed about it. People should not think I am someone to photograph. I do not understand that reaction. Your English culture is different, perhaps from mine?'

'No,' Claire said gently. 'That wasn't why those newspaper people treated you like a celebrity. I'll explain why it happened in a little while.'

But another thought suddenly alarmed Maria.

'I have made things worse for myself!' she said. 'All this time in England, I have tried to live very quietly and not be discovered...' She paused, trying to control her emotions. 'But now...those tablets....' She paused at the painful recollection. 'I have spoilt my plan. What will happen now?'

Her question seemed not to be directed to Claire, but to her own mind.

'Well,' Claire began in her quiet, comfortable tone, 'Things have certainly changed, but perhaps for the better. Do you remember Lord Ploughdon?'

'Yes! I did not like that man, when he came here. I thought he might report me to the immigration people!'

To Maria's bewilderment, Claire laughed.

'Then I've got a big surprise for you! I'll give you a few minutes to get settled in here. I moved your belongings from the cottage, but you'll want to arrange your things as you like, of course. Just make yourself at home. While you're doing that, I'll make us some coffee. Then - the surprise!'

Ten minutes later, Maria joined Claire in her sitting room.

'Oh, you are watching television!' Maria said.

'No. We're going to see something I recorded yesterday evening, from the ten o'clock news. The news was extended specially.'

'But... the surprise?' Maria sounded disappointed.

Claire zapped quickly through earlier items, then set the video to play. Maria was bewildered.

'What is this strange place? So ornate! So much red and gold!'

'The House of Lords,' Claire answered, 'The Upper House of our Parliament.'

Suddenly, Maria's attention was riveted.

'That old man! He looks like that man I did not like when he came...'

'Yes,' Claire said mildly. 'That's Lord Ploughdon. Listen now!'

Two weeks ago, I met a young asylum seeker. She was looking after the garden of a friend of mine in the Yorkshire Dales.... She is the daughter of a well-known dissident writer in Alborus...'

Maria watched, astounded, as she listened to Lord Ploughdon's account of her journey to England, her asylum application and its rejection, and his outline of her experience in Yorkshire, culminating in her overdose. Her first reaction was dismay.

'But everyone who saw this programme will know all about me! The immigration authorities will find me! I must go away! It is even more necessary than before!'

'No,' Claire said. 'The situation is quite different now. Because your story has been made so public, the Government will have to be careful what they do. There will probably be a strong public reaction in support of you. If so, the Government won't want to go against public opinion.'

Maria looked incredulous for a few moments. then she said, 'I was forgetting - this is a democratic country! So this is how it works?'

'Well, the party in power would lose the next election if the majority of the country didn't support their policies.'

'But,' Maria said, 'Not everyone in Britain supports asylum seekers. I have heard some criticism, even here at Wildwood House. Some people on courses here think we are all scroungers, trying to benefit unfairly from your social services.'

'Yes,' Claire agreed, ' Some do think that. But many people here don't understand the situation. If people realised how harshly many asylum seekers are treated, they wouldn't be so rigid in their views. Unfortunately, some people prefer not to know what is going on.'

'To keep their consciences clear?' Maria asked.

Claire nodded. 'I imagine so.'

They were both absorbed in thought for a while.

'Now,' said Claire, ' let's get back to your situation. Now that your circumstances have become widely known to the public, I think you stand a much better chance of being granted asylum. So, when the photographers and journalists come, smile! Their reporting may do you a lot of good!'

Maria looked more relaxed now.

'May I see this programme from the beginning?' she asked. 'I would like to hear what the other speakers said.'

'Yes, of course,' Claire said, setting the video to rewind. 'And you might see someone else you recognise! At the beginning, before the speeches start.'

'Do you know many Lords?' Maria asked, somewhat awed.

'No, only Lord Ploughdon. Now, look carefully when the camera shows the people in the public gallery.'

'Yes! - That man at the end of the front row - It is your husband, Aidan! But why was he there?'

'We were talking about this debate the day before, and I said I'd love to be there, but I couldn't leave the College. So Aidan said he'd go instead, and tell me all about it. We didn't know, then, that it was to be filmed and shown on television.'

'I wish I had not thought badly of Lord Ploughdon. He has spoken so kindly for me. I will write a letter to him very soon,' Maria said.

****

The unprecedented media interest in Lord Ploughdon's speech gave rise to much anxious conferring at Government level. The Home Office realised that a bland announcement to the effect that no one with a justified fear of persecution would be sent back to their country of origin, could not be trotted out again this time. Concerned members of the public, including church representatives and members of the legal profession, were becoming vociferous in reminding the Government of Britain's commitment to the United Nations Convention concerning refugees, and pointing out how it was being flouted, despite the rhetoric. They drew attention to the plight of families with young children who had been taken from their homes in the small hours, and hustled away to Removal Centres, with no time to collect belongings, and kept in cramped conditions, deprived of medical care - although, according to official claims, there was always a doctor on the premises. Letters detailing other specific cases appeared in major newspapers. And perhaps most importantly of all, because this was probably the fate of the biggest number of asylum seekers, they brought to the notice of a wider public the desperate plight of the many thousands of people who had been refused asylum, and either could not be returned to their own countries, or would not return, for fear of the persecution from which they had sought a safe haven in Britain, and who were now destitute, dependent on the kindness of concerned individuals.

The Home Office quickly issued yet another announcement that strenuous efforts were being made to improve the asylum process, and it was made known to the public that Maria Petrova had now been granted a temporary residence permit for two months, while her case was reconsidered.

Chapter 38

Two weeks later, at Morning Service on Sunday in her church on the Yorkshire Wolds, Jessica's small congregation was doubled by strangers to the village.

Towards the end of the service, Jessica said, 'We are very happy to have with us today Maria and Hugh and a good number of their friends. Some have travelled quite a long way to be here, because this is a very special day. Maria and Hugh recently became engaged, and we offer them our warmest congratulations.'

Jessica paused for a moment, and there was a small ripple of applause which stopped suddenly. 'Yes. Do applaud if you like,' she said with a smile, and there followed a burst of clapping.

'There is however a difficulty,' Jessica resumed. 'Maria is waiting to know whether she will be allowed to stay in Britain, and she and Hugh can't make arrangements for their wedding until that is settled. This could take some time.'

Again, Jessica paused. She was not surprised to notice that two dark heads near the back nodded. The Somali couple who were living in her house knew what waiting for an asylum decision was like. They were still waiting for theirs.

'In the meantime,' she continued, 'Hugh and Maria have asked me to give a blessing to their life together. I am now going to say a short prayer, and I would like everyone who agrees with what I say to join me in saying *Amen* at the end.'

'We ask you, Lord,' she began after a short silence, 'to bless the union of Maria and Hugh. We pray that their problems will be solved, and that they will be strong to face whatever difficulties may lie ahead. We look forward, as they do, to their wedding, and we ask that their lives together will be happy and fulfilling.'

Maria was startled by the volume of sound with which the *Amen* was expressed. Jessica smiled again.

'We shall now sing a hymn that Hugh and Maria have chosen - one which is often sung at weddings, but which seems especially appropriate to them:

"*Lead us, Heavenly Father, lead us*
 O'er the world's tempestuous sea..."'

****

When they emerged into the sunlight, Hugh and Maria were touched to see that the local churchgoers had waited to shake hands and wish them well. Jessica introduced them both to the Somali couple. Although commiserating with each others' long wait for a reply to their asylum applications, they agreed that they had each been unusually lucky in finding kind hospitality during the prolonged delay.

Maria felt sorry for Giles, after Hugh had introduced them to each other. Vera had declined the invitation to attend the service and the lunch to celebrate their engagement. 'It would be just too much,' she had replied. But Maria was sorry that the boy had had to travel most of the way from Sheffield on his own, probably thinking mixed thoughts about his father's planned remarriage, and pessimistic about his stepmother-to-be. Now, however, Giles seemed to be in his element. People were flocking round him to sign up to sponsor him in the London-to-Paris cycle ride. Jessica had mentioned this to her parishioners before the service, and several were responding kindly, as were the guests.

Gradually, Maria, Hugh and their friends walked the short distance to the village pub, noted for its catering. Over the pre-lunch drinks, Maria was delighted to renew her friendship with Sandy, who had arrived with Rex from a few days spent visiting Hadrian's Wall. She wasn't surprised to notice that Sandy was wearing an engagement ring, a sapphire, like hers.

'Not really official until Rex's divorce comes through,' Sandy confided. 'So, like you and Hugh, we're a sort of provisional couple.'

No mention was made of Sandy's tablets and their fate, each woman having privately decided that the subject was best left alone.

'Rhoda!' Maria exclaimed, surprised that she and Ted had taken the trouble to come, but, as Ted explained, Grimsby wasn't far from this part of the Wolds.

Rhoda hugged Maria emotionally, almost tearfully.

'I remember feeling sorry for you on that walk, when you were all on your own. None of us spoke to you, because Claire had said you might be upset if we asked you any questions...'

'I remember that, and how kind you were to me, Rhoda. I hadn't forgotten, and I won't forget.'

Another group Maria hadn't expected to come was the Alboruvian family from Bradford, Ursula and Lev and their two daughters. Maria was delighted to meet Ursula again, feeling a special gratitude for her help in her very early days in England.

'I felt so helpless!' she said, when Ursula made light of her kindness. 'I couldn't have coped without your help - taking me to Liverpool to register for asylum. That cost you two rail fares - yours and mine! And even when you got an allowance for my board and lodging, it wasn't nearly enough.'

'Oh, nonsense!' Ursula tried to make light of her own kindness.

'And you found somewhere for me to get a job, when I wanted to go away with no plans - when I got frightened that I would be caught by the authorities. And,' she added quickly, to prevent further remonstrations, 'You've sent some letters on to me at Wildwood House. One of them was a lovely letter from Nina, the old lady I told you about, who I travelled with in that container. We kept each others' spirits up.' Then she said, 'Your girls look happy, don't they?'

'Yes,' Ursula answered, 'but we had to bribe them with those new dresses to persuade them to come! Rather garish, and much too short. Don't they look dreadful?'

Maria laughed. 'Well, they're very bright, but that is OK for teenagers, I think'.

****

'Here's something for you two!' Claire said, when she found Hugh and Maria.

'It arrived just this morning at Wildwood House,' she said, ' delivered by hand.'

'Who's it from? ' Hugh asked, taking the big envelope and looking at the handwritten address.

'You open this one,' said Maria.

It was a card from the staff of Wildwood, with a photograph of the House on the front. Inside, they had all signed, Geoff in a big bold hand, then the two cooks, and even the women who did just a few hours' work there each week, whom Maria hardly knew.

'To Maria and Hugh,' it said, 'Congratulations on your engagement. Lots of love from us all'

'We should have invited them!' Maria said, regretting the omission.

'If they'd come, I'd have had to stay at the House and I wouldn't have missed this for anything!' Claire exclaimed.

'There's a letter here, too,' she said, opening her bag and handing Maria a more formal-looking envelope.

'It's from Jason!' she said. You know - my solicitor in Bradford. He worked so hard for my asylum case.'

Inside was a letter and a small card. The card offered congratulations and was signed by Jason and Caroline.

'Jason is offering to provide his legal services, without charge, if I need more help,' Maria said, after perusing the letter. 'He says Lord Ploughdon telephoned him before the House of Lords debate, to ask him about my case...'

'Yes,' Claire said. 'Jason is the solicitor Lord Ploughdon mentioned in his speech.'

'Oh yes, of course!' Maria said. ' Jason thinks we may well win, this time, now that the public have heard about me!'

She smiled, but after a few moments' reflection, she looked perturbed.

'But,' she said, 'it does not seem fair! If I am treated better now, it will be because of those moments of weakness, when I despaired of what to do, and swallowed those tablets! If I had continued trying to be brave and not drawing any attention to myself, I would not have succeeded, would I?'

She looked earnestly at Hugh, then at Claire, then Aidan.

'Maybe not,' Claire said, 'but that doesn't make you any less deserving. And all this publicity may eventually bring about some improvements in the way asylum seekers are treated,'

Aidan doubted that, but this was no time to say that there seemed to be little hope of much improvement in the foreseeable future. There was a huge backlog of cases to be considered, and the current world financial crisis could only make things more difficult. The influx of strangers would continue, and many more would be added to the thousands of destitute people living rough in Britain's towns and cities, hungry, humiliated and disillusioned by the country in which they had put their trust.

Much later that day, Maria and Hugh were walking beside the River Wharfe at Buckden. Even more than the reunion with friends at Jessica's village, Maria had wanted to come here today, after the church blessing. It was almost dusk as they came to the spot she'd longed to see again. The old sycamore, bare of any leaves of its own, was conspicuous among the fresh summer foliage. But the young ash-tree shoot, with its pairs of delicate light green leaves, still pointed confidently skywards from the fork between the dead branches. Maria and Hugh stood for a long time, embraced, silent. Then, without a word, they walked back to Hugh's car in the village, then drove to their home in Grassington.

****

At the same time, Jonquil was feeling exceptionally happy. Claire, Aidan, Rory and herself were on their way to York, where, for the first time in many months, they would all stay the night together in the family home. Since some years ago, Jonquil had been aware of the tenseness and friction between her parents, but for several weeks now, a happier ambience had prevailed, and, especially today, she'd noticed a more relaxed and friendly mood, and she knew that Rory had sensed it too. It had coincided with her father's purposeful resumption of writing for newspapers, as she remembered him doing when she was quite small. Their mother, too, could relax more, now that the College was several weeks old, and could already be regarded as a success. Soon, Rory and herself would move on to higher education. All four of them were launching out on new ventures, but wherever these might lead them, they would always remember this summer, and Maria, who had, ever since Claire had found her in the shed, imperceptibly changed each of their lives, in some way, for the better.

Lightning Source UK Ltd.
Milton Keynes UK
25 May 2010

154646UK00001B/30/P